THE WHATNOT

THE WHATNOT

STEFAN BACHMANN

GREENWILLOW BOOKS

An Imprint of HarperCollins*Publishers*

The Whatnot

The text of this book is set in 13-point Mrs Eaves.
Book design by Paul Zakris

Library of Congress Cataloging-in-Publication Data
Bachmann, Stefan, 1993–
The whatnot / by Stefan Bachmann.
pages cm
"Greenwillow Books."
Companion book to: The Peculiar.
Summary: Bartholomew Kettle, unable to save his sister, Hettie, when she was pushed into the faery Old Country, promised he would find her but sinister forces are still at work and he must rely on Pikey, who would do almost anything to escape his past, to help find her.
ISBN 978-0-06-219521-0 (hardback)
ISBN 978-0-06-228630-7 (intl. bdg.)
[1. Fairies—Fiction. 2. Changelings—Fiction. 3. Magic—Fiction. 4. England—Fiction. 5. Fantasy. 6. Youths' writings.] I. Title.
PZ7.B132173Wh 2013 [Fic]—dc23 2013015023
13 14 15 16 17 CG/RRDH 10 9 8 7 6 5 4 3 2 1
First Edition

 Greenwillow Books

To my family,
who made me who I am
~

CONTENTS

Prologue

No one noticed the soldier. He stood in the middle of the ballroom, dark and hunched against the blazing lights, and no one saw. Brightly colored frocks whirled around him. Coattails spun past. The laughter and the chatter filled the air, and the clockwork maids sped right up to him with their heavy trays of glasses and red currant tarts, but he never moved. His face was white as bone. Blue shadows stood out under his eyes, and his uniform was blotted with mud.

Mr. Jelliby did not notice him either, not at first. He was busy being worried and a little bit irritated, leaning against the fireplace and watching the guests as they moved toward the dancing floor. The gentlemen were in full uniform, jangling with swords and medals of bravery, though most had not seen a day of battle. Red sashes slashed down their chests. The ladies smiled and whispered. *Such bright birds,* Mr. Jelliby thought. *So happy. For tonight.*

It was hot in the ballroom. The great windows were edged with ice, but inside it was a furnace. Candles were lit, the fire stoked, and the chandeliers burned so bright that the air around them rippled and the ceiling was heavy with smoke. Mr. Jelliby rubbed the hair above his ear, as if to scratch away the silver that was appearing there. He could smell the red currant tarts as they skimmed past. He could smell oil from the servants' joints, and the damp wraps and overshoes lying in steaming heaps in the neighboring room. The orchestra was tuning up. Dear Ophelia was stooped over a sofa, trying to placate Lady Halifax, who seemed in constant peril of exploding. Mr. Jelliby felt he needed to sit down. He turned away from the mantel, looking for the most convenient escape. . . .

That was when he spotted the soldier.

Good heavens. Mr. Jelliby squinted. What were things coming to that you could get into a lord's house dressed like *that*? The lad's coat was filthy. The wool was sodden, the buttons dull, and the collar was black with who-knew-what. Had he been fresh off the battlefields it might have made some sense to Mr. Jelliby, but the Wyndhammer Ball was the going-off celebration. The war had not even started yet.

"Dashing good bash, this," Lord Gristlewood said, sidling up to Mr. Jelliby and interrupting his thoughts. Mr. Jelliby jumped a little. *Drat.*

Lord Gristlewood was a droopy, fleshy man with pale, swollen hands that made Mr. Jelliby think of dead things soaking in jars of chemicals. Worse yet, Lord Gristlewood was the sort of man who thought everyone liked him even though no one actually did.

"Dashing good," Mr. Jelliby said. He scanned the crowd, making a point to ignore the other man.

Lord Gristlewood did not take the hint. "Ah, would you look at them. . . . Brave lads, every one.

The pride of England. Why, a thousand bellowing trolls could not frighten these men."

Mr. Jelliby pressed his lips together.

"Well, don't you think?" Lord Gristlewood asked.

"No, I don't usually." Mr. Jelliby spoke quietly, into his glass, hoping Lord Gristlewood wouldn't hear.

"I beg your pardon?"

"Oh—That is—I certainly hope so!"

Lord Gristlewood smiled. "Of course you do! Cheer up, old chap. It's a celebration, after all."

"Indeed." Mr. Jelliby set his glass down sharply on the mantel. "Well, *old chap*, if I'm to be honest with you, I see no reason to celebrate. We are entering into a civil war."

Lord Gristlewood's smile slipped a little bit.

Mr. Jelliby didn't stop. "Tomorrow all you'll hear is, 'Hand in your wife's jewels!' and 'Enlist your footman!' and 'All for the good of the empire!' and other such bunk. And then the bodies will start coming back in sacks and wagons, and one will be your footman, and no one will be dancing then. It's not a funny thing, fighting faeries."

"Oh, but you are gloomful," Lord Gristlewood said. "Come now. It'll never go so far. The faeries are wild! They are leaderless and unorganized, and we shall settle them the way we settled the French. With our superior intellect. Let them come, I say. Let them strike us with all they've got. We won't fall." Lord Gristlewood gave an uneasy laugh and slid away, apparently deciding to grace a less depressing person with his presence.

Mr. Jelliby sighed. He picked up his glass again, turning it slowly. He took a sip. Over the glinting rim he saw the soldier, standing dark and solitary among the dancers.

Mr. Jelliby watched him a second. Then he smiled. *Of course. The boy is shy!* Why had he not thought of it before? No doubt the young soldier was frightened out of his wits and wondering how best to ask one of the ladies for a dance. Mr. Jelliby decided to go and rescue him. There was bound to be some equally unhappy nobleman's daughter about, ideally lacking a sense of smell.

Mr. Jelliby pushed off into the crowd, setting course for the dancing floor at the center of the room. It was like navigating a sea of cotton candy, pressing between all those frocks. More and more couples were moving toward the dancing. In fact, the room seemed to be getting fuller by the second, not with people exactly, but with heat and laughter. Mr. Jelliby's head began to buzz.

He had not gone ten steps when Lady Maribeth Skimpshaw—who moved within her very own atmosphere of rosy perfume—intercepted him, grabbing his arm and smiling. She had a very pink, gummy smile of the sort that comes with false teeth. Mr. Jelliby had heard she'd had her beginnings in London's theater district, so doubtless all her real teeth had been traded for poppy potions and illegal faery droughts.

"Lord Jelliby! How perfectly delightful that I've found you. Your wife's arm is going to fall off. She should stop fanning that odious Lady Halifax. The fool thinks someone's stolen one of her gems, but she probably just forgot how many she put on this evening. No matter. I've kidnapped you and that's what is important." Her smile stretched. "Now. I know you are terribly busy managing your estates and counting your money and all that, but I absolutely *must* speak to you very urgently."

"Oh dear, I hope not."

"What?"

"I hope Ophelia's arm doesn't fall off. Shall I get you a tart?"

"No, Lord Jelliby, are you listening to me?" Her fingers tightened around his arm. "It's about young Master Skimpshaw. I want to ask you a favor for him."

Oh, drat again. People were always asking favors of Mr. Jelliby now that he was a lord. They asked for positions in government, or good words slipped to admirals, or whether he had any nonmechanical servants to spare. It drove him to distraction. Just because he had saved London from utter destruction and the Queen had given him a house and some stony fields in a distant corner of Lancashire did not mean he wanted to spend the rest of his life being charitable to aristocrats. Anyway, one would think they could handle their own problems.

"Terribly sorry, my lady, but you will have to find me later. Someone is in need of my assistance now, and"—Mr. Jelliby broke free of Maribeth Skimpshaw's clutches—"and I really must be *going*." He set off again toward the young soldier, trailing rose scent in ribbons behind him.

The orchestra was in full tilt now, sweeping everyone up in a glorious, whirling waltz. Mr. Jelliby could hardly see the soldier anymore. Only snatches of him, in between the spinning figures and bright gowns. His face was chalky. Drained, almost.

"Lord Jelliby? Oh, Arthur Jelliby!" someone called from across the room.

Mr. Jelliby walked faster.

And then, all at once, a rustle passed through the crowd, a disturbance, like the wind in the treetops before a storm. It started on the dancing floor and spread out until it had reached the farthest corners of the ballroom. The rustle swelled. Shouts, then a shriek, and then people were peeling away from Mr. Jelliby, backing up against the walls.

Mr. Jelliby stopped in his tracks.

The young soldier stood directly in front of him, not five paces away. He was alone, all alone on the polished floorboards. His hand was raised, stretched out in front of him. In it was clutched a bloody rag.

Mr. Jelliby let out a little cough.

The rag was blue, the color of England, the color of her army. Shreds of a red sash still clung to it. A spattered medal. The young soldier's mouth opened, but no sound came out. He simply stared at the rag in his hand, a look of mild surprise on his white, white face.

The ballroom had gone deathly still. No one spoke. No one moved. The clockwork maids had all creaked to a halt. The old ladies were staring so hard their eyes seemed about to pop from their heads. Lady Halifax lay sprawled over a fainting couch, face red as an apple.

Mr. Jelliby's first thought was, *Good heavens, he's killed someone,* but he couldn't see anyone hurt. No one seemed to be missing a piece of his uniform, nor were there any wounds visible among the swaths of lace and satin.

"Young man," Mr. Jelliby started to say, unsteadily, taking a step toward the soldier. "Young man, what in—"

But he didn't have time to say anything else, because suddenly the soldier began to change. As Mr. Jelliby watched, blood came up between the soldier's teeth and gushed down his chin in a crimson sheet. Bright holes tore themselves through the fabric of his uniform. He spasmed, once, twice, as if being hit by some great, invisible force.

And then he began to fall, so slowly. Petals of black pulled away from his coat, his arms, and the side of his face as he descended through the air. There was a sound like distant guns. And before he struck the floor, he seemed to disintegrate, turn to ash and smoke and black powder.

Then he was gone, and the ladies were screaming.

Mr. Jelliby heard glass breaking. The lights were so hot now, so raging hot. He couldn't smell the tarts anymore. Only the fear, thick as river mud in the rippling air.

CHAPTER I
Snatchers

PIKEY Thomas dreamed of plums and caramel apples the night the faery-with-the-peeling-face stole his left eye.

It was a wonderful dream. He wasn't in the bitter chill of his hole under the chemist's shop anymore. The old wooden signboard with its painted hands and hawthorn leaves no longer creaked overhead, and the ice wasn't crusting his face. In his sleep Pikey was warm, curled up by an iron stove, and the plums were drifting out of the dark, and he was eating a caramel apple that never seemed to get any smaller.

He always dreamed of caramel apples when he could help it. And iron stoves, too, in the winter. And plums and pies and loud, happy voices calling his name.

Tap-tap. Tap-tap. *Far, far away on the other side of his eye-lids, a figure entered the frozen alley.*

Pikey bit down on his apple. He heard the footsteps, but he tried not to worry. Whoever it was would be gone soon. Folk were always stumbling into the chemist's alley from Bell Lane, from the gutters and sluiceways and all the other fissures between the old houses of Spitalfields. None of them ever stayed for long.

Tap-tap. Tap-tap.

Pikey squirmed inside his blankets. Go away, *he thought.* Don't wake me up. *But the footsteps kept coming, limping slowly across the cobbles.*

Tap-tap. Tap-tap.*Pikey didn't feel warm anymore. The plums still fell, but they stung now as they touched his skin, spitting, icy cold. He tried to take another bite of his apple. It turned to wind and cinders, and blew away.*

Tap-tap. Tap-tap.

Snow was falling. Not plums. Snow. It gusted into his little hole, and suddenly Pikey's nose was filled with the stench of old water and deep and mossy wells. A racket kicked up, old Rinshi straining against her chain, barking at something and then stopping, sharp-like. There was a grating, a scrape of metal.

Pikey saw the blood before he saw the figure, always the blood trickling toward him between the stones. Then the alley was filled with screams.

Pikey Thomas was running for his life.

It was a clear day, sharp and cold as a knife, but he couldn't see a thing. The string that held the patch over his bad eye was slipping. The square of ancient leather slapped his face, disorienting him. He bounced off a drainpipe, did an ungainly whirl, kept running. Behind him, he heard the sound of a bell, coming after him, clanging furiously. Ahead was a gutter. He leaped into it and whistled over the frozen grime, sliding fast as anything. The gutter ended in a rusting grate. Pikey hurled himself over it, struck the cobbles running. His fingers went to the patch, trying desperately to tighten the string, but it wouldn't stay, and he couldn't stop. It was only about to get worse.

The cobble faery tripped him in Bluebottle Street.

There Pikey was, a knob of black bread clutched inside his jacket, pounding up a street that was as empty and icy as any in London. His pursuer was still two or three corners behind him. Pikey was sure he would get away. And then he felt the tremor in the ground beneath him, the rattle of the cobbles as a tiny faery raced through its secret tunnels. It popped up the stone just as Pikey's foot was flying toward it.

Pikey let out a yelp and went careering into the wall of a house. His head knocked against stone. Pain shuddered through him, and he heard a wicked little voice sing, "Clumsy-patty, clumsy-patty, who's a clumsy pitty-patty?"

Pikey spun, pushing himself away from the wall.

The faery was peeking out from under the lifted cobblestone, black-bead eyes glittering. It was a spryte, not three inches from head to toe. Bits of frosty branches grew behind its pointed ears and a dreadful grin was on its face, stretching halfway around. It was a very yellow grin, full of prickly little teeth.

"Shut up," Pikey hissed. He ran at it, determined to smash it into a stringy mess. Too slow. The faery pulled down the cobble like a hat and was gone.

Pikey froze. He glanced back down the street,

listening, making sure he still had some seconds to spare. Then he struck his boot heel against the ground three times, getting softer with each strike so that it would sound like he was walking away. The faery shot back up, still grinning. And Pikey leaped, straight onto the cobble. There was a squeak. The cobble smashed back into place. The faery's hand twitched where it was pinched in.

"Serves you right, too," Pikey said, but he had no time to enjoy his little victory. The bell was close now, echoing up between the buildings. An instant later, a huge officer in blue and crimson skidded into the street. A leadface.

"Thief!" the leadface shouted, his voice oddly flat and dull inside his iron half-helmet. *"Thief!"* But before he could see Pikey, Pikey was moving again, slipping under an archway and down a steep flight of steps, heart hammering.

The leadface charged up Bluebottle Street, flailing his bell. Pikey flattened himself against the gritty stone of the stairwell, just far enough down so that he could still see the street. He saw the black boots go by.

He allowed himself a careful smile. The officer was running straight for the cobble faery. In five steps he would be flat on his face. *Three. Two* . . . And the officer kept right on running, hurtling toward the end of Bluebottle Street and the sooty flow of traffic on Aldersgate.

Oh. Pikey wiped his nose. *Must have stomped that faery harder than I thought.*

He leaned back against the slimy wall, waiting for the sound of the bell to become lost in the noise of the steam coaches and crowds. Then he strode up the steps and into the street, hands in his pockets, looking for all the world as if he had just gotten up and was off to sell matches or shine shoes or squawk the news at unsuspecting pedestrians.

Of course, he wasn't. He had just snatched his supper and now he was going to find a quiet spot where he could eat it. Leadfaces were inconvenient; so were cobble sprytes, especially since they had supposedly been banned from the city months ago together with all the other faeries. But they were nothing Pikey Thomas couldn't handle.

He picked his way back toward Spitalfields, careful to avoid the places where the leadfaces prowled and where the war agents sat at their painted recruiting booths. They were everywhere these days, and they went after most anyone they saw. "For Queen and Country!" they liked to bellow into their loudening horns. "For England, to eradicate the faery threat! Step right up, all men of hardy constitution!"

Pikey didn't know if he had a hardy constitution, but he knew he couldn't go to war. A year ago he would have. He was only twelve, but he would have signed up in an instant. The army had bread. It had thick coats and colorful banners and great bashing songs that made your feet want to march even if they didn't know where they were going. And you got a musket, too, for shooting faeries, which sounded good to Pikey. But that was before. Before the snowy night in the chemist's alley, and the blood between the cobbles, and the feet limping closer, straight toward him no matter how far he pressed himself into the dark. Before everything changed and he didn't know what he was anymore.

From an alley, Pikey watched as a group of boys not fourteen hunched over a war agent's table and signed their Xs on squares of brown card paper. When they had finished, the leadface handed them each a coat and a pair of huge scuffed boots. Then the boys were loaded into a wagon and it creaked away.

The leadface at the booth began scanning the passersby again, eyes invisible behind the dark holes of his helmet. Pikey hurried on. Those boys would be fighting soon, somewhere in the North. Fighting forests and rivers and whispery magic nonsense. He wondered if their boots would come back to London afterward, when they were gone, and be given to other boys.

He went up street after street, ducking into alleys when he heard the leadfaces' shouts, hurrying beneath the drooping, blackened houses. They had been the mansions of the faery silk weavers once. Now they were the houses of pickpockets and bloodletters and the poorest of the poor. Sometimes a woman leaning out of a window, or another boy in the street, would spot Pikey and shout, "Oy, pikey!" in a not-very-nice voice. Pikey always hurried faster then.

Pikey wasn't his real name. Or Thomas, either, for that matter. "Pikeys" were what folks called foreigners, and because Pikey had a face as brown as an old penny (whether from dirt or because he actually *was* a foreigner not even he knew), the name had stuck. As for Thomas, it was the name on the box he had come in, twelve years ago on a doorstep in Putney: *Thomas Ltd. Crackers and Biscuits. Premium quality.*

People had thought that funny once, coming from a cracker box. Pikey didn't think it was funny at all.

In the pigeon-choked space in front of St. Paul's Cathedral, a gang of boys accosted him.

"Give you a ha'penny if you show us your socket," the oldest and tallest one snarled. He wore a blue coat with brass buttons, much too big for him, and a pair of boots with popped toes. He looked like the leader.

The other boys crowded around, prodding Pikey, dirty faces pressing in. "Yeh, show us your socket! What happened, eh? Did you see something you weren't supposed to? Did Jenny Greenteeth pluck it out and string it up for a necklace?"

If Pikey'd had a socket he would have taken the boys' offer in an instant. A ha'penny could buy him a proper meal, let him sit in the warmth and stink of an inn and eat potatoes and gravy and gray boiled mutton until he burst. But he didn't have a socket, and the boys wouldn't like what they saw.

"Shove off. Leave me alone."

"Aw, come on, piker. Just a peek? Whada you say, fellas, you think we can see his brains through it? What say I pull off the patch and we get a look-see at his brains, all yellow and squishy inside."

The boys murmured their assent, some more readily than others. The gang leader stepped forward, reaching for Pikey's patch. Pikey braced himself for a fight.

"I said, shove *off!*" His voice went hard like a proper street rat's, but he was too short to make it count. The boy in the brass-button coat kept coming.

Pikey ducked away, ready to run, but two of the boys grabbed his arms and pinned them behind his back.

"You stay where you're put at," one of them whispered, close next to his ear.

"Help!" Pikey croaked. There were people everywhere. *Someone* would hear him. Or see. The spot in front of St. Paul's was one of the busiest in London, even in winter, even with the sky going black overhead. Costermongers shouted from their pushcarts, offering lettuces and cabbages and suspicious-looking roots. Peddlers haggled, servants bought. A red-and-gold striped cider booth stood not ten paces away, with a whole line of people waiting in front of it. They couldn't all be deaf.

"Help, *thief*!" he cried.

No one even glanced at him.

"Stop cryin' like a little pansy. We only want a quick look. Shut up, I say. Shut up, or you'll get us all in trouble." The leader planted a heavy fist in Pikey's stomach, and his next shout came out in a puff of white breath.

He hung for a second, gasping, his arms still clamped behind him. He felt the leader's fingers undoing the string of the eye patch, pulling it off.

"We only want a quick look—"

Pikey shut his eyes hard and threw himself back with all his strength. His head thudded against the head of the boy behind him and they both went down, rolling over the cobbles. Pikey landed on the other boy's stomach with a satisfying squelch and sprang back up, one hand covering the place where the patch had been, the other swinging wildly.

The leader struggled to his feet and spat. "You little cog splinter. I'll beat you blue—" He came at Pikey swiftly, the hobnails in his boots snapping against the ground.

"Pound 'im!" the boys shouted, jostling, forming a ring. "Pound 'is other eye out!"

Pikey didn't have time to think. He flung up both hands to protect himself. . . .

The boy in the brass-button coat stopped dead in his tracks. The other boys went silent.

Too late Pikey realized what he had done. The eye where the patch had been was bared for all to see. He felt the cold sliding against it. He knew how it looked, what they all saw—a flat, empty orb, gray as the frozen sky. No pupil. Nothing like a regular blind eye. Only endless, swirling gray.

For a moment Pikey was looking into two places at once and his brain practically screamed with the effort. London was on one side, cold and dark and swarming with people like so many shadow ants. But on the other side was a different place, a great, dead forest rising out of the snow. He couldn't hear anything of that world. He still heard London, though. Shouts. The clatter of a gas trolley. The gang leader cursing, backing away.

"Faery-touched," said the boy in the brass-button coat. *"Faery-touched, is this one!"*

Now people were paying attention. Pikey whirled, saw folks slowing their steps, staring, a veiled woman in black bombazine, one gloved hand clapped over her mouth. The whispers spread, fanning out around him. From the corner of his good eye, Pikey saw men slipping toward the spiderweb of streets that went off St. Paul's Church Yard, to the entrance of Fleet Street where the leadfaces stood. Somewhere not far away, a bell began to ring.

Pikey pushed his fist into his clouded eye. *Not again,* he thought. *Not twice in one day.* And then he ran, smashing between the people, toward the widest street he could see. Four leadfaces marched quickly past him in the opposite direction, toward the yells and the growing panic. Pikey had lost his patch, left it behind in the hand of the boy in the brass-button coat, but he didn't care. Not then. He put his head down and ran as fast and as hard as he could.

He ran until his breath rattled inside his ribcage. He ran until his muscles burned and his legs felt like bags of water. And when he finally raised his eyes from the cobbles, he found himself in a part of London he had never seen before.

He had gone in entirely the wrong direction. He must be miles from Spitalfields now, miles from the chemist's shop. Night was falling. The streets were emptying of the regular people, filling with the irregular, the debauched, the drunk, the gaudily dressed fops and hoop-skirted ladies painted up so heavily they resembled nightmarish clowns. Overhead, the streetlamps cast dim reddish halos.

The flame faeries that had been inside the lamps before the Ban had been replaced by brimstone bulbs, and these produced an ugly, bloody-looking light, but at least there was no more knocking and spitting, no more glowing faery faces trying to get the attention of the people below. Pikey was glad for it.

Stupid faeries. It served them right they had been sent away. He remembered how, a long time ago, Spitalfields had been swarming with them—faeries with spines, faeries with inky eyes and onion-white skin, with heads of barnacles and thorns, and so many fingers. You couldn't go anywhere without seeing one, and Pikey had lost count of all the times he had woken in his hole under the chemist's shop with his bootlaces knotted together, or with nettles wound into his hair. Well, now the faeries were being kicked out, and he hoped they all landed in bramble patches.

He continued to hurry, peering at everyone and wiping his nose. The pubs were bursting with light and riotous war songs. Some ways up ahead a door opened and a great fist punched out holding a filthy jabbering fool by the collar and depositing him in the green-tinged ice of a gutter. Closer, a street circus was setting up its hoops and props. An organ-grinder was playing a jangling, off-key tune. Pikey spotted a lady pulling a miniature hot-air balloon beside her, its basket filled with opera glasses and a fan and other necessaries. He saw someone wearing a pair of newfangled shoes, built of clockwork and powered by coal, that lifted your feet so that you didn't have to lift them yourself. The man who wore them was galumphing about like a two-ton elephant, and Pikey was careful to give him a wide berth.

He slowed to a walk, fishing in his pocket for the bread. His hand had dropped from his clouded eye, but he didn't care. He doubted he would be the first person noticed here. The streets were becoming wider. The crowds dwindled away and all went very quiet, the air somehow heavy, as if all the snow that was waiting to fall was pressing down on it, compacting it over the city. Only the occasional steam coach passed by now. Pikey looked up at the soaring stone buildings, with their spires and gables and wrought iron anti-faery gates.

He rounded a corner. He didn't know where he was, but it must have been a rich place. The houses here seemed absolutely bursting with light. It was almost as if there were no floors or walls inside them and they were simply great hollow shells, little suns burning within.

Traffic had picked up again. Well-bundled ladies and gentlemen were coming up the street, canes swinging, gowns whispering beneath heavy furs. Steam coaches and mechanical horse-and-fours rattled past, leaving swaths of coal smoke behind them. All were headed to the same destination—a great palace of a house, four floors and a green metal roof, and all of its windows, all the way to the roof, lit, punching golden holes in the night.

Pikey approached the house, gnawing at his bread. He watched from behind a lamppost as a great fat lady went up the steps to the door. She wore a delicate hat shaped like a fly and was practically dripping with diamonds. But she didn't look happy. In fact, she looked downright peeved. Pikey wondered how anyone could be peeved when they had so many diamonds. And going into such a bright, warm house. . . .

"Ah, the Wyndhammer War Ball," said a droopy, tucked-up gentleman, passing close by the lamppost. A very tall lady walked at his side, and he was hurrying to keep up. "What a dashing good bash this will be, don't you think, dear? Don't you?"

After a while, Pikey spotted the telltale red-and-blue of a leadface and slipped behind a coach wheel, walking along with it as it rumbled over the cobbles. The coach wheel was taller than he was and hid him right to the top of his head. The leadface marched past. As soon as he was gone, Pikey hurried back to the huge house and swung over the iron railing, onto the steps that went down to the servants' entrance. He didn't want to leave yet. It was getting colder, but the lights from the windows were so cheery. They shone down onto his face and he imagined he could almost feel their warmth. The panes were fogged right over it was so hot inside.

He sat down on the fourth step from the top and bit away at his bread. It was hard as a rock and full of gritty kernels that probably weren't flour. Pikey liked it quite a lot. The last carriage left. Faintly the sound of an orchestra drifted into the street. He heard muffled laughter and loud, happy voices.

And then he heard a different sound from the shadows at the bottom of the stairs. A scuttling, scraping noise, like knives dragging swiftly over stone. He sat up.

Was it a rat? The windows of the servants' hall were dark. No doubt everyone was in the kitchens, wiping and boiling and building towering platters of pork chops and hothouse fruits.

A steam coach turned onto the street, headlamps blazing. The light sliced through the railings, sending spokes of shadow spinning along the wall. In the blackness at the bottom of the steps, a pair of eyes glimmered. Two huge silver globes, there for a second, then gone.

Faery.

Pikey scooted up one step, muscles tense, ready to run. The noise came again, the sharp flutter, and this time it was accompanied by a weeping, thin and high, like a child crying.

Another steam coach coughed and sputtered up the street. The two globes lit again as the headlamps passed, then vanished into the dark. Whatever was at the bottom of the steps began to move.

It approached slowly, painfully, a pale slender thing dragging heavy black wings behind it like a cloak.

Pikey's heart skipped a beat. *That weren't no cobble spryte.*

The wings were huge, ruffled with dark, spiny feathers, and the blue-lipped mouth was riddled with teeth. A black tongue flicked from it every few seconds. But when Pikey peered at the faery it didn't look as if it were about to gnaw his leg off. Rather, it looked as if it were about to drip into a puddle. One of its wings hung limp, the feathers smashed. The bone was bent at a hideous angle.

Pikey eyed the creature as it pulled itself up the stairs, keeping his bread safely behind his back. The faery might not *seem* dangerous, but faeries could look however they wanted to look if it suited their fancy.

He wasn't about to fall for any hookem-snivey.

"Boy?" it said in a high, whistling voice. *"Boy?"*

Just like a baby, Pikey thought. He frowned.

"Boy?" It had reached the seventh step. It stretched a thin-fingered hand up toward Pikey, pleading.

"What d'you want?" Pikey asked gruffly. He shoved the bread into his pocket and glanced around to make sure no one was near. Fraternizing with faeries was dangerous. If anyone so much as smelled of spells or piskie herbs, it was off to Newgate, and Pikey had heard there was a kindly looking old man there in a butcher's apron, and he was always weeping, and he would weep and weep as he pulled your fingernails out, but he would interrogate you until you'd say anything. Then you'd be sent to a different prison. Or hanged. Whatever the case, you were in for it. Pikey had been in for it all day, and he'd had enough.

The faery continued up the steps, its round eyes locked on his.

"What?" Pikey snapped. "You can't have my bread if that's what you want. I ran a long way for it. Go away."

"Boy," it said, yet again. *"Wing."*

"Yeh, looks broken to me. Rotten luck." Some servant in the downstairs had probably caught it stealing and had smashed it with a frying pan. Served it right, too.

"Help." The faery was on the step below Pikey now, looking up at him with great mirror eyes that seemed to grow larger with every breath.

"I ain't helping you." Pikey turned his face away. His gaze flickered back. He didn't want to be awful. But he wasn't about to put his neck out for a faery. Someone might be watching from one of those glowing windows. A street sweeper might pass just in that instant. Pikey couldn't be seen with it. It was hard enough staying alive with one eye looking like a puddle of rain.

"Please help?" The voice was so human now; it sent a little stab through Pikey's heart despite himself. The faery was just bones, a few thin sticks wrapped in papery skin. And it was hurting. He wouldn't leave a dog like that. He wouldn't even leave a leadface like that.

He frowned harder and joggled his knee. Then he leaned forward and took the damaged wing in his hand. The faery shied ever so slightly at his touch, but it did not pull away.

"Fine," Pikey said. "But if someone sees, I'm going to shove you at 'em and get outta here, you hear me?"

The feathers felt smooth and oily between Pikey's fingers, strangely immaterial, like smoke. He felt gently along the bone. He didn't know a great deal about doctoring, but Bobby Blacktop, the old chemist's boy, had gotten run over by a gas trolley a year ago and had both his legs broken. Pikey had learned a few things from that.

Suddenly the faery sat up, ears twitching, as if picking up a sound only it could hear. *"Quickly,"* it hissed. *"Quickly!"*

"Ow, aren't you one to make demands. What's the hurry, then? Where you gotta be?" Pikey's fingers found the joint, clicked it back in place. "It was just banged out o' the socket is all. Is that better? Does it work now?"

The faery's eyelids snapped, once, across its eyes.

In a flash its wings unfurled, faster than Pikey would have thought possible. He jerked back. The faery peered at him a second longer, its tongue slithering between its teeth. Then it whirled, wrapping itself in its feathers. There was a brush of wind, a chorus of whispers, like many little voices calling to one another, and then the faery was gone.

It didn't exactly vanish. Pikey thought it might have, but it was more as if it had moved into a pocket, as if the stairs and the street and all of London were painted on the thinnest of veils and the faery had simply slipped behind it.

Pikey stared at the place where it had been. Then he stood quickly. Lights were coming on in the servants' hall below. He could hear voices raised in excitement, the clatter of metal. A hand began to fiddle with the lacy curtains over the window.

Time to go, Pikey thought. He vaulted over the railing and set off briskly along the side of the street.

But he had only taken a few steps when a deep, skull-shivering shudder almost tossed him from his feet. He stumbled. The shudder grew in strength, pounding and stamping louder than all the steam engines of King's Cross station, all going at once.

Pikey turned. It was the house. Fissures were racing up the windows, splitting smaller and smaller. The walls shook and swelled, as if something were straining against them from inside. And then, with an almighty shriek, every window in the house burst outward. All those bright windows, exploding into the night in sprays of gold. The roof blew into the sky. Stone rained down, glass and green metal and shreds of colored silk. Pikey yelled and raced into the street, dodging the falling debris.

An oil trolley skidded around him. Steam coaches honked, belching fumes. Men leaned out of vehicles, ready to shout at Pikey, but their words stuck in their throats. All eyes turned to Wyndhammer House.

Piercing wails were coming from within, swooping down the winter street. There another resounding *boom*. And then the house began to fall.

CHAPTER II
Hettie in the Land of Night

Six days and six nights Hettie and the faery butler had walked under the leafless branches of the Old Country, and still the cottage looked no closer than when they had first laid eyes on it.

Of course, Hettie didn't *know* if it had been six nights. It always felt like night in this place, or at least a gray sort of evening. The sky was always gloomy. The moon faded and grew, but it never went away. She trudged after the wool-jacketed faery, over roots and snowdrifts, and the little stone cottage remained in the distance, unreachable. A light burned in its window. The black trees formed a small clearing around it. Sometimes Hettie thought she saw smoke rising from the chimney, but whenever she really looked, there was nothing there.

"Where are we going?" she demanded, for the hundredth time since their arrival. She made her voice hard and flat so that the faery butler wouldn't think she was frightened. He better think she could smack him if she wanted to. He better.

The faery ignored her. He walked on, coattails flapping in the wind.

Hettie glared and kicked a spray of snow after him. Sometimes she wondered if he even knew. She suspected he didn't. She suspected that behind the clockwork that encased one side of his face, behind the cogs and the green glass goggle, he was just as lost and afraid as she was. But she didn't feel sorry for him. *Stupid faery.* It was his fault she was here. His fault she hadn't jumped when her brother Bartholomew had shouted for her. She might have leaped to safety that night in Wapping, leaped back into the warehouse and England. She might have gone home.

She wrapped her arms around herself, feeling

the red lines through the sleeves of her nightgown, feeling the imprints the faeries had put there so she could be a door. *Home.* The word made her want to cry. She pictured Mother sitting on her chair in their rooms in Old Crow Alley, head in her hands. She pictured Bartholomew, the coal scuttle, the cupboard bed. The herbs, drying above the potbellied stove. Pumpkin in her checkered dress. *Stupid faeries. Stupid butler and stupid Mr. Lickerish and stupid doorways that led into other places and didn't let you out again.*

She paused to catch her breath and noticed she had been clamping her teeth shut so hard they hurt. She wiped her nose on the back of her hand and looked up.

The cottage was still far away. The woods were very quiet. The faery butler barely made any sound at all as he walked, and when Hettie's own loud feet had stopped, the whole snowbound world seemed utterly silent.

She squinted, straining to make out the details of the cottage. There was something about it. Something not right. The light in the window did nothing to dispel the hollow, deserted look of the place. And the way the trees seemed to curl away from it . . . She closed her eyes, listening to her heartbeat and the whispering wind. She imagined walking forward under the trees, hurrying and spinning, gathering speed. Her back was to the cottage. Then she was facing it, and for an instant she was sure it was not a house at all, but a rusting, toothy mousetrap with a candle burning in it, winking, like a lure.

"Come *on*." The faery butler was at her side, dragging her along. "We haven't got all of forever. Come on, I say!"

She stumbled after him. The cottage was normal again, silent and forbidding in its clearing.

"I can walk by myself," Hettie snapped, jerking away her arm. But she was careful not to stray too far from his side. They really didn't have all of forever. In fact, Hettie wondered how much longer they could go on like this. They had nothing to eat but the powdery gray mushrooms that grew in the hollows of the trees, and even those were becoming scarcer as they went. There were no streams in this wood, so all they had to drink was the snow. They melted it in their hands and licked the icy water as it ran over their wrists. It tasted of earth and made Hettie's teeth chatter, but it was better than no water at all.

Hettie crossed another snarl of black roots, stomped over another stretch of crusty snow. She was so hungry. She was used to that from Bath, but there it was different. Her mother was in Bath, washing and scrubbing and making cabbage tea, and Hettie had always known that she'd never let her and Bartholomew starve. Hettie doubted the faery butler would care much if she starved to death. He didn't give her anything. He hadn't told her to eat the mushrooms or melt the snow. She had watched him and had stuck her nose up at him, and then she had gotten so hungry she'd *had* to copy him. But what would happen when there were no mushrooms left? What would happen when the snow all melted?

When she felt she couldn't walk another step, she stopped.

"I'm tired," she said in the sharp, nettled voice that back home would have gotten her a pat on the head from Mother and a silly face from Barthy. "Let's stop. Let's stay here for tonight. We're not getting any closer to that dumpy old house and I want to sleep."

The faery kept walking. He didn't even glance back.

She bounded after him. "You know, what if someone lives in that cottage? Have you thought about that? And what if they don't like us? What'll happen then?"

The faery kept his eyes locked straight ahead. "I suspect we'll die. Of boredom. I've heard tell there's a little girl in these woods, and she follows folk about and jabbers at them until their ears shrivel up and they go deaf."

Hettie slowed, frowning at the faery's back. She hoped he would drown in a bog.

She thought about that for a while. If he did—drown in a bog—it would be frightening. He would lie under the water, and his long white face and white hands would be all that showed out of the murk. And perhaps his green eye, too, glowing even a thousand years after he was dead. She wouldn't want to see it, but she didn't suppose she would object much if it happened. This was his fault, after all.

Finally, when even the faery butler was breathless and dragging his feet, they stopped. Hettie collapsed in a heap in the snow. The faery butler sat against a tree. The woods were dead-dark now. On her first night in the Old Country, Hettie had slept against a tree, too, thinking that the roots might be warmer than the ground, trees being alive and all. She soon learned better. The trees here weren't like English trees. They weren't rough and mossy like the oak in Scattercopper Lane. They were cold and smooth as polished stone, and she had woken with the ghastly feeling that the roots had begun to wrap around her while she slept, as if to swallow her up.

The snow was cold, but at least she was not in danger of being eaten by a tree. She curled up for the seventh time and went to sleep.

The sound of footfalls woke her.

At first she thought the faery butler must be up again, pacing, but when she peered around the tree, she saw he was lying still. His gangly legs were propped up akimbo, long white hands limp in the snow. He made only very small sounds as he slept, little wheezing breaths that formed clouds in the air.

Hettie sat bolt upright. Something was moving through the trees, quickly and stealthily toward them.

Tap-tap, snick-snick. Hard little feet on roots, then on snow, limping closer.

She remembered the faeries she had seen the day they had arrived in the Old Country, the wild, hungry ones with their round, bright eyes. They had all leaped and swarmed around her, poking and prodding until the faery butler had chased them off with a knife. For a few nights they had followed, slinking along at the edge of sight, darting around the trees and giggling, but after a while they had seemed to tire of the strangers and had vanished back into the woods.

Only the cottage remained.

Hettie crawled around the tree trunk. The faery butler was still asleep. She poked him in his ribs, hard.

He grunted. Slowly his face turned toward her, but his eye remained shut. The green-glass one was dull, tarnished lenses loose across its frame. Hettie shivered.

She looked back around the tree.

And found herself staring straight into the red-coal eyes of a gray and peeling face.

"Meshvilla getu?" it said, and placed one long finger to its lips.

Hettie made a little noise in her throat. The skin of its cheeks curled like ash from a burned-up log. Its breath was cold, colder than the air. It blew against her, and she could feel it freezing in a slick sheen on her nose. It smelled rotten, wet, like a slimy gutter.

"Meshvilla?"

She wanted to run, to scream. Panic welled in her lungs. She couldn't tell if the gray thing's voice was threatening or wheedling, but it was without doubt a dark voice, a quiet, windy voice that prickled up her arms.

"No," she squeaked, because back in Bath that had

always been the right answer for changelings like her. "No, go away."

The creature pushed closer, eyeing her. Then its horrid hands were feeling over her cheeks, running through the branches that grew from her head. Bone-cold fingers came to rest on her eyes.

Hettie screamed. She screamed louder than she had ever screamed in her life, but in that vast black forest it was just a little baby's wail. It was enough to wake the faery butler, though. He sat up with a start, green clockwork eye clicking to life. It swiveled once, focused on the gray-faced faery.

The faery butler jerked himself to his feet. "*Valentu! Ismeltik relisanyel?*"

The gray face turned, its teeth bared. Hettie heard it hiss. "*Misalka,*" it said. "Englisher. Leave her. Leave her to me."

Hettie began to shake. The long, cold fingers were pressing down. An ache sprang up behind her eyes. She knew she should fight, lash out with all her might, but she could not make herself move.

The faery butler had no such troubles. A knife

dropped from inside his sleeve and he swung it in a brilliant arc toward the other faery, who let out a grunt of surprise. It was all Hettie needed. She threw herself to the ground and began to crawl desperately around the base of the tree. Once on the other side, she wrapped her arms around the trunk and peered in terror at the battling faeries.

They moved back and forth across the snow, swift and silent. The faery butler was fast. Faster than rain. She had seen him fight back in London, seen him use that cruel knife on Bartholomew, but right now she was glad for his skill. He moved his long limbs with grace, whirling and slashing, liquid in the moon- light. The blade spun, streaking down over and over again toward the other faery, who barely managed to get out of its path.

"No!" it screamed, in English. "You fool and trai- tor, what are you—?"

The knife grazed it. Bits of gray skin flew away on the wind. Hettie saw that underneath there was only black, like new coal.

She turned her face into the tree, squeezing her

eyes shut. She heard a shriek, a dull thud. Then a whispering sound and a long, long breath fading away. After that, there was nothing.

It was a long time before Hettie dared peek around the trunk. She listened to the faery butler, pacing in the snow and panting. She wondered if she should say something to him, but she didn't dare do that either. He seemed suddenly frightening and dangerous. After a while she heard him lean against the tree, and after another while, his slow, whistling breaths. Only then did she inch from her hiding place.

The faery butler was still again, his green eye dark. The snow between the roots was trampled. At the faery's feet lay what looked like a heap of ashes and old clothes. Already they sparkled with frost.

She edged over to the heap. It didn't look like a faery anymore. It didn't look like anything, really. Nothing to be afraid of. She nudged the pile with her toe. It rustled and gave way, the jerkin and boots collapsing over a delicate shell of cinders.

She wondered what sort of creature it had been.

She didn't know if it had been a woman-faery or a man-faery. She had never seen a faery like it in Bath, falling to ashes.

The moon was out like every night, and it shone through the branches, glinting on something in the clothes. Hettie knelt and shuffled about in the pile. Her fingers touched warmth. She jerked back, wiping her hand violently on her sleeve. *Blood? Was it blood?* But it couldn't be. If there was frost, the blood would have gone cold by now. She leaned in again, brushing away the rest of the ashes with the hem of her nightgown. Her hand closed around the warmth. She brought it up to her eye, examining it . . . and found herself looking into another eye—a wet, brown eye with a black pupil.

Hettie let out a muffled shriek. She almost dropped it. But it was only a necklace. The eye was some sort of stone, set into a pendant, a pockmarked disk on a frail chain. The pendant lay heavily in her palm, the warmth seeping into her fingers.

She stared at it. She hadn't felt anything warm in so long. She ran her thumb over the stone. It looked precisely like a human eye. There was even a spark in it, a knowing little light like the sort in a real person's eye. She couldn't tell what its expression was, because there were no eyebrows or face to go with it, but she thought it looked sad somehow. Lonely.

She peered even closer.

Behind her the faery butler shifted, white hands scraping over the snow. Somewhere in the woods, branches skittered.

Hettie tucked the pendant into the neck of her dress and darted back around the tree. She went to sleep then, and the eye kept her warm the whole night long.

The next morning, when she woke, the forest seemed to have lightened several shades, fading, like the pictures on coffee tins when they were left too long in the sun. The clouds no longer hung so low in the sky. The trees didn't look so close together. The cottage was still a hundred strides away, but when Hettie and the faery butler took their first step toward it, it was quite distinctly only ninety-nine. A short while later they were halfway there.

No light burned in the window anymore. The door hung open on its hinges, showing blackness. The house appeared even emptier and more desolate than before.

When they were only a few steps away, Hettie glanced back over her shoulder. What she saw made her whirl all the way around and stare.

Their footprints extended back in a thin line into the woods. And then the forest floor became packed with them. Thousands upon thousands of prints, winding between the trees—her small ones, and the faery butler's long, narrow ones—going back and forth and round and round, trampling one another and never arriving anywhere.

A tangle of footprints under the very same trees.

CHAPTER III
The Sylph's Gift

GOBLINS were in the walls of Wyndhammer House—two of them, hurtling down the servants' corridor that hid behind the polished paneling of the ballroom. They streaked under fizzing oil lamps, quick as winks in the dimness. The corridor was hot, narrow, barely wide enough for the goblins to run in single file. Spools of wire lay on the floor. Iron bells lined the ceiling. It was an old precaution, meant to frighten off invading faeries, but it had been for naught. The wires had all been snipped.

The goblins were breathing hard, gasping as much from the thick air as from excitement.

"Did you see their faces?" the shorter one exclaimed, in a sort of breathless chuckle. His skin was cracked and brown like the bark of a tree, and he wore a red leather jerkin with copper bottles clinking all along the belt. The bottles were labeled such things as *Soldier Illusion, Needlewoman Illusion, Weeping Waifs Illusion. . . .*

The other goblin grunted. He was gaunt and pointy, the precise opposite of the short one. "Made 'em scared right enough," he said, leaping a tangle of wire. "It's what we came for. If'n we get out of here before the servants come, it'll all be a good night's work."

The short goblin chuckled again, then wheezed. "A good night's work, he says. A good night's work. I should say it was a good night's work. All those puffed-up pigeons, all pinned up with bottle caps. Won't be going off to battle so happily, will they be? Not so happily at all."

The goblins skidded around a corner and pounded down a flight of steep, worm-eaten stairs. The walls went from brass and gleaming wood to damp, mossy stone. At the bottom of the stairs was a long, dripping cellar, disappearing into blackness.

The short goblin wouldn't stop talking. "The Sly King'll be very pleased with us, don't you think? Don't you, Nettles? Most all of London's up there. All the important parts, at least. All frightened so bad the wax in their whiskers melted. Shouldn't wonder if the Sly King pays us a small fortune when we get back. Shouldn't wonder."

The goblins dashed to the end of the cellar and into a vaulted room, footsteps echoing. Wine barrels lined the walls. Somewhere high above in the house, they could hear a commotion, banging and thuds and raised voices. Then screams.

"Oh, the Sly King, the Sly King, in his towers of ash and wind," the short goblin sang under his breath. "How much d'you think he'll pay, Nettles? How much d'you—"

The goblin named Nettles spun and knocked the shorter one firmly on the head. *"Don't* count your frogs before they're hatched. Nobody knows what the Sly King'll do. Nobody sees. We'll know what we get once we're safe on our way. *Milkblood?*" His voice was suddenly loud, booming under the stone vault. "Milkblood, get us out of here!"

Slowly a small, hunched shape slid out of the shadows.

"Has all gone well?" it whispered. "Will he be pleased with us?"

Knuckly branches grew from its head instead of hair. At first it seemed to be a child, all bones and huge, hungry eyes. But as it approached, the lines became visible around its mouth, the grooves in its corpse-white skin. It was an old woman. An ancient Peculiar.

The short goblin shuddered in disgust. Even Nettles darkened, his brows pinching.

"Not if we're caught," he growled, and opened his mouth wide. One cheek was swollen, the inside pressing against the rows of teeth. A box had been mounted there, grown into the red flesh. Both his hands went for it, and he fiddled with it, coughing. A small glass bottle rolled onto his tongue and he spat it out. It was filled with a dark, luminous liquid. He sent it spinning through the air. "Drink. Fast. Get us away from here."

The Peculiar's hand shot out, snatching the bottle. Her fingers were filthy. All of her was filthy, slicked with a layer of grime. Her bare feet stuck out from under a ragged ball gown. Her arms were stamped with wriggling red lines, like tattoos.

"He'll be pleased with me. Oh, he'll be pleased with me." She sounded as if she were begging.

She uncorked the bottle and gulped it down. Black liquid dribbled over her chin. When there was nothing left, she took a deep breath, dragging in the air. Then she smashed the bottle to pieces at her feet.

Nettles glanced over his shoulder, shifting from foot to foot. They would be searching soon—servants, lords, Englishers, leadfaces. They would search the house, corridor by corridor. They would come here. He barely blinked as an inky line began to trace itself along the pale woman's form. It whispered all the way around her. Then it pulled away. The air shivered, as if being beaten by invisible wings. A door appeared, a very small one, only a foot wide on either side of her. Nettles could just glimpse a seascape behind her, black cliffs and rolling, white-capped waves and a midnight sky full of stars.

"By *stone*, you're getting worse by the day," the short goblin said. "Soon we'll be crawling into the Old Country on hands and knees."

"Shut up, Grout," said Nettles, but his scowl went even deeper.

The woman made a pitiful face, twisting her hands through the soiled lace of her gown. "Yes, watch your mouth. Watch who you're speaking to."

Grout spat. "Oh, and who's that? You're just a slave. You're worse than a slave. You're a *Peculiar*."

"I am the King's servant!" the old woman cried. "Show me the dignity!" But that only seemed to goad Grout further and he started prancing, rattling his bottles.

"You're just a sla-ave!" he sang, hopping around her. "Just a slave, just a slave, just a *rotten slave*."

The pale woman looked to Nettles, her eyes drooping and watery. "Make him stop!" she said.

"Slave, slave, slave!" Grout screeched.

The old woman's eyes became imploring. "I used to be his favorite."

That was that. Nettles's lips twisted into a sneer. "Well, you're obviously not anymore," he said, and it was as if he had slapped the old woman.

She drew back, staring. "How dare you?" she said. "How dare you *both*?" She began to shake. She was so small and old, but she was trembling with fury.

And then suddenly a door banged open at the far end of the cellar and voices echoed, loud as gunshots. Lamplight danced along the walls, coming closer.

"I'll show you," the pale woman snarled. "I'll show you what I can do." She stepped toward the goblins.

"No!" Nettles barked, but too late.

A cold wind whipped into the cellar. And suddenly the space was filled with wings. They slashed past Nettles's face. With a lurch, the door expanded.

"Enough!" he screamed over the flapping wings. He dashed forward, through the door, onto the cliffs. "Come on, both of you, or we're all dead!"

The old woman started to walk. "Say you're sorry!" she shrieked. "Say you're sorry!" With every step she took, the door grew, the feathers whirling wilder and darker. The blackness had reached the ceiling. Bits of dust and stone sifted down. The stars of the Old Country shone into the cellar, glimmering in the puddles on the floor.

"*Now*, you dimwits! D'you want the whole house coming down on our heads? Get in!"

Shouts. The glow of the lamps grew, spreading. Shadows appeared on the walls. The shadows began to run.

Even Grout looked frightened now. "I—I didn't mean nothing by it! I didn't, I'm sorry!"

But the pale woman wasn't listening. "I used to be his favorite," she said. "I am the Door to Bath. I am the greatest door of the age. He'll be pleased with me again."

She began to run, straight toward the oncoming English.

"Come back!" Nettles shouted. "Come back!"

The wings swelled, darker than night. The ceiling gave a wrenching grunt. Grout leaped onto the cliffs.

A deafening screech filled the cellar. It came from

Wyndhammer House above and the hall full of heat and dancers. Feet, hundreds of them, battered the floor, pounding on and on like thunder.

Wyndhammer House began to fall.

The bells of St. Paul's were tolling thirty-five minutes past midnight, but Pikey was not even thinking about going to bed. He scratched through the ankle-deep mud, his shoulders up around his ears to keep them from freezing. He didn't count the strikes of the bells.

There was no moon in the sky. The clouds drifted, black and endless, snagging on the spires of St. Paul's, on weather vanes and gable tips. It was so dark.

Only dead folk and the fay come out on moonless nights. Dead folk and those soon to be dead. Anyone wanting to keep the blood inside his veins and the coat on his back would not be found alone in the streets after eleven o'clock. But Pikey didn't have a choice. He *needed* to find his patch.

After the fall of Wyndhammer House he had fled straight back to the square in front of St. Paul's. He had searched for hours, bent double, picking through the muddy cobbles like an old farmer seeding a field. He was on his seventh time now. The cold was sinking into his bones. His legs had gone stiff as posts. But he couldn't find his patch. It was gone, taken away or trampled deep. When a gang of draft dodgers came, whooping and shouting into the square, Pikey ran off in a fright.

He limped toward the warren of alleys that led to Spitalfields, rubbing his hands to keep the dull ache of the cold away. He tried to stay in the shadows, darting from doorway to doorway, running whenever he heard footsteps. He didn't know what had happened at Wyndhammer House, but he would bet his boots it had something to do with faeries, and he was beginning to be afraid. What if someone had seen him there? What if they were following him, right now? He couldn't be caught like this. Not with his bad eye in full sight.

He tried to go faster. The city became a beast after dark; the streets were its throats and the graveyards were its bellies, and ever since things had started going rotten between the English and the faeries the beast had gotten hungrier. The leadfaces had appeared first, hired by Parliament to chase the faeries from the city and then gather soldiers to fight them once they'd fled. After them had come the highwaymen and gunslingers, the thugs and ruffians and faery hunters with their iron teeth and packs full of knives and nets. Since the Ban had been declared they had been popping up in London like mushrooms. They set about in the night, searching for any fay that had not already left. Sometimes they found one. Just last week Pikey had heard of a whole colony of nymphs and water sprytes discovered in the Whitechapel sewers, hiding in the green and stagnant water. Where they were now Pikey didn't know, but he did not want to join them.

He was just turning the corner at Glockner's Inn, shuffling along the edge of the gutter, when he saw the girl.

His heart stopped, just like that, as if it had frozen stiff.

She was standing about ten feet away, staring

at him. But she was not in the street. Not with the cobbles under her feet and the houses and blackened chimneys of London at her back. Behind her were trees and snow. *Moonlight.*

"Wot the—" Pikey breathed. In all the time he'd had the clouded eye, he had only ever seen three things through it: a long wooden staircase with a guttering light at its top; a gray-and-peeling face, leaning close, leering with red-coal eyes; and snowy woods. There had never been a girl before. Never a child in only a nightgown, standing barefoot in the snow as if it were nothing.

The girl took a step toward him.

Pikey's brain made an odd, twisting lurch as it tried to grasp what was happening. She seemed to be above him, and he on the ground, looking up. For a second he was not sure if he was standing or falling.

He leaned against the inn's wall, head down, gasping lungsful of frigid air. When he looked up she was hurrying toward him, her nightgown flapping. She was so pale. She seemed to glow in the darkness. One of her nightgown sleeves was crumpled and pulled up her arm, and Pikey saw that the skin underneath was twined with red lines, like tattoos. He jerked back. She stooped down.

It made him sick all over again. His stomach lurched, and he shut his eyes as hard as he could. When he opened them, she was so close he could see every pore and vessel in her papery skin. She lifted one finger and brushed it over his clouded eye.

He tried to dodge her, scraping his back on the rough stones. He tried to swat her, to tell her to keep her bleeming fingers to herself, but his hand only swept the smoky air of the street.

She was just a child, he saw, even younger than he was. She had twigs for hair, and eyes so large and black they looked like drops of ink, and—

Oh no.

He knew what she was. Not a human child.

"Get out of here," he said, his voice strangled. "Shove off, before—"

Please, please don't let a leadface come now. . . .

The girl reached for him again. He could actually feel her thumb this time, flat against his eye. He lurched forward, fists swinging.

Her hand was still on his eye, but she was not there, not in London. She did not flinch at his onslaught, and though he moved forward several steps she was still in front of him. He gritted his teeth, shouldered toward her, tried to push her. She didn't even blink.

Then, somewhere behind her in the dark wood, Pikey saw movement, a silent rushing. The girl's face wrinkled with fear. Her other hand came up, little fingers reaching straight for his eye.

The moon vanished. So did the trees. He was alone again in a dark and empty street.

Pikey ran all the way back to the chemist's alley, ignoring the pain in his legs. He crawled into his hole and wrapped himself in his old blankets. The air was cold enough to freeze the skin off his cheeks, but he barely felt it. He lay in the dark, shivering and worrying. When he could bear to, he opened his clouded eye and looked out.

The girl wasn't there anymore. Neither were the woods. All he saw was blackness and the occasional slash of light. He put his hand over the eye again and tried to think of stoves and hams and happy, smiling faces.

Finally he slept.

A sound in the alley woke him. For an instant a deep pit opened in his stomach and he was hearing the feet again, *tap-tap, tap-tap,* limping toward him across the cobbles. He smelled the frost and the moss and the haunting burned-sugar scent of caramel apples. He saw the blood. . . .

He shook himself and sat up an inch, careful not to knock his head on the boards. It was still night. He couldn't have been asleep more than an hour. Keeping his blanket around his ears, he peeked out of the hole. He slept in his clothes of course, in his cap and jacket and three pairs of socks. But he had been cold before he had even woken up. Now he was freezing. All the warm, foul-smelling air slipped from under his bedding in a flicker of steam.

He scanned the alley, shivering. The cobbles were

slick with ice, the air clear and frozen. He waited, straining to see what might have woken him.

Suddenly the dark lantern swung over the chemist's door.

Pikey started. Something was there. Not slow and limping, but quick, moving in bursts of speed, a ragged shadow on the wall, then closer, at the newel stone of the shop.

He jerked himself back into his hole. He opened his mouth, ready to shout for the chemist, his wife, the lock picker up the lane, everyone in Spitalfields. But then he saw it.

It was the faery. The faery from Wyndhammer House. It came swooping up to the entrance of Pikey's hole, inky feathers flowing behind it. It paused, its head snapping to and fro, sniffing. Then it focused on Pikey, and its mouth opened in a smile that was all needle teeth and sickly black tongue.

Pikey sat bolt upright, and this time he did knock his head against the ceiling.

"*Boy*," it said. Not a question anymore. A confirmation. It had found him.

"What is it you *want*?" Pikey hissed, shooting a look at the chemist's door. The orange light was gone from around it. That meant the fire was out. That meant it was well past four in the morning. The chemist would be waking soon.

"Go away!" Pikey flapped his hands at the creature. "*Shoo!* If someone sees you here, I'm dead. We're both dead, and it'll be your fault."

He thought of the leadfaces. The chemist with his blunderbuss, and the faery hunters with their mouths full of spikes. A horrid panic began to tighten around his lungs.

The faery didn't move. It stood in the entrance to the hole, still smiling that ghastly, uneven smile.

"Look," Pikey whispered, backing up into his blankets. "I helped you at that big house and that's all fine now, all right? No debts. You don't have to be visiting." He lowered his voice even further. "A faery hunter'll come. If someone sees you, he'll come, and he'll put you through a meat grinder. Faeries are *banned* in London. Banned!"

The faery cocked its head, still smiling. Then it

opened one thin-fingered hand and held something out to Pikey.

It was pitch-black in Pikey's hole. The lantern above the shop door had long gone out, but he didn't need it. Because the faery held in its hand a gem, large as a goose's egg, and it seemed to fill the freezing space with its own cold, gray light. Tendrils of silver filigree wrapped around it. Its insides were deep purple, veined and splintered. Its outside was smooth as glass.

Pikey stared at the gem. *Oh, that's worth a dozen pounds, that gleamer is. Or a hundred.* He could buy a caramel apple with it. He could buy a *bushel* of caramel apples. He could march right up to one of those pretty painted carts with the steam curling off it and the apples behind the glass, and he could buy the whole thing, aprons and all.

Pikey reached out and ran a finger over the stone.

"Boy," the faery said again, and this time it took Pikey's hand and wrapped it around the gem. Pikey looked from stone to faery and back again. His heart was making odd little bumps against his ribs.

"It's for me?" he breathed. He could already see it all: running away, finding someplace good, someplace where there were thick warm socks and a stove and people who didn't only kick at him and shoo him away when he walked too close, and—

Coach wheels rattled in Bell Lane. Iron horseshoes hammered the cobbles. The faery's smile vanished. It looked at Pikey an instant longer, its mirror-eyes wide and limpid. Then it whirled, black wings sweeping, and disappeared down the alley.

Pikey watched it go, the gemstone heavy in his hand. The gem was very cold. But it was solid, too, reassuring like nothing he had ever held before. He wanted to laugh, holding it. He wanted to whoop and yell and dance up the alley, and tell all the few people he knew that he was richer than them and the landlord put together. He stared at the gem a second longer, cupping it in his hands and watching his breath cloud around it. Then, with a start, he realized what he was holding and clutched it to his chest. He looked sharply up the alley. He wriggled into his hole and wrapped himself in his blankets, the gem hard against his heart, like a piece of good luck.

He did not dream of apples that night, as much as he would have liked to. He dreamed of the branch-haired girl. The huge dark trees surrounded her, leaning down. Her flimsy nightgown flapped in the wind. She was walking, bent and weary, straight toward him, but she never seemed to get any closer. And she looked so sad. So sad and alone under those soaring black trees.

CHAPTER IV
The Merry Company

IN a shadowy castle at the edge of a sounding sea, a figure sat in a chair where four halls met. Water and starlight splashed through unglazed windows, but none of it touched him. The chair was high, and its back was turned so that you could not see the figure sitting in it unless you stood on tiptoe and peeked around its edge.

Nettles and Grout would not have dared peek around its edge for anything in England or the Old Country. They waited nervously, shuffling their feet, and all they saw of the figure were his long, pale fingers, toying with something glinting like glass.

"*Mi Sathir?*" said Nettles at last. "*Mi Sathir*, we did as you told us. The illusion in Wyndhammer House? All done, just the way you wanted it."

The pale hands fell still.

"Yessir," said Grout, trying to sound brave. He nudged Nettles in the ribs. "Very satisfactrilly, too, if I daresay. There weren't a fellow in the room what weren't afraid of his own shadow. And all them generals and lieutenants in *Her Majesty's Army* . . ." He spoke the words with exaggerated contempt. "All standing there gawping. Oh, they'll make a sight on the battle-field. They'll be too frightened to lift a gun against you, *Sathir*. Won't be much of a fight."

The figure in the chair laughed, a high, clear sound, like a bell. Then he spoke, his voice soft and lively. "No. It won't be, will it. They will not fight because half of them are dead, yes? You killed them when you let my little Milkblood open her door under Wyndhammer House. She's dead, too, by the way. The leadfaces found her body under the rubble." The figure laughed again, quietly, to himself.

The goblins exchanged looks, and if their

bark-brown skin could go pallid, it did. Nettles tried to say something, choked.

"*Sathir,*" he stammered. "*Sathir,* we didn't, we—"

"You were supposed to frighten the English," the figure in the chair said. "That is what I told you to do. A parlor trick to give them a taste of what was to come. I did *not* tell you to fuel the patriotic fires of the entire country by blowing up half their aristocracy. You've rather ruined everything."

He sounded as if he were smiling, as if he found it all unbearably droll.

Grout's eyes darted to Nettles. Then he began to jabber. "No, *Sathir,* oh no, we didn't fuel no fires! Leastaways, *I* didn't. It was Nettles here as did. *He* was being horrid to the old Peculiar, called her all sorts of awful names. Oh, *Sathir,* it weren't me, I swear it weren't!"

"Go away." The figure in the chair laughed, and the sound echoed down the four halls, chilly and gray. "Go away, I've heard enough."

His long fingers snapped together. At the end of one of the halls, two women materialized, richly dressed and wearing beaked masks. One had six pale arms. The other had a key protruding from her back. They glided forward without a sound.

"What shall we do with them, *Sathir*?" they said, and the voices that came from behind the masks crackled like sparks.

Another laugh. One slender white hand lifted the glass object again, spinning it idly. "I don't know. What does one do these days with people one doesn't like? Something ghastly, I hope. Something truly ghastly."

Hettie and the faery butler stayed in the cottage for what felt like a very long time. Hettie couldn't decide exactly *how* long. There were no clocks in the Old Country, or train schedules, and even if there had been, Hettie suspected they wouldn't have made any sense. Time in these woods seemed to run a different path. Every night Hettie would go to sleep, and every night she would wake up and wander through the house, and watch the sky go from black to very black, but it didn't really *feel* like days were going by.

Outside in the forest, the seasons never changed. The snow was always on the ground, and no new snow ever fell. Hettie could still see their tracks whenever she looked out a lead-paned window. The labyrinth of tracks going round and round to nowhere.

Ever since the fight with the gray-faced creature, the faery butler had become very silent. The first day they had set foot in the cottage he had propped himself up against the wall just inside the door. He had barely stirred since. To begin with, Hettie had stayed with him, close to his knife and his pale sinewy arms. But as the days went by and all he did was creep out to drink snow and eat the gray mushrooms from the cracks in the trees, Hettie decided *she* ought to do something else. Bartholomew would come for her eventually, but until he did she thought it would be better to be busy. And she might as well be busy exploring the cottage. The thing that had lived here was dead, after all. It was a heap of ash a hundred steps away and perhaps already completely carried off by the wind. There was nothing to be afraid of.

So one morning, while the faery butler was

outside, Hettie went to the end of the passage. It was beam-and-plaster of the sort one would find in a regular cottage. At the end were two doors and a steep wooden staircase leading up. One door was painted blue. The other was painted red.

She tried the blue door first. It opened into a little room that probably ought to have been a kitchen but was utterly bare. There was a stone fireplace, which explained the chimney, and nothing else. The floor was perfectly swept. The walls, though cracked and pitted, were whitewashed. Not even the flat Hettie had lived in back in England had been so bare. At least there had been *things* in it, bottles and bowls and Mother's wash wringer and Mother. Even just a spiderweb in a corner. But not here. Hettie hadn't seen a spider since the day she had arrived. Not even a beetle. Not even a bird in the iron gray sky.

Why would such an ugly faery have such a very neat house? Hettie wondered what it had done for a living.

She walked around the room several times, looked out the window, peered up the chimney, and satisfied that it really was a bare, empty room, went back into the passage. She tried the red door next. It opened into a low, filthy room, as black as the inside of a chimney. Rubbish lay heaped in the corners. The light that forced its way through the grimy window barely penetrated the dark at all, and the air was close and foul. It smelled of moss and brackish water.

She took a few steps in. She could dimly make out a wooden chair in the middle of the room, in front of a wooden table. She took a few more steps, and looked back over her shoulder to make sure the door was still open. It seemed suddenly very far away. She approached the table. Tools covered it, and it dripped with what looked like seaweed. Hettie's eyes narrowed. There were hammers and pliers and odd hooked instruments, and many pieces of thick, wrinkled old paper. A gust came through the door suddenly, rustling the papers, and Hettie saw that they were scrawled with writing and pictures. Pictures of eyes, eyes from all angles, whirls of ink, the veins and nerves like gnarled branches. They seemed to watch her, frowning and glaring and weeping. Hettie shivered and pushed all the papers into a heap and fled, closing the red door tightly behind her.

She didn't go into that room after that. She would have gone into the blue room often. She asked the faery butler to come in and build a fire. He didn't. She sat down next to him in the passage and told him he might build some chairs and a table, too, but he never answered.

Hettie didn't mind. As long as the red door stayed closed, she was all right on her own. The necklace she had picked from the gray face's remains was always inside her nightgown, flat against her skin, and it reminded her that the thing that had lived here was gone and would not appear suddenly in a corner or hurry down the shadowy staircase. Sometimes, when the cottage felt particularly lonely and the faery butler wouldn't say a word, or even look at her, she took to clutching the pendant to keep from being frightened.

The metal was always cold to the touch, but the stone . . . It was always warm.

〜〜〜

Hettie found the light when she went to the top of the stairs. At least, she felt fairly certain it was the light she had seen. She had first spotted it in London, in the warehouse. The light had been twinkling in the cottage's front window then, only a few feet above the ground. Now it was at the top of a long, winding stair, in a window that looked down onto the forest from what seemed like a hundred feet up. The light had come from a candle and something had blown it out.

The candle was yellow and greasy looking. Reddish veins ran just under its surface. Hettie wondered what would happen if she lit it again. She thought of having the candle downstairs to keep the night away.

She reached out to touch it.

And then she heard a sound. *Bells.* Bells, ringing in the woods.

Her eyes went wide as teacups. "Someone's coming," she whispered. And in a wink she was running for the stairs, down, down into the cottage.

"Someone's coming!" she shouted, leaping the last five steps. The faery butler was still propped against

the wall. He didn't move at the sound of her voice.
She barreled past him.

*Barthy. It has to be Barthy. He's had weeks and weeks to find
me. . . .*

The bells were nearer now, almost in the clearing.
She heard the sound of hooves, crunching through
snow, and voices, and high and windy laughter. She
slid back the bolt and opened the door a crack.

Not Bartholomew's voice.

She peeked out.

Not Bartholomew.

A company of riders was coming through the trees
toward the cottage. They looked all black-and-white
at first—black riders on white steeds, or white riders
on black steeds—and with the dark branches interlac-
ing behind them and the snow beneath their hooves,
it was as if they were a living extension of the forest
itself, like stitchery in a pillowcase.

Hettie hadn't seen much during her short life in
Old Crow Alley, but she knew how horses were supposed to look, and it was not like that. These steeds
had four legs and long necks, *almost* like horses,

but their bones were more delicate and their faces sharper, and their manes and tails seemed to be made of water or seaweed or molten glass.

Pale, pointy-faced people sat on their backs. Some were tall and lean like the faery butler. Some were small like Mr. Lickerish, the wicked Sidhe gentleman who had turned her into a door back in London.

The men wore black waistcoats and black overcoats just like English gentlemen did. The ladies wore gowns of dewdrops, or dresses made of open, flutter-paged books. One, a wizened old woman, was wrapped in so many swaths of black that she looked nearly swallowed up. Her head was bent and her hands were knotted tightly through the mane of her steed.

At the head of the company sat a small faery lady with a strange smile on her face. It was not a happy smile, but it was very wide. The lady wore a dress of fish bones, sewn together with what looked like spiderwebs, and as the riders came into the clearing and halted to dismount, Hettie was a little bit afraid all the threads in the lady's dress would snap and the whole costume would unravel at her feet.

Nothing like that happened.

The faery lady did not dismount. Instead, her steed shrank beneath her, bones grinding and re-jointing, until in its place stood a tall, mischievous-looking youth with sharply slanted eyes. He held the lady in his arms and then placed her daintily on the snow. The other steeds did the same.

The lady in the fish-bone dress looked about briefly, chin tilted to a haughty angle. Then she strode toward the cottage.

Hettie spun away from the door. "They're coming here," she whispered, hurrying back to the faery butler. "Get your knife! Get your knife, do something, they're *coming*!"

Still the butler did not move. For a moment Hettie thought he was pondering something, but then she saw his face. His skin was stretched and ashen. Little muscles twitched in his cheek, and his green eye was wide and dull. He wasn't going to move, Hettie realized, and her heart dropped. He was frightened out of his wits.

She glanced back at the door. Through the crack, she could see the hem of the faery lady's dress sweeping forward across the frozen earth. She gave the butler one last angry shake. Then she slipped down the corridor and up the stairs.

She heard the faery lady knock on the open door, three sharp raps. "Belusite Number 14!" the faery called. "We come to collect." The hinges protested.

Hettie ran, up, up toward the window and the candle. Below, feet tramped. She could hear voices everywhere suddenly, under the wooden treads, floating up the stairs after her. Doors slammed. After a few seconds the voices turned to angry shouts.

They wanted the person who lived here. And the person was not here.

At last Hettie came to the high window and scrambled up onto the sill. She looked down through the black branches at the scene below.

The faery lady had come out of the cottage and was swirling here and there, as if she were at a garden party and not in the middle of a vast, dead forest. Three gentleman-faeries were standing behind her, all in a line, not moving, and as far as Hettie could tell, not speaking. The old, old woman in her shawls and wraps was hunched against the roots of a tree.

And the faery butler . . . ? Two horse-people had him by the jacket and were dragging him out of the cottage, his long legs trailing in the snow.

Hettie gasped. *Why didn't you run?* she thought desperately. *You could have hidden! You could have hidden* somewhere!

The horse-people threw him to the ground. One held him in the snow with a bony, sharp-toed foot, and the other kicked him, right in the stomach. Hettie heard the scream, saw blood spatter the whiteness.

She didn't wait to see more. Whirling, she ran from the window and down the stairs. The treads flew by beneath her feet. She didn't like the faery butler. Usually she hated him. But he was the only thing she had left of England and home, and she wasn't going to let him die. She reached the beam-and-plaster passageway. She crashed through the front door.

"Stop!" she shouted, leaping out into the clearing. "Stop, leave him be!"

Twelve pairs of black eyes turned to stare at her. She froze. The faery butler lifted his head. A flicker of green, almost like surprise, passed behind his clockwork eye. Then the lady in the fish-bone dress strode up to Hettie and looked her in the face. She was only a bit taller than Hettie, and she resembled a pompous little child.

"English." It was a statement, spoken with a faint, precise accent that no English person would ever use.

"Yes," Hettie said, her boldness fading a little. Her hands went to her nightgown, and she looked down, suddenly shy.

"Are you an accomplice to this faery?"

"I— No. But I don't want you to hurt him. What are you going to do with him?"

"This faery"—the lady said, waving a hand in the butler's direction—"has been found guilty of murdering one of His Majesty the Sly King's most valued servants. He will be put to death, of course. Drowned in a bog, I think."

"Oh," breathed Hettie.

"And you?"

"Yes, miss."

"Who *are* you?" The lady punctuated the *are* with one sharply raised eyebrow.

"I'm not anybody."

"Yes, I can see that, but what sort of nobody? You are the strangest-looking faery I've ever seen. And no hair, or I'd think you simply a particularly ugly human."

Hettie knew better than to tell her she was a changeling. The daughter of a human mother and a faery father. Something in-between. English people didn't like changelings, but she had always been told faeries liked them even less.

"Oh, I *am* a faery, miss. Only . . . See, I come from England and I've lived there my whole life, and—well, I s'pose I picked up a bit of their looks."

Twelve pairs of eyes met across her head. There was a long pause in which the frosty air seemed to fill up and become heavy with all sorts of unspoken words and laughter.

Then the lady in the fish-bone dress let out a high, musical laugh that set everyone else to laughing, too, and the horse-people laughed, and the old woman laughed, and even the silver bells seem to tinkle with their own merry notes.

"She is so exquisitely funny," the faery lady said.

"Ex-*quisitely*," one of the horse-people mimicked, and that set them all to laughing again.

The fish-bone lady's mouth twitched. Her eyes went a little blacker, and her brows seemed to become even sharper. Then she laughed again, too, louder than anyone.

"John?" she said, turning to a horse-person with white hair and white skin that glittered as if with frost. "John, let her ride upon you. We shall take her with us."

"What?" The creature named John looked perfectly horrified. "That *thing*? On *me*?"

"Oh, no, I—" Panic gripped Hettie. It wrapped around her throat, made her breath escape in little gasps. "Please, I mustn't—"

They were all staring at her, all those black eyes, sparks of amusement in their depths, sparks of malice. She couldn't go with them. She couldn't be taken away from these woods, or the cottage. This was where the door had opened and where she had arrived, and this was where Bartholomew would find her when he came for her. *But what will he do if I'm not here?*

The thought made her sick.

"Please, miss," she said, taking a step toward the faery lady. "Please don't make me leave."

The faery lady did not even look at her. "You must. You will be my Whatnot. Or I will snip out your tongue. Don't be tiresome."

Hettie closed her mouth with a plop.

"Now," said the faery lady, whirling away. "Vizalia? Send a dispatch to the King. One of his Belusites has been killed. The wrongdoer has been dealt with. Nothing was found. You needn't say anything of my little bauble."

And the next thing Hettie knew, she was on the back of a white horse with hair like wisps of snowy wind. Everything was confusion, stomping hooves and whispering cloaks. Her steed began to gallop, away into the woods. *The faery butler.* Hettie looked frantically at the other riders. *Where is he? He isn't here!* With a little shiver, she glanced back over her shoulder.

Three figures had stayed behind in front of the cottage. The faery butler was on the ground, kneeling, his chin on his chest. Two horse-people stood over him, their faces strangely thin and hungry. And just before the company went over a rise and the cottage was lost from view, Hettie saw the horse-people begin to change again and their teeth grow long as needles and their eyes glow red as they looked down on the faery butler. Then Hettie was over the hill, riding away into the shadows and the snow.

CHAPTER V
Mr. Millipede and the Faery

PIKEY was able to avoid the chemist and the chemist's wife and almost everyone else for two long, cold nights. His luck ran out on the third, as he was returning from Fleet Street. He was slinking down the alley, past the shop door, soft as a shadow, and then the nails in his boots clanked against the stones and the sound echoed all the way up to the chimneys.

He winced.

"Oy! Whozat? Pikey?"

Orange light flickered around the door.

"Yeh." Pikey's voice was rough as bark. He dashed toward the hole under the shop, his hand tight around the gem in his pocket. "Yeh, it's me, Jem."

The bolt scraped. Pikey pulled in his feet and lay still.

"Oy!" the chemist said again, when he found the alley empty. He had a deep voice, but it was sloppy and wet now, and Pikey knew Jeremiah Jackinpots had been in his bottles again. Jem wasn't a bad man. Pikey liked him more than most folks. But he was slow-brained and weak, and gin did nothing to improve his wits.

"So quick into yer mouse hole, boy?" Pikey heard Jem take a few heavy steps toward the hole. Then a hacking spit. "No words for me? No talk? What 'ave the oil of earthworm prices gone to? Has the war started yet?"

Pikey remained perfectly still. "I don't know," he lied. "I didn't hear. Weren't no one around to tell me nuthin'." He *had* heard. The town crier had been on Fleet Street as always, reading the news and the prices to the illiterates that flocked around him. Pikey had been there, too, poking his head between the dirty waistcoats. He went every day to Fleet Street to listen and make sure the herb-and-root sellers didn't cheat Jem when they came to the shop. It was why Jem let him stay in the hole, why the aid ladies hadn't come by in their black bonnets and hoop skirts and taken Pikey to the workhouse. He hoped Jem would forgive him, just this once. *Just one more day.*

"I'm dreadful tired, Jem," Pikey called. "I'll tell it all in the morning, promise my boots, I will."

Jem grunted. There was the clink of a bottle and the smack of lips. Then grumbling as he staggered back toward the shop. The door banged. The alley became silent again.

Pushing himself as far into the hole as he could, Pikey wound himself into a ball, all arms and legs and rank-smelling wool. He was pressing his luck. He knew he was. Tonight Jeremiah Jackinpots was too sullen and too drunk, but he wouldn't be in the morning. In the morning Pikey had to be gone.

Sell the gemstone, get an eye patch, leave the city. I'll go southward. Away from the war. Away from leadfaces and cities and bleemin' faeries.

He had been repeating it like a spell the last three

days, hour after hour until he fell asleep. Though it *had* changed a bit since that first morning. Then it had been more like, *Buy a caramel apple. Then buy lemonade and ginger-rocks, and six—no, seven meat pies. Then go back to the caramel apples and buy the whole lot.*

He would still get that caramel apple. But he was more practical now.

He shivered and stuffed his blanket down the front of his jacket to keep out the chill. His hole was set inside the foundations of the shop, flat on the dirt. Four feet long. Half that high. Above him, through the floorboards, he could hear Jem and his wife snapping at each other. He had to pull in his knees and bend his neck to fit, and the winter could come right in at the door.

But it didn't matter. He was leaving. Things would only get worse in London once the fighting started in the North. And anyway he didn't *want* to stay here, in a hole in Spitalfields. Someday he wanted to be somewhere else, somewhere green perhaps, with plums and pies and the voices he had dreamed about, the loud, happy voices.

Pikey fell asleep, and dreamed of them all over again.

The next morning, he made himself a badly sagging patch out of one of his socks and tied it over his bad eye. Then, pushing the gem deep into the one pocket that still had all its stitches, he wriggled out of his hole.

The foot with only two socks instead of three noticed its diminished state almost at once. It went numb, then unfeeling. Pikey felt sure it did so out of spite. But better a frozen foot than holding a hand over his eye all day like a simpleton, and so he ignored it and hurried up the alley toward Bell Lane.

The chemist's door creaked as he passed it. The bolt scraped, then the hinges. Pikey knew who it was before she even stepped into the alley. Not Jeremiah, this time. Worse.

"What you got there, laddy?" Missus Jackinpots could coo like a dove to her little one, but to everyone else she was worse than a crow.

"Nuthin'." Pikey's hand tightened around the gem

in his pocket. He took a few more hurried steps, his frozen foot jarring against the ground.

"Jem says he's seen not hide nor hair of you for almost three days. Where's the news? What are the prices at? You know the deal, and you oughta keep it. Prices and news six times a week, else there's no point keeping *you*."

Pikey turned a little, his glance skipping over Missus Jackinpots for the briefest instant. She was a small, buxom woman with a stained, flowered handkerchief tied over hair like stringy black joint oil. There were smudges under her eyes. Pikey looked at the ground.

Missus Jackinpots didn't. She eyed him steadily, hands on hips. "Jem's too soft, he is. I'd have 'ad you out from under our shop the moment we found you, and off to the workhouse, make no mistake."

You didn't find me, Pikey thought. Anger rushed up suddenly, hot behind his ribs. *I lived here before you did. The old chemist let me stay here. It's my* right. He gritted his teeth.

"What's the matter? Goblin ate your tongue? Look at me, boy!"

"Old Marty said I could stay here," Pikey said. His voice was dull and sullen. "And so did Jem." He focused on a sickly thread of grass pressing up between two cobbles. He didn't want to look at the hard, flat face staring at him, the smudges under her eyes.

"You call him *Mister* Jackinpots," she hissed, taking a step toward him. "Or sir. It's his place now. Old Marty's dead. He's dead, and don't you forget it."

Blood, dripping between the stones.

Pikey stumbled toward Bell Lane, but Missus Jackinpots lunged forward, blocking his escape.

"Come on, ma'am, lemme go," he said. "I ain't got nothing."

Missus Jackinpots was looking at his pocket. "Oh, you've got something. What're you hiding, boy? Bloody *roses*, if you're keeping things from me, I swear I'll—" Suddenly she froze, and such a rage came over her face that Pikey felt his own anger evaporate. He took a step back, startled.

"That eye patch," she said slowly. "Let me see that. That ain't yours. It's my Jem's sock, it is. On your filthy *face*! I knitted that! My own hands knitted that and you've been *pinching*—"

Pikey shoved past her and pelted into Bell Lane, ignoring her screams as they bounced up the houses behind him. He didn't stop running until he was halfway to Ludgate. Then he stooped down under the window of a tailor's shop and felt in his pocket for the gem. His hand closed around it and he let out a sigh.

Away from the war. Away from leadfaces and faeries. Away from horrid people like Missus Jackinpots.

He was going to do it. He was going to get out of here and he was never coming back.

The walk from Spitalfields to anywhere respectable was a long one. He trudged for miles, out of the slums and along the slow, greenish river toward the wide streets and straight-backed houses of St. James's. One hand he kept under his arm, trying to stop his fingers from cracking off. The other stayed in his pocket, clamped tight around the gem.

Every time he thought of it there he felt a little thrill, a pleasure at its weight. It would turn into so many shillings and sovereigns for him. A whole stack of them. He would sell it and fill his pockets, and then he would leave London behind him once and for all.

An hour later he was in the part of the city that folks called Mayfair, on a big, noisy street full of shops and carriages. He walked along, darting around bicycles and the frozen brooms of the mechanical street sweepers. The horses and gas trolleys meant that the air was somewhat less icy than in the more old-fashioned parts of the city, but it was still cold enough to make Pikey's teeth chatter. A squadron of soldiers marched by, real grown-up ones in splendid red-and-blue uniforms. They stomped in formation, and a whistle at their head played a jaunty tune. Pikey watched them as they passed.

He stopped in front of a tall, gray-stone shop. The sign above the door read, *Jeffreyhue H. Millipede, Jeweler*, but to Pikey it was only a lot of flourishes and lines. A plate-glass window spanned the shop's front, so clean you might smack flat into it before you even knew it was there. And behind it was a wall of jewels. Row upon row of winking, glittering stones, pinned to the swaths of black velvet like so many brilliant insects. There were diamond necklaces and iridescent combs. There were strands of pearls, opals curled in silver, emeralds green as the verdigris on the old clock tower in Rot-Apple Street. They all looked so huge and polished. Pikey was suddenly afraid his own gem might not be good enough, that his dirty fingers had smudged it and that when he took it from his pocket it would look dull and flat, plain as a river stone.

No, he told himself firmly. He had come this far and he wasn't going to turn back now. He knew a caramel apple seller on the way out of the city. He could already taste it. He could feel the brown, sticky sweetness dripping over his fingers, warming them as he walked away into the country.

Pikey squared his shoulders and pushed through the cut-glass door into the shop.

A tinkling of golden bells, and one great iron bell to scare him off in case he was a faery, signaled his entrance. Three ladies in enormous feathered hats turned languorously to glance at him. A shopkeeper's assistant did the same, and so did a bald, waistcoated gentleman standing behind a glass table. The table was filled with bulbous red necklaces, and the way the man stood with his large, milk-white hands spread over it made him look rather sinister.

Pikey felt his heart flutter as they looked at him, but he didn't hesitate. He marched toward the waist-coated gentleman, who he thought looked the most important, and said, "G'day, guvn'or. I have something for you. Are you the swanbolly?"

Pikey tried making his voice as deep and rough as he could, the way the men in Spitalfields did when they wanted something their way. Then he looked the man in the eye and waited, hoping he had done a good job of it.

"I beg your pardon?"

"Are you the swanbolly?" Pikey asked again, and this time his voice slipped up a bit and squeaked.

The man sniffed. "No, I'm quite sure that I am not. And if you do not state your business within three ticks, I'll have you dragged to the workhouse. What is it you want?"

Pikey almost bolted at that. Almost. But he was

so close to getting away, away from wars and faery hunters and horrid people like Missus Jackinpots. He wasn't going to give up now.

Forcing down his fear, he said, "I do have business, guvn'or. I got something to sell to you." And then he opened his hand and held up the gem for all to see. It came to light, pale gray and glimmering. Beautiful as ever.

The gentleman leaned in. The three ladies did as well, and they smelled like such a draft of pomegranates and cold soap and powdered petals that for an instant Pikey thought he might sneeze. Then Mr. Millipede (because that was who the gentleman was) plucked the gem from Pikey's hand. He pulled a mechanical monocle from a little drawer behind the counter and fitted it to his eye. The monocle clicked as it focused, the lenses swiveling and realigning. The ladies stepped back, whispering among themselves.

Mr. Millipede stared through the lenses for several seconds. His tongue darted out, running over his lips. Then he took the monocle from his eye and snapped it shut.

"Where did you get this?" he asked. His voice was very high and very strained.

The question made Pikey's arms go to gooseflesh. He hadn't really thought that anyone would ask him this. If he had stolen the gem, he would have understood. Then he would have been guilty and he would have invented a whole web of lies and tales to protect himself. But he *hadn't* stolen the gem. He hadn't done anything wrong. He was suddenly aware of how he must look to the gentleman, to the shopkeeper's assistant and the ladies. All muddy and snowy and pathetically hungry. His heart pounded. He hoped they couldn't see it beating against the filthy wool of his jacket.

"Someone gave it to me," he said. "As a gift."

Mr. Millipede arched an eyebrow. "A gift. Of course. Well, you must be quite the wonderful boy to get such a fine gift. Do follow me, and let's do business."

That was more like it. It *was* quite a fine gem, after all, and if Mr. Millipede was too good to pay for it, Pikey could always bring it to a different jeweler.

Pikey followed the gentleman, stalking past the

three ladies with as much dignity as he could gather. They turned their heads to watch him pass, the feathers in their hats fluttering.

"This way, if you please," Mr. Millipede said, ushering Pikey down a corridor, past a great brass speaking machine. "To the money room." They stopped at a door at the end of the corridor. The jeweler unlocked it and gave a little bow as it creaked open.

Pikey peered in. The room was dark and square and very small. One grimy window looked out from high up in the wall. The floor was a jumble of old crates and chairs and portraits wrapped in string and wax paper.

Money room, my foot.

Pikey turned to tell the gentleman exactly that, and then Mr. Millipede shoved him. Pikey flew forward, banging to his knees. The door slammed behind him and the key clanked in the lock.

"Hoy!" Pikey shouted, whirling and beating his fists against the door. "Hoy, what—Help! Kidnappers, *help me!*"

He kicked and yelled and rattled the handle. The ladies would hear. They were such a little ways away. They couldn't possibly *not* hear him.

He leaned his head against the door, listening. No sound. No sound of ladies hurrying down the corridor to rescue him. No shrieks, or shouts of shock and outrage. The only thing he heard was the whirr of the speaking machine as Mr. Millipede cranked its handle, and the brass *ping* as the call went through.

"Yes. Yes, Mr. Millipede's, Number 41, Dover Street." The gentleman's voice had lost all its politeness. It was brisk and businesslike, and it made Pikey want to punch the jeweler in his horrid, false face. "A guttersnipe brought it in. . . . Lady Halifax's . . . stolen . . . Come right away."

Then Pikey wanted to punch himself.

Idiot.

He slid down the door and closed his eyes.

Idiot, fool, boggle-eyed fish-brained dunderhead.

Of course it was stolen. That black-winged faery had snatched it somewhere and given it to Pikey, likely as a joke. And Pikey had fallen for it. He thought he could march in and sell a gem that was worth all of Spitalfields and several streets of Fenchurch as well, a gem worth more money than most men earned in their entire lives? What had he expected? That the jeweler would believe him? That Pikey could strut and put on a deep voice, and everyone would ignore his filthy clothes and his smell of mud and frozen alleys?

Well, now he *was* in for it. Now he was dead. Forget caramel apples. Forget his stupid dreams. The officers would come. They would see his eye, and the war was starting soon. A faery-touched boy in the middle of London would be spirited away in a blink. To the lockup, or the workhouse, or worse . . . a faery prison.

The mouthpiece clattered into its cradle. Footsteps receded down the corridor. Pikey heard a high flutter of giggles. Then nothing.

He leaned his head against the door, his hair sticking unpleasantly to the cold wood. He knew he should move, look for a weapon, look for a way to escape, but he barely felt he could. He had been so close. For three days he'd had a path laid out in front of him, a gem in his pocket and a spring in his step, and suddenly the happy voices and the warm stove had seemed very near indeed. But now Mr. Millipede had dropped the gem into his waistcoat pocket, and that was where it would stay until Pikey was well on his way to being locked up and to disappear and—

Disappear. The word brought him back with a sharp twist of panic. That would be the end, then. He would be dead, and that would be all.

He pushed himself off the floor and glanced about. The lock on the door was strong and old, and he had never been good at picking locks anyway. The only other way out was the window. He looked up at it. Veins of lead crisscrossed it, and it was high above his head. But not too high.

He snatched one of the rickety chairs and dragged it up under the window. He clambered onto it, careful to keep his feet on either side of the brittle straw seat. Then he pulled his sleeve over one hand and knocked it against the glass. The panes were thick. So thick they distorted the alley outside into bluish waves and whorls. Well, he didn't have a choice. He balled his fist to smash it—

"Don't," said a voice.

Pikey froze.

The door had not opened. No one had come in. The voice had been soft, and dark, and spoken with the faintest hint of a laugh.

Slowly Pikey turned to face the room. The chair wobbled under him.

A tall, thin figure stood in the shadows, next to a stack of canvasses and empty picture frames. Pikey couldn't see its face or eyes—only a silhouette—and for a moment he wondered if it was a statue and he had imagined the voice. But then a long-fingered hand unfurled from the shadows, and the voice spoke again: "Come to me. Come quickly. We mustn't have you in trouble."

Pikey leaped off the chair and backed up against the wall, his hands flat on the stone. "Stay away," he hissed. "Who're you? Stay away!" His voice sounded small and sharp, a little boy's voice.

"They will catch you." The thin figure laughed softly. "They will *kill* you."

Beyond the door, the jeweler's shop was no longer

silent. Bells jangled, long and insistently. Then heavy footsteps, in the shop, in the corridor. *Boots.* They were coming for him.

"Do you want that? Do you want them to make you disappear like you never existed? They will see your eye. They will drag you to one of their faery prisons in the wilds, and no one *ever* comes back from those. No one like you, at least." Another laugh, so quiet it was just a breath. "Take my hand."

Pikey looked at the hand, then at the figure in the shadows. He couldn't see its face. He couldn't see *anything.*

The boots had reached the door. A key clicked into the lock. *Turning, turning.*

The figure flicked its fingers, beckoning him. The door opened with a squeal.

Pikey gripped the hand.

It was cold. Cold and stiff as a dead man's hand. It pulled Pikey into the dark.

Behind him he heard a shout. The figure clutched Pikey. It whispered under its breath, and the shadows seemed to fly like ravens out of the corners and wrap around them. Leadfaces were in the room, hurling picture frames, poking into everything, but suddenly the sound of them was far away, as if on the other side of a velvet curtain. Mr. Millipede stood in the doorway, his mouth agape. Pikey saw it all. Then the thin figure said another word, and Pikey was swept forward, past the jeweler, out the door, carried on an invisible wind. They flew out of the shop, up the street, faster and faster, and no one seemed to see. Houses sped past, steam coaches and automatons, and hundreds of people in hats and hoop skirts. They crossed the river, so quick Pikey didn't know if they had been on a bridge or if they had simply floated right above the water. And then the figure let go of his hand. Everything screeched to a halt.

Pikey gasped, wobbling on his legs. He looked about. He was back in the squalor of Spitalfields, in a little court behind a butcher's shop. An old, old tree called the Gallows Tree arched over him, its branches gnarled and black.

"Now," the tall figure said. "Do not be foolish again. You are no use when you are dead."

It did not wait for a response. It spoke another word, and the Gallows Tree seemed to untwist and open like a gaping mouth. Wind flew at Pikey. Not the heavy, ash-filled wind of London, but a sharp, wet wind that smelled of salt. It ruffled his hair, dampened his lips. Through the tree, as if through a telescope, he saw a seashore, dark cliffs and waves crashing over a bone-white beach. It was all so close; he could practically feel the spray flying up around him and spattering his cheeks. The figure gave him a wink and a nod, and stepped into the tree. There was a snapping sound. Pikey felt a pain in his head, a dark, sharp spark stealing his vision. And when he could see again he was alone in the court. The Gallows Tree stood silent and still, just as it always had. Only the slightest hint of a laugh hung in the air, fading into the snow.

Pikey did not go back to the chemist's shop. He didn't know where to go. He spent the night in the corner of a frozen alley, covered with a few issues of *The London Standard,* and wondered what would become of him.

Pikey woke the next morning surrounded by glittering things.

He sat up slowly, rubbing the grit from his eyes. They were all around him, scattered over the cobbles in wide circle. Diamonds and opals and poppy-red brocade in crumpled rolls. A complete set of silver flatware, a cup wrought with leaves, a wooden box spilling pearls. A mantle of frost lay over everything.

Pikey squinted, blurring his vision to see if it would all fade into the smoke and frozen grime of the alley. It didn't. Everything was sharp and clear, sparkling in the cold. A single black feather fluttered, caught in the prongs of a silver fork.

Pikey sat up with a start.

Oh no. Stupid faery. Stupid, stupid faery—

But it was too late to run. And someone was there. Several someones. In the alley. Standing over him. Three leadfaces.

"Got you now," one of them spat, so close Pikey could see the spittle strike the cobbles. "Now you're in for it. *Thief.*"

CHAPTER VI
The Belusites

HETTIE soon learned a few things, traveling through the woods with the company. She learned that laughing and smiling did not necessarily mean the Sidhe were pleased about anything. She learned that some words left them sulking, and others made the darkness pool around them like a drenched cloak, and still others made them turn odd, shadowy, and gaunt and glare at one another with glinting eyes. But mostly Hettie learned to disappear. She sat on the back of the snowy-haired horse, trying to make herself as small as possible, trying not to make a sound lest one of those long, pale faces turn to look at her. In Old Crow Alley, she had barely ever left Mother's kitchen; she hadn't been allowed to be seen, because to be seen meant she would die. And now she was riding with an entire company of faeries into some strange country, on her way to some strange place. . . .

It'll be all right, she told herself over and over. *Don't be afraid. Don't be a baby.* But she was afraid. The faery butler had been her kidnapper. He had been a wicked, snappish creature who would never stop walking when she told him to, and—well, she had known him, at least. Back in England she had known him. He had been like a piece of that place, like a colored thread that coiled all the way back home. Now even that was gone.

Hettie knotted her hands into her nightgown. *The cottage.* She wouldn't be there anymore when Barthy came. He would call for her, but she would be far away. He would go into the cottage and find everything silent and empty. Perhaps he would see the blood on the snow and leave again, and not look for her any longer because he thought it was her blood and she was dead.

Hettie sat up so straight her steed wrenched its neck about and glared at her. *No,* she thought fiercely. *Not my brother. My brother won't ever give up. I'll get home one day.*

After what felt like hours of riding, they entered a darker, deeper part of the wood. The great trees formed a tunnel around the company, the branches thick as chimneys. Hettie saw they were on the remains of an ancient road, bits of paving stones sticking up like broken teeth out of the snow. The ground became softer. The hooves of the horse-people sank in farther than before, releasing with a wet sound instead of a sharp one. And then, all at once, the snow was gone. The horses' hooves were squelching through turf and moss, and the trees were no longer black, but green and leafy, their trunks rough with cracked bark.

A faery riding close to Hettie let out a sigh. "Ah," she said. "At last. We are out of Deepest Winter."

Hettie looked back over her shoulder. The snowy wood had simply ended. As if it were an entirely different world. As if there were an invisible line, and everything on one side was desolate and dead, and everything on the other side was alive and growing.

"I do detest it," the faery said to no one in particular.

Hettie peeked at her. She was not as pretty as the fish-bone lady. She had a very round face like a moon, or a dinner plate, and huge watery eyes. Her dress was sewn from giant rose petals. Her skin was still deathly pale, but somehow she didn't look quite as sinister as some of the other faeries. Hettie decided to ask her a question.

Leaning off the back of her steed a little, she said, "What did you say? Where are we now?"

Hettie had meant it to be so quiet that only the petal faery would hear, but she wasn't so lucky.

"Where?" the faery repeated, so loud the entire forest seemed to echo the question. "The ugly one asks where! Why, in Brightest Summer, of course! Silly thing!"

Everyone in the company turned to stare at Hettie. Then they started laughing.

"Hollow head," said the old crone, her eyes glittering.

"Numbskull," said the lady in the book dress.

"What a dimwit," said the fish-bone lady happily.

Hettie shrank into the streaming white mane of her steed and waited for them to be done. They were, after not too long. Hettie remembered how back home she had heard Mother sighing about how faeries had tempers like spring weather, always changing, never good, and perhaps they did, but they certainly did not stay interested in things for long.

When the faeries had all been diverted by one thing or another, Hettie looked about at the new woods. *It doesn't* look *like Brightest Summer,* she thought spitefully. *Not to me.* You're *the hollow heads.* Summer in Bath meant stinking streets, stuffy rooms, and stairs so hot the wood sweated and the nailheads burned when you touched them. Here it wasn't even warm. The air was heavy and wet. It smelled of damp and fog and green things, but it wasn't warm. In fact, there was not a drop more light than there had been before, and all was still shadowy, gloomy, and gray.

They rode through this new wood for some time, under drooping branches and through silent hollows. A mist lay over the ground. Hettie saw that some of the riders had changed as well, along with the trees. The plate-faced lady looked slightly more luminous, the petals of her rose-dress a deeper red. Another lady was covered in sapphire-blue butterflies, all now emerged from the chrysalises sewn to her gown. The old woman—the tiny shriveled-up one who had been sitting so bent—was pale and slender and very young now, fresh as a summer apple. Her black shawls and blankets had become gauzy scarves. The gray coils of her hair were long and corn-gold. Hettie thought she looked very pretty.

At last the company came to the edge of the woods and rode into a dewy green field. It, too, was swathed in fog.

A huge house lay a few hundred strides from the forest. It was nothing like the cottage of the gray-faced faery. It was large and sprawling, and from every angle it looked a bit different, depending on how Hettie turned her head.

One side appeared like a great farmhouse with painted shutters and gingerbread trim. Another side was a soaring castle with towers and battlements and gargoyles watching from around diamond-paned windows. Another side was a palace, all glass and domed winter gardens.

Fog enveloped everything beyond the house. Hettie wondered what the country looked like farther on. For all she knew there *was* nothing. For all she knew the faery world ended here and everything after the house was simply a foggy green field forever and ever. She didn't like the thought of that.

The company stopped in front of a great, worm-eaten door carved with bears. Hettie had half expected them to go to a stable or a barn, but she had forgotten that it wasn't really horses they were riding. Likely the horse-people slept on sheets and ate with forks just like the English did. Below her, Hettie felt the bones of her steed begin to jerk and snap. She gasped. He was shifting, his skeleton making horrid little jolts against his hide. The other horse-people were doing the same. Their riders were set carefully on the ground. Hettie was dropped.

"Ow!" she cried, pushing herself up off the grass. She was about to shout at the glittery-skinned boy and tell him what a wicked, bad-mannered creature he was, but he had already stalked off.

"Ow," she said again, a little quieter this time.

No one else was paying her any attention either. They had not even bothered to laugh at her fall. The lady in the fish-bone dress stood in front of the great door, and the others were waiting impatiently behind her. She said a single word, sharp as a sewing pin, and the door shook and opened, very suddenly, as if it had been startled.

The riders stepped through first, then the horse-people. No one waited for Hettie, and so she went in last of all, rubbing her back and scowling. She found herself in a dim, dusty room that had no ceiling, but went up and up into the dark. Ropes hung down out of the gloom. Against one wall stood a clock with faces where its numbers should have been, and on the far wall was a complicated red curtain, like a miniature theater curtain, framed in chipped and fading gilt. Nothing else. The room would never have been able to hold the entire company had they waited, but the young woman with her corn-gold hair slipped behind the curtain, and the horse-people skittered up the walls, and soon there was no one left but Hettie, the lady in the fish-bone dress, and three small gentlemen.

The gentlemen were speaking to one another, eyes half closed. The lady had her nose in the air. Her gaze was fixed on the clock, and her hands were picking at a fish bone in her bodice.

Hettie glanced at each of the faeries in turn. Now would be the time to run. The faeries were all very small. Not much taller than herself. Behind her, the door was still open. She could knock them right over and dash back across the green field and into the woods. Then she could eat mushrooms and drink snow and follow the horse-people's tracks until she was at the cottage. *And then—*

Then they would find her. They knew the woods better than she did. They knew the whole country, and they had killed the faery butler though he'd only been protecting her. They would kill her, too. These dreadful little people would as soon lop off her hand as shake it, and if they ever found out she was a Peculiar, they would lop off her *head*. The thought made her angry.

She stamped her foot. "What are we *waiting* for?" It came out in a sort of loud squeak. The three faery gentlemen turned to look at her, their eyes still half closed.

The fish-bone lady did not look at her at all. "*We* are waiting for our passage to be ready," she said. "And you are waiting for us."

Behind Hettie, the worm-eaten door closed with a boom. She jumped. And then the clock bonged, and the fish-bone lady reached forward and pulled a golden cord. The red curtain folded upward in ripples, revealing a long, opulent hallway, paneled in white and gold. The faery lady stepped into it. The faery gentlemen followed her, and Hettie followed the gentlemen. She stared about, trying to keep up. There was definitely something odd about the hallway. It was lined with doors, but they were only painted on, even the handles. Up ahead there appeared to be a panel missing in the wall. She passed it, peering through. She gasped. For a second she saw a vast gloomy space, pulleys and wires and little orange lamps extending into the distance. She saw that the walls of the hallway were only an inch thick and made of paste. And then a faery in a harness swooped out of the dark and slammed the panel into place, and the hallway looked real again. Hettie could still hear the creak of the pulleys on the other side of the wall, though. She wondered what sort of strange house this was.

The group walked on, never speaking. Their footsteps tapped dully against the floor, as if they were inside a box. At length the gentlemen disappeared behind doors. Hettie felt odd following the fish-bone lady all alone, especially since the faery seemed to have forgotten she was even there.

"Where are we going?" Hettie asked, just to remind her. "Miss, I have to—"

"Hush!" hissed the fish-bone lady, and looked quickly about, as if someone might be watching.

Finally the hallway ended in a pair of tall, paneled doors. The fish-bone lady opened them, and they entered a long, soaring room, full of shadows. Beams arched overhead like branches. Hundreds of portraits hung from the walls. A high-backed chair stood at the far end. Above the chair were two windows that looked almost exactly like thin slices of lemon. Hettie thought that was clever at first, because the windows made the gray light from outside look warm and lemony as well. But then she saw the bright faces pressed against the yellow glass from the other side. *Lamp faeries.* The windows were false, too.

The lady locked the doors with a toothy key, three ribbons, and a sprig of something green and alive.

"Ah," she said, when she had finished. "On solid ground at last. Come." And she practically dragged Hettie to the end of the room and deposited her on a footstool. The faery lady clambered up onto the chair. Then she arranged herself and looked down at Hettie expectantly.

Hettie sat very still and looked at her toes.

After a while the lady clapped her hands together.

"I shall call you Maud," she announced, and giggled. "I always wanted to call someone that."

Hettie looked up sharply. "I don't want to be called Maud," she said, before she could stop herself. "I want to be called Hettie. That's my name. Hettie."

The lady barely glanced at her. "Hettie? Hettie is a dull name. It sounds like broomsticks and straw. Maud, on the other hand, sounds like violets and dust and melancholy. It is far more suitable."

"I don't like it."

"Well, nobody asked you," the lady said, swinging her legs like a child.

Hettie blinked at her.

"Now, Maud, be a darling and bow whenever someone important sees you. I want them to be impressed with me." Her smile left. The corner of her mouth twitched. "Is that clear?"

Hettie was staring at the picture behind the lady's head. It had begun to move. Figures were emerging from the painted woods in the distance and dancing across a meadow. Something dark was creeping toward them from a bloody patch in the corner. *Something dark and—*

"Maud!" The lady's voice was sharp.

"Oh— Yes, miss."

"Excuse me, silly thing, I am not a *miss.* I am the Duchess of Yearn-by-the-Woods, Daughter of the Ponds, and Lady of the Hall of Hatpins. You will call me 'milady.'"

The faery leaned over. Abruptly her face crinkled into a smile. "But when no one is here you can call me Piscaltine." She winked conspiratorially. "Oh, we'll be such *friends.*"

Hettie didn't want to be friends with this strange creature, but she doubted it would be a good idea to tell Piscaltine that. "Yes, milady," she said, and a second later the doors groaned open and an entire crowd of faeries swept into the room.

Hettie started. Piscaltine scooted a little straighter in her chair. "Oh, dear," she whispered. "Oh, they weren't supposed to come tonight. I *told* the reconstructionists to keep them in the Dragonfly Wing and to turn all the passageways around on them if they decided to leave!"

Hettie had no idea what reconstructionists were, but she wished they had been more obedient. Because the creatures advancing on her now were the strangest, most dreadful bunch Hettie had ever seen, stranger even than Piscaltine's riding party. There was a lady who had small curtained windows where her eyes should have been and a wooden door for a mouth. There was another who was exquisitely beautiful on the front, with a great pleated gown and a dark, high-boned face, and a back like a hollow tree, gnarled and crawling with beetles. There was a man with a huge black spider for a head, its long legs curling around his shoulders. There was a water-fay. She floated in an upright tank, its wheels pushed by two tiny sprytes barely a foot from head to toe. There were many others, and all of them were dressed in rich clothes and complicated dancing dresses; all were bizarre in some way, misshapen or mad-looking. One had a key protruding from her back.

They rustled forward, and Hettie and Piscaltine watched them approach, the faery lady poised in her chair like a statue. "Don't say anything," she hissed, her lips barely moving. "Not a word."

The creatures came within five steps of the chair and formed a half circle. Hettie heard Piscaltine take a breath.

"Ooh," said a tall, pale lady with a hooked nose when she caught sight of Hettie. "Ooh my, what is *that*?" There were white, wriggling maggots sewn all over the lady's skirts, and every few seconds she would squish one between her fingers and eat it.

"Why, Piscaltine, it is positively *grotesque*," gurgled the water-fay from inside her tank. Perfect little bubbles plumed from her mouth with every word.

All of Piscaltine's air went out of her in a burst. "What?" she cried, dragging Hettie up into her lap. "No, she is a rarity! A curio and a peculiarity! She is going to be my Whatnot. Her name is Maud and she's from the Smoke Lands. All the way from London, can you imagine?"

"Uncivilized."

"Uneducated."

"Horribly vulgar."

Piscaltine put her nose in the air, but her mouth was

starting to twitch again. "As if any of *you* would know."

The lady with the maggot dress waved her hand dismissively. "Silly, of course we know. We're the King's people, don't forget. Most of us have been there. To London. To Darmstadt, and Prague, and St. Petersburg. Completing our little tasks. Putting our fingers in the pie and making sure the humans are doing things just the way he wants them to. It is the most difficult place to get to, not to mention the journey through the wings always fills my shoes full of *feathers.*" She laughed and looked around at the others to make sure they were laughing, too. They were not, but the lady with window-eyes reached up obligingly and opened her door-mouth, and a little red bird sprang out on a brass wire and twittered. The maggot-lady turned back to Piscaltine. "You see?" she said. "Which is why none of us would want one so close to us. Contagions, you know."

All the ladies began nodding and whispering at once, then, and every few seconds Piscaltine would wriggle and try to say something over Hettie's shoulder.

And then Hettie noticed that two of the women in the group were not speaking. They were standing very, very still, a little ways apart from the others, watching Hettie. They were both incredibly tall, and they wore matching dresses of thick, crimson velvet. Their faces were glazed like dolls' faces, one porcelain white, and the other black and smooth as the trees in Deepest Winter. Their eyes were empty holes, rimmed in red. They both stared, silent and unblinking, at Hettie.

Suddenly the pale twin spoke. "Where did you get her?" she asked, her voice sliding above the prattle. It was a flat, hollow voice. Instantly everyone in the hall went silent.

"What?" said Piscaltine. "I found her. It isn't any of your business."

"Everything is our business. *Where* did you find her?" The dark twin spoke now, too, at exactly the same time as the pale one. Hettie shivered.

"At—in the woods. In Deepest Winter. No one was there. She was all alone, and she's quite useless and pointless; she said so herself."

"You would tell us, of course, if the creature would be of interest to our King. You would not keep it from him." It was not a question. Hettie noticed that the other creatures seemed to be just as afraid of the red twins as Piscaltine was. They all stood stock-still.

"Oh. Of course not! What a thought. Anyway, she's nothing so special. Just a curious little stray." Piscaltine laughed, too brightly.

"Have her roll up her sleeves." The twins stepped toward the chair, both at the same time.

"What?" Piscaltine wrapped her arms around Hettie and squeezed her so hard that Hettie gasped.

"Have her roll them up," the women said again.

Piscaltine frowned. Then she hunched over Hettie and struggled with the sleeve of her nightgown. The fabric rolled up an inch. *Strands of red, winding and winding over pale skin. Eleven. Eleven. Eleven, they said in the language of the faeries.* Piscaltine saw. Hettie didn't know if the red twins saw, but she was sure no one else did, because in a wink Piscaltine had pulled the sleeve back down and was searching Hettie's face. Her eyes were not angry. They were wide and quivering and very,

very frightened. Behind her, Hettie knew everyone was staring, stretching those long white necks for a glimpse.

Piscaltine shoved Hettie off her lap. "Maud? Leave." She faced the others. "I think we should all go to the Hall of Intemperance and eat wild goblin until we're sick. Don't you agree? My hunters caught it almost a fortnight ago. It will be delightfully decayed."

Hettie didn't bow to anyone. She broke into a run. Behind her, Piscaltine was talking, going on and on in a quick, annoying voice, and the red twins were staring at Hettie, and so was everyone else. She reached the door. It was heavy, but it was no longer locked. She pushed against it, out. It closed behind her with a solid *clank*.

Hettie let go a long, slow breath. What had all *that* been? What had they been talking about? Hettie didn't like the way those twins had stared at her, and she didn't like the way everyone talked about her as if she wasn't there. She didn't like this place. She had to get out.

The painted hallway was no longer on the other side of the door. Instead, she was standing on a huge, dark staircase that went up and down and was carpeted with wine-red carpets that were faded and threadbare in some patches and dusty everywhere. She looked up the stairs. She looked down them. Then she hurried to the banisters and looked over the edge. She was very high up. Above her, she dimly saw the roof, but everything below it was a tangle of construction. She saw rooms being built, others being dismantled, drawing rooms and sleeping rooms and ballrooms being fitted together like puzzles. Rooms hung from ropes and chains or were set on top of one another in teetering stacks. Doors opened into nothing. Hallways simply ended. And all around, creaking through the dark on little metal swings and harnesses, were goblins and gnomes, building, hammering, hauling.

Someone who might have been a maid hurried down the stairs, carrying in her arms a load of panels painted to look like a kitchen. She stopped long enough to stare at Hettie.

"Oh," Hettie said when she saw her. "Oh, excuse me, ma'am, could you help me?"

The maid jumped at the sound of Hettie's voice, as if she hadn't expected Hettie would actually be able to speak.

Hettie didn't notice. "I'm Lady Piscaltine's . . . well . . . I'm her Whatnot. And I need to know where a door to the outside is. I need to leave."

"Leave?" the maid whispered, and her eyeballs practically popped from her head. "Oh, you can't leave. Nobody can." She began to hurry on down the steps, murmuring anxiously to herself.

"What? Wait, don't go!" Hettie chased her. "What d'you mean, nobody can? *I* can. I just need to know where a door is! Can't you answer my question?" She felt the hard little knot of anger growing in her stomach. *Stupid faeries. Stupid Piscaltine, and her stupid house.*

"No!" the maid shouted over shoulder. "Ask a troll. Ask the pity-faeries when they're hungry. It will be better for you in the end."

Hettie stopped, glaring after her. She turned in a circle on the step. Then she decided to go up and became utterly, hopelessly lost. The house was vast, and it didn't help that it was always changing. Sometimes she would step into a hallway that was being reconstructed and would discover a wall behind her where seconds before there had been a door, or that all the panels had been flipped and what had looked like a regular corridor before now looked like a deep forest of red and rust-colored mushrooms. Some passageways were only a foot wide and she had to go down them sideways, squeezing between the plaster walls. Others were decaying, sagging on their chains and swinging dangerously. She wandered until her legs ached, up staircases and along peeling galleries full of cobwebs. She didn't meet many faeries. The few she did all looked startled when they saw her and disappeared before she could come near.

When she began looking in doors she regretted it rather quickly. The rooms were mostly false and flat, made to look like drawing rooms and dining rooms. At first glance, some of them appeared to be full of faeries and Hettie shrank back in fear, but the figures were only cutouts, silhouettes that ran on tracks in the floor. It was as if Piscaltine were pretending her house was busy and alive, even though it wasn't. One door led into a room full of toys, too-large rocking horses and colorful blocks. Another opened on a room hung with nothing but bells, from little silver ones to great, big, ear-splitting ones. None of the doors led outside.

At last Hettie gave up, and finding herself a real window seat in a real wall, she curled up against the cold panes.

Outside, the sky was tarnishing like old silver, going black. It would be full night soon. She told herself she didn't want to be escaping now anyway, but she did. She wanted to be home. She wanted to be in her cupboard bed, and she wanted her doll even though it was really just a handkerchief, and she wanted Mother who was always tired and a little bit sad and who loved Hettie very much. She wanted her brother most of all—her brother who would go looking for her no matter how far away she went, who would never give up. Perhaps he was already in the

Old Country, following her tracks, coming to the cottage. Finding nothing. *Nothing but blood on the snow . . .*

Hettie closed her eyes. Her hand went to the pendant inside her nightgown. She held it up. The eye set into the dark metal looked alive as ever, glistening wet and bright. She stared into it, trying not to cry.

"What am I going to do?" she asked it softly. "Do you know? How am I going to get home?"

"Who are you talking to?"

Hettie flinched so hard her shoulder blades knocked together. The twins—the tall, tall pale one and the tall, tall dark one—stood directly behind her in their red dresses. She hadn't heard them approach. She might have sworn there had not been a sound in the hallway since she had climbed onto the window seat.

"Oh . . ." she said quickly, dropping the pendant back inside her nightgown. She was sitting with her back to them. She hoped they had not seen. "Nothing. No one, I mean."

They stared at her. They looked just like dolls, Hettie thought. Not like her doll in Old Crow Alley, but like real china dolls that someone had punched the eyes out of.

"Who?" they asked again, and their heads tilted suddenly.

"No one!" She hunched up to hide the shape of the pendant under the thin fabric of her nightgown. "Who are you?"

The twins blinked at her, both at the same time. "We are Florence La Bellina."

"Oh." Hettie's eyes flicked from one to the other. "Well—which one's Florence and which one's La Bellina?"

"What do you mean, *which one*?" They leaned toward her, and Hettie couldn't tell if the pale one had spoken, or the dark one, or if both had spoken at once. "We, together, are Florence La Bellina. There is no *which one*."

"Oh," Hettie said again. *Go away. Please go away.*

The pale twin lifted her hand, and Hettie saw there was something in it, a hook on the end of a long ivory handle. Florence La Bellina slipped it under Hettie's sleeve, delicately, as if touching a slug. She started to pull back the fabric. But just before the red lines were uncovered, a voice sounded from far down the hallway—

"Maud?" it echoed. "Maud, for stone's *sake*!" It was Piscaltine.

The pale twin drew back. The sleeve slipped into place. And as Hettie watched, the two women came together, linking arms and merging, until there was only one woman, one side of her face white, and the other side black, black as a lacquered box.

Florence La Bellina stared at Hettie for several heartbeats, those red-rimmed eyes bottomless and empty. Then she turned and glided away into the shadows of the house, her skirts rippling like blood in the dark.

CHAPTER VII
The Birds

A madwoman was locked in the cell across from Pikey's. Across the dripping corridor, beyond the backs of the scratching rats and the tufts of moss, she sat hunched against the dank wall. He could hear her muttering to herself in the dark, hour after hour, whispering words that made no sense.

"We knew," she said, and her voice grated like an old hinge. "We knew he would clip their wings and put their heads in the earth. But it *was* sad."

Pikey scooted out of his corner and peered through the bars. The rats scattered. The woman did not look up. She sat as she always did, huddled in shadow. Her hair was lank and straggling, hanging over her face. Sometimes, when she said a word particularly loudly, the strands would fly away from her mouth. Pikey could not see her eyes, but he knew she wasn't looking at him. She wasn't looking at anyone.

"The water is black there, you know." Her hands went to her ears, covering them. "Black and green and sharp as turpentine, and the hammers fall all the night through."

Pikey coughed and crawled back into his corner. There was a patch of straw there, damp and black with age. High in the wall, on the level of the street, was a barred window with not even a shutter to stop the snow and the wind from blowing in. The cell was set a little way underground, and the walls were always wet. Some days, when the air in the street was not as cold, and the steam coaches were more numerous, the snow would melt and the water would flow down the stone in rivulets. Moss grew out of cracks in the stones. All Pikey could see through the window were feet, passing by in an endless, pounding parade.

"Don't let him see," the madwoman hissed from her cell. "Don't let him see!"

Some of the feet were slopping by in filthy, broken boots like his own. Others wore fine, ebony overshoes, waxed and waterproofed and polished to mirrors. Still others were pinched into pointy, button-up ladies' boots that peeked out from skirts held up over the muck.

To amuse himself, Pikey tried to imagine what sort of faces belonged to the feet passing outside. The fine overshoes, he decided, belonged to pale, bushy-browed gentlemen with warts on their noses and gold watches in their hands, gentlemen who worked in banks and smoked cigars until their lungs turned black and they coughed up little puffs of ash. The worn boots belonged to kinder men, busy and tired, like Jem when he wasn't drunk. The dainty boots and the colorful children's shoes were good people's, sweet ladies and happy boys and girls. Those were Pikey's favorite to think about.

"And the others?" The madwoman's voice rang out suddenly, sharp in the depths of the jail. "The others

in their pretty clothes? All gone? All broken?"

Pikey shut out her cries and moved a little closer to the window. He decided to see if any of his guesses were correct. He touched the sock that hid his clouded eye, making sure it was still in place. When a particularly fine pair of green velvet boots passed by, he scurried to the base of the window and peered up.

The boots belonged to an elderly lady. She wore clothes all in green, with a hat and muffler of silver fox fur. When she saw him staring up at her through the bars, she let out a gasp and picked her way over the slush to the other side of the street.

Pikey watched her go. *Well,* he thought. *That weren't how I imagined her at all.*

The others were no better. Nobody's faces seemed to match the boots they wore. The polished over-shoes often belonged to perfectly normal gentlemen with beards and top hats, not coughing up ash at all. The children's shoes were usually on the feet of stiff, buttoned-up boys and girls with sickly faces. They always walked faster when they saw him staring up at them. After a while, Pikey decided he didn't like his game anymore and burrowed into the straw, laying his head on his fist. He tried to sleep, but the madwoman would not shut up.

"A tower of blood," she sang to a wavering, sliding tune. "A tower of blood and a tower of bone. A tower of ash and a tower of stone. Who's at the top of them, who's in the dark? Who climbs the stairs without leaving a mark?"

Pikey woke cold and clammy. He didn't know how long he had been asleep, but the madwoman had stopped singing. The prison keeper was walking between the cells. He whistled as he went and rattled his billyclub against the bars.

"Dinnertime, me lovelies," he shouted, sloshing a bowl of something gray and lumpy. "Or . . . me one lovely. So little to do with the faeries all gone. It's right desolate down 'ere!"

So little to do with all the lads out of London fighting in the war, Pikey thought, but he didn't say anything. He sat up, shivering. He had flopped into one of the puddles while he slept, and moss was squashed all over the skin of his neck.

The prison keeper came up to Pikey's cell and pushed the bowl between the bars. It was gruel. Porridge and water and anything else that was in grabbing distance of the one who stirred it. Pikey hoped there had been a duck or a cow wandering nearby at the time, but he couldn't see any of it in the bowl. No parsnips or meat. Not even a bone.

"Looks tasty, don't it," the prison keeper said, grinning, and Pikey snatched up the bowl and began to pour its contents down his throat. It was cold as wet plaster.

The prison keeper watched him. Pikey saw he had that look in his eye, a sad, wondering look, as if he pitied Pikey. Pikey didn't want to be pitied.

He finished the gruel and set the bowl down with a snap. "Well?" he said, looking the prison keeper square in the face. "Aren't you gonna give the batty lady any?"

The prison keeper pulled Pikey's bowl through the bars. He drummed a quick rhythm on its side with his fingernails. Then he shook his head. "She don't eat."

Pikey scowled at him. "She don't eat. . . . Everybody
eats, 'specially in jails, because you're not allowed to
let us starve like when we're on the streets."

"It's no fib!" the prison keeper said, loud and a
little bit pleading, as if he couldn't bear it that Pikey
didn't believe him. "The story's been all over London,
all over the presses, and in the *Times* and the *Globe* and
the *Morning Bugle*." He counted the newspapers off on
his fingers. "Six months she's been 'ere, since the
first spriggan riots up in Leeds, and she hasn't had
a bite to eat nor a drop to drink since then. Not *one*
bite." The prison keeper leaned toward Pikey. "They
say the faeries are feeding her."

Pikey snorted and pushed himself back into the
cell. The prison keeper *was* fibbing. Telling him a
stupid tale to cheer him up, like he was a little boy.
Well, he didn't want to be cheered up. And he wasn't
a little boy. "That's daft. I don't believe you."

"It's the truth, I swear 'tis!" The prison keeper
threw up his hands as if to ward off the accusation.
"It's why she was put here. Everyone was saying she
was a witch, always disappearing for days on end, or

years, always casting spells on folk, even after the laws was passed. She's from a village in the North, and folks are keener there. Sharper-eyed and more afraid. One day they caught her conversin' with a dead tree in a dark wood and put her in an iron carriage to London, and she's been here ever since. Waiting for a trial. Like you. Only she doesn't eat. No food, no water. And she's no worse than the day she arrived, if you can believe it."

The prison keeper wasn't smiling anymore. He clicked his nail one last time against the bowl. Then he set off down the passage.

"I *can't* believe it," Pikey shouted after him, but the prison keeper just kept walking. Pikey slumped against the wall, staring at the hunched shape in the other cell.

She sat as she always did, huddled and shivering, muttering to herself. She sounded different now, though. As if she were crying.

"I know," she whispered, her voice breaking, becoming a sob. "I know what they've done. But *they* don't, the poor dears. They don't know what they've started."

Her voice echoed in the empty cells. After a bit, the sad words became harsh, then sly. The woman laughed sometimes, a high, fluttering laugh. Many hours later, when Pikey had almost dozed off again, he thought he heard other sounds from the mad- woman's cell, quick footsteps and the brush of hands on stone, as if she were walking or dancing. But when he dragged himself to the bars and peered through them, she was still sitting in the gloom, whispering, her hair hanging over her eyes.

The next day Pikey gave up listening to the mad- woman. She did nothing but cry now, anyway, wretched sobs that hurt his head. He gave up watch- ing the shoes that shuffled by in the street. He barely looked out the window at all anymore.

She's waiting for a trial, the prison keeper had said. *Like you,* and the very thought of it was enough to make Pikey's stomach go watery. He had known a trial was coming from the moment the leadfaces had dragged him out from under the newspapers. A pauper's court was the sort of thing all gutter boys had to face at one point or another. But regular gutter boys were never caught with heaps of gems. Regular gutter boys didn't end up with silver flatware from the finest houses in London and not a single smashed window-pane or broken lock to show for it. Regular gutter boys didn't have faery eyes.

Every day, the prison keeper came to deliver the bowl of gruel, but he wouldn't say anything useful. With a sinking feeling, Pikey began to wonder if he would have to stay here as long as the madwoman had. Months and months in the dark and damp. He might go mad himself, then. He'd be dotty as a handkerchief. At times he caught himself staring into the shadows, half hoping to see that pale hand again, the long fingers beckoning, sweeping him away to freedom.

No one came. No one he saw, at least. But the sounds in the madwoman's cell continued, footsteps and laughs and whispers, and all the while the mad-woman sat in the dark and wept.

On Pikey's twenty-fourth day in the cell, a tremen-dous squawking brought his attention back to the window. What he saw made him leap to his feet and clamber up so that his face was flat against the bars.

The sky was full of birds. So many birds they seemed to darken all of London. They swarmed under the lid of clouds—crows and jackdaws, ravens, sparrows, and even swans, flowing across the city in a vast hissing flock. The street turned black as night. People screamed and threw themselves into doorways and under stopped vehicles. Gentlemen held down their top hats and scurried for cover.

As Pikey watched, a gaggle of geese waddled frantically up the street and past the prison, flapping and honking. Three leadfaces came at them, ringing their bells, forming a wall. The geese didn't stop. They seemed almost frenzied, their tiny eyes a sharp, vicious black. They arched their necks and screeched, dodging the officers. One goose bit a leadface in the leg, so hard it left a bloody gash. Then the gaggle hurried on, around the corner and northward toward the edge of the city.

In barely sixty seconds it was over. The sky returned to its still, dull gray. A single raven flew screaming across the rooftops. People began to peek from the shelter of barrels and steam coaches, their jackets grimy with soot and vinegar. Pikey dropped down from the window and plunked himself onto the floor.

Faery magic. He knew it was. Only faery magic could get a pack of geese walking that quick all on its own.

They're going north, he thought. *They're all going north.*

The faeries were calling, and the birds were answering. The war had begun.

CHAPTER VIII
The Insurgent's House

"MAUD! My shawl. We should have been in the lower house yesternight."

Hettie dashed to a little dresser and shuffled through the heap of shawls that lay on it. *Spiderwebs, onionskin, poppy seed* . . . "Which one, Piscaltine? I don't know which one you want."

"The green one, silly! Look at the weather." The faery stood before a mirror, fixing a wreath of wilted flowers behind her ears. The mirror reflected a little box of a room painted to look like a study, and a window that was really only a picture of gloomy hills and rain. Hettie didn't think a *picture* of rain counted as weather, but she snatched the greenest shawl she could see and went to Piscaltine's side.

Piscaltine looked down at it. "That isn't green. That is striped."

Hettie squinted at it. She didn't see any stripes. "It looks green to me."

"Maud, don't be *contrary*! It is green and the stripes are green as well. Anyway, I asked for lilac. Get me lilac."

Hettie didn't glare. Hettie didn't fuss. She kept her face still and went back to the dresser. She felt very wise. Piscaltine seemed to think she was her little servant, and so the other night Hettie had decided she would play along. The faery lady was bound to grow bored of her soon. Then Hettie would leave, and when she did it would be better to be on good terms with the faery lady.

She picked up a length of dull purple cloth and brought it back to Piscaltine. Piscaltine accepted it with a smirk and sailed out of the room.

"So!" she said as they went down the corridor. It was being built as they walked, and in the darkness ahead Hettie saw the reconstruction faeries swinging on their harnesses, pounding the floors and walls into place with frantic haste. "We are supposed to be practicing bell immunity, but of course we won't. We must simply be very careful now, because the King's people are in my house."

"The King's people? You mean those fancy people?" Hettie asked, snatching up Piscaltine's frock before it could snag on a heap of tools that had been forgotten on the inside of the corridor.

Piscaltine ignored her.

Hettie squinted at the faery a second. Then she said sweetly, "You're very pretty, Piscaltine."

Piscaltine smiled. "Yes, the King's people. They watch everything, the wicked creatures. And they tell everything to *him*."

"Why? Who are they?"

"They are his Belusites, of course! His menagerie of curious creatures. He collects them, you see. Just like I do!" Piscaltine clapped her hands delightedly and patted Hettie on her branches.

Hettie didn't know what to say to that. She didn't

really understand the way the faery lady talked of *collecting* people and then snipping out their tongues, but she didn't have time to think about it because just then they turned a corner and stepped into a hallway made entirely of cloth. Hettie very nearly fell on her face. The whole length of the hall was made of cloth, the floor and the walls and the ceiling, and whenever Hettie or the faery lady took a step the construction jounced and juddered. It was like walking inside a hanging tent. The stuff didn't seem particularly thick, and Hettie was afraid it would rip and she and the faery lady would tumble into the dark and break their necks. But Piscaltine struggled along, and Hettie struggled after her, and soon they were at the other end, clambering up into the safety of a wooden doorframe.

"Where are we going?" Hettie asked, gasping for breath. "I've—I've never been through *that* before."

"To the hearth room," Piscaltine announced, not out of breath at all. "I had it built in the Mildew Wing today. They won't ever look there. They think I am such an obedient little duchess, but I'm really not."

She smiled a sharp-toothed smiled and started down a staircase.

Hettie hurried after her. "Piscaltine, why don't you do what the King tells you? Don't you like him? Is he a bad king?"

"He is a king. Of course he's bad. Our Country never had kings. When you call people kings they tend to believe you, and so we always only had lords and duchesses and people like me." She primped, adjusting the flowers behind her ears. "You see, we each had our own little place to govern. Before."

"Before what?"

Piscaltine bobbed her head about, nose in the air, pretending to admire a badly painted wall of vases and flowers.

"I also like your shoes," Hettie said, glancing at the tips of the violet slippers as they darted out from under Piscaltine's frock.

"Before the Sly King!" Piscaltine answered. "Before he took everything, and he put all the low faeries underground, and everyone he didn't like, and forced them to build weapons and such nonsense. Because it is wartime, he says. Because we must all do our part. Well, I simply want to *rule* my part. Brightest Summer was wonderful before he came. There was no fog, and I had so many servants and so many courtiers and jugglers and entertainers, and oh, the *feasts*. It's so dreadful now." The faery lady shuddered.

Hettie thought she agreed. "Couldn't you go somewhere else? Couldn't you go to a different part of the Old Country?"

"Of course not. There are only four places to go, and they're all bare and desolate now, anyway. Winter is the largest part, because doesn't it just stretch on and on when you're in it? And then there's Summer. I have a little piece of Summer. Belinda Blue has a piece, though she never leaves her tower anymore. Don't tell anyone, but I suspect it's because she's dead. The rest of Summer is simply wild now. Then there's Spring and Fall, and both are very small and very colorful and very difficult to find. I've never been to them. I'm not sure even the Sly King has. I've only ever been to Deepest Winter. That's why the Belusites say, 'Oh, silly little Piscaltine. Doesn't know anything of the world.' But what are they? Servants. Servants and slaves." Her voice was bitter, and she clutched the lilac shawl so tightly Hettie could see all the bones in her hand.

They arrived at the hearth room. Piscaltine pushed through the door. Again she locked it with ribbons and a sprig of green, only this time she added a bone and spoke a word and waved her hand over the old, ornate lock. Then she turned to Hettie and sighed.

"There. We're safe now. All the other faeries are in the immunity rooms, down to the last boot-scraper, having their innards unsettled by iron-sounding things, and here we are just having a *delightful* time!"

"We might get in trouble," Hettie said. "I mean, if someone tells, and he's king and all, he might be angry. He might chop off your head."

That seemed to annoy Piscaltine. "Well, if he chops off my head, I'll make sure he chops off yours, too. Anyway, he'll never know. And don't be such a worrywart! There are many of us who don't do as he says. Whole *houses.* It's horrid having a king. Especially

one like him. He makes us wear dresses and ride
Virduger and speak English. He wants things just so,
and most faeries don't want things any way at all. So
some of us don't follow him. And some of us die, but
I'm not going to. I'm far too pretty for dying. Now.
Before anything else, are you hungry?"

"Oh, yes, please!" exclaimed Hettie. In an instant,
she all but forgot about disliking the faery lady, and
about being crafty and clever. She had eaten nothing but mushrooms for ages, and she was more than
ready for some proper food. She hoped it was stew.
Or cabbage tea. Or black bread with carrot mash.

Piscaltine giggled and glided over to a silver dish
that sat waiting atop a claw-foot table. She lifted the
lid. Hettie hurried to her side and peered in. At the
bottom of the dish were six perfect black cakes, like
very dark chocolate. Swirls of buttercream had been
piped on top, and they were decorated with glossy
sugar pearls and threads of toffee. They looked so
scrumptious. Hettie let out a gasp.

"Have one," said Piscaltine, holding the dish under
Hettie's nose. She had a glint in her eye, but Hettie

didn't see it. All she saw were sugar pearls and butter-cream, and cakes like ones she would never, ever be able to eat in England. She picked one up carefully, as if she were afraid she might drop it. She admired it a second. Then she bit into it, one great, round bite.

Piscaltine snapped the lid back onto the dish. The claw-footed table vanished. So did the dish. "Excellent," she said. "Now you have eaten of our food. Faery bread and faery butter. You will not be able to leave this house. You'll be my friend forever and ever. Oh, I can't *wait*."

"What?" Suddenly the cake tasted like dirt in Hettie's mouth. The cream clogged her throat, too sweet. "What—?"

"What, what," Piscaltine said, sitting herself in a chair and smoothing her skirts. "I can't have you running away. I want you to listen to me and follow my orders and tell me stories and cheer me when I'm sad, and you are an Englisher. Englishers can be very wicked."

Hettie felt dizzy. Blood pounded in her ears. *This isn't true. Oh, this isn't true.*

"But it is!" the faery said, as if Hettie's thoughts were a book that she could read. "You are part of the house now. Part of the inventory. No door will open for you. No window will break. And since all the reconstructionists have strict orders not to let you too near the outer walls, you won't get out. Ever. I would have to be dead before you could leave this house."

Hettie spat the cake onto the floor, but it was too late. It was far, far too late. She couldn't be sure, but she already felt a little heavier, a little duller, as if her feet were weighted with lead.

"No," she said. And then louder, "No, I have to go home! My brother's looking for me, you can't keep me here. He'll never find me. He'll never find me here!"

"Well, good, I don't want him to find you." Piscaltine's voice had been very calm before, but it was getting pointier now, and she kept glancing at Hettie, little hurt glances. "He would take you away from me, and I don't want him to!"

Suddenly, at the end of the room, a quiet knock sounded on the door.

Piscaltine went very still. Hettie didn't. She didn't care. She didn't care about Sly Kings, or skipping bell immunity, or stupid faery rebellions. She didn't care if Piscaltine's head was chopped off right that instant. "No, Piscaltine, make it go back. Make it not work. I have to leave, I *have* to!"

The knock sounded again, a tapping—porcelain fingers on wood.

"Be *silent*," Piscaltine hissed. "Silence, I say!"

"No!" shrieked Hettie. "No, let me go! Help! Help, Piscaltine's in here! Piscaltine's in here!"

The knocking turned into a slow, steady beat.

Piscaltine rose, her hands fluttering. She looked as if she were about to slap Hettie. The knocking grew louder. Piscaltine whirled to the door. "Oh, it might be the Belusites. They might have inspected the immunity rooms." She spun back to Hettie. Her eyes narrowed. "Get out. Hide. They mustn't see you again."

A sharp command sounded from the other side of the door. The ribbons and sprig frizzled away to nothing. The bone snapped.

"It never *works!*" Piscaltine whined, and then she shoved Hettie viciously toward the chimney. "*Out.* And Maud? You will be my friend, or I will kill you."

The door clanked open.

For a second Hettie thought about facing the Belusites, if it was them. Perhaps *they* would help her. But then she glimpsed the two hands pushing the door, one black and one white, and she saw the red skirts. She felt a sudden jerk of panic. She stepped into the cold fireplace just before Florence La Bellina swept into the room, and swung herself up by the bar, hanging from it like a little pig about to be roasted.

"Piscaltine," Florence said, and Hettie could imagine her striding closer, one half of her face white, and the other black. She pulled herself onto the top of the bar and stood on it, hardly breathing.

"Yes?" Piscaltine said. "Hello, Florence La Bellina. If this is about bell immunity, I was just about to go."

"This is not about bell immunity, Piscaltine. This is about the child we saw yesternight. We wish to inspect her."

Hettie stood so, so still, the bar cutting into her bare feet. *Inspect me?* She didn't want to be inspected. And suddenly she was almost grateful to horrid Piscaltine for coming down the hallway that night at the window seat, for frightening the Belusite away.

"A child?" Piscaltine was saying. "What child? I don't know what you mean. You've probably lost your mind. You should go look for it. I suggest starting at the top of the house and working your way down, and don't forget the sinks and the linen cupboards."

"Where is she, Piscaltine."

Hettie had to get out of there. She had to get out of there *now*. She began to scramble up the chimney as fast as she could. She made a terrible noise. She gasped and grunted and sent falls of soot down into the hearth, but she couldn't bother with that now. A few feet above her was a ledge. *If I can only reach it.* Her toes found the seams in the stone, her fingers gripped a little hole, and she pulled herself up, rolling over onto her back just as two faces appeared below and peered up.

"What was that?" Florence La Bellina asked. "What is in your chimney?"

"Rats!" called Piscaltine. "And spiders. And roaches and toads and horseradishes. They're all so *noisy*."

Hettie lay on the ledge, utterly silent. Seconds passed, and nothing stirred down in the fireplace. Then she heard Piscaltine and Florence La Bellina retreating into the hearth room. Hettie lifted her head and looked about. It smelled of rat droppings up here, and something sharp that scratched the back of her throat. There was almost no light, but even in the gloom she could see that the chimney branched in many directions, like a tree. She felt a draft of air against her cheek.

She scooted toward it and found a crack in the stones, just a foot wide and smaller at the bottom than at the top. She squeezed through it into pitch blackness. The draft stirred her branches. She began to crawl. Suppose she could get out of the house this way? Suppose there were broken parts and she could just drop out of a hole and run away? She hoped she could. She hoped it wasn't true, what Piscaltine had said about the cakes, that it was just a lie and a joke.

On and on she went, through the dark, on hands and knees, into spaces so narrow she could hardly fit. And then, at last, she saw light below her. She dropped down. She wasn't outside. She was on a cold hearth, in a room made of mirrors. The floor was mirrors and so was the ceiling, and they all showed a little person in a little nightgown, who was utterly and completely black, her branches sticking up like a charred broom.

CHAPTER IX
The Pale Boy

ON his twenty-seventh day in prison, Pikey started looking out the barred window again, and on the thirtieth, a pair of overshoes passed by belonging to a tall, pleasant-faced gentleman with curly golden hair that was turning gray over his ears. His arm was wrapped in a linen sling. Someone was walking at his side. Pikey couldn't see who it was, but he could see the boots—fine black boots, clotted with snow and mud. Like police boots, only small, with silver buckles up the sides wrought in the shapes of feathers.

"My dear boy, I understand you perfectly," the gentleman was saying, his voice snatching at Pikey's ears. "But it won't do any good! I can assure you, anything this woman may have done is entirely . . ."

The gentleman's voice faded again. Other feet sloshed by, spattering Pikey's face with dirt and sludge. But when Pikey flattened himself to the wall and looked up through the bars, he could see that the two figures had halted at the door of the prison, only a few paces farther down the street. They were going to come in.

Minutes passed. Pikey heard hinges creaking, the prison keeper speaking in a loud, friendly voice, and then the jangle and scratch of keys as a door was opened.

Pikey scrabbled up to the bars. Three figures stood in the gloom. One was the curly-haired gentleman, hat in hand. The second was the prison keeper. The third was the one in the buckled boots. He wore a cloak and a hood that hid his face. He was barely four feet tall.

The three figures started up the passageway. They stopped in front of the madwoman's cell.

"Here she is, sirs, alive and kicking. Except for

the kicking bit." The prison keeper's voice was still cheerful, but his eyes kept darting from the gentleman to the hooded figure and back again.

Pikey was looking, too. He sat crouched on the ground, and so as the group passed him, Pikey glimpsed up under the short one's hood, saw pale skin and dark eyes. They were deep eyes, deep as a wishing well.

"Unlock the gate, please," the hooded figure said. "Let me speak to her."

Pikey held his breath. That wasn't a man's voice. It was soft and reedy. A boy's voice.

The hooded figure waited for the prison keeper to unlock the gate, then darted into the madwoman's cell. The curly-haired gentleman remained in the corridor, back straight, looking strikingly out of place in his embroidered waistcoat and red brocade cravat. He glanced about, at the low vaulted ceiling, the moss on the stones, and the puddles on the floor, pretending to find them very interesting. Pikey thought the gentleman was very bad at not looking suspicious.

"That's all, thank you," the pale boy said, without looking at the prison keeper. "Wait for us at the end of the passage, please, at the door."

The curly-haired gentleman stopped his examination of a puddle and looked up, startled. The prison keeper's reaction was much the same.

"Wait for us at the door, please," the pale boy said again. "We'll be safe."

The gentleman nodded uneasily, and the prison keeper lumbered off, shaking his head. The boy waited for him to reach the end of the corridor. Then he stooped quickly in front of the madwoman.

"Hello," the boy said. He spoke so softly; Pikey had to strain to hear him. Pikey inched closer to the bars. The gentleman hadn't noticed him yet. If the pale boy had, he made no indication of it. "I've discovered from several reliable sources that you are in contact with faeries in the Old Country. I need to know if it's true. Do they come to you? Do they come through a door?"

The madwoman did not look up.

"Do they?" The boy's voice was still low, but it

held an edge now, sharp as a leadface's sword.

The gentleman stopped shuffling. Water dripped in a distant hollow, but there was no other sound. Every lock and stone and lung seemed to be holding its breath.

Suddenly the madwoman snorted. "I'll not tell," she said. "Johnny and Lucy and Black Jack Pudding said, 'Don't tell, sweet lady, don't tell. It would be very bad for all of us.' So I'll not tell a soul."

The pale boy let his breath out slowly. "I need to know," he said. Pikey leaned his head against the rusting metal. He could hear the words clearly now. "I'm searching for a door into the Old Country. I know they exist. Little holes and passageways. Please, madam, I need your help."

That was when the madwoman looked up. "Why?" she asked. It was a simple word, but she spoke it with a sort of smug malice, like the meow of a cat. Pikey wondered if the pale boy would slap her. When folks in the streets spoke that way they were usually slapped for it.

The pale boy remained perfectly still. "My sister's

there. Years now. She's stuck there, and I need to get her back."

The madwoman dropped her head again. "They said not to tell," she said. "My little friends from the hedges and the hilltops. 'Dangerous,' they said, 'dangerous,' so I mustn't say. No, I mustn't say."

"Then I'll wait," the pale boy said. "I'll wait here and see for myself."

The gentleman gave the boy a warning look. "Bartholomew," he said quietly, reaching through the bars to lay a hand on the boy's arm. "You tried. This will get you nowhere. It's no use."

The boy shook him off, but the madwoman sat up. "You should listen to that one. It *is* no use. My friends will not come if you are here. You will frighten them. *Changeling.*"

Pikey flinched at the word. Changeling. Half blood. A Peculiar, right here in London. The pale boy could thank his lucky stars the prison keeper didn't know. Or the leadfaces up in the street. He would be packed off to a faery prison before he counted to three.

And it was then that Pikey had an idea. The boy named Bartholomew was looking for his sister. Stuck in the faery world, he'd said. Pikey had seen something like that. A girl in a dark forest, not in London. Suppose he could use that? He had to do *something*. When the pauper's court came, no one would believe him when he told them a sylph had stolen all those things. They would think Pikey had, slipping into houses and vanishing again like a shadow. *Faery-touched*, they would say. *Just look at that eye. Wouldn't wonder if he can work all sorts of spells. Let's dip him in a pond and find out.*

If Pikey stayed here, he was dead. One way or another. But if he could convince these folks that he could help them . . . He would have to be quick.

Bartholomew was half standing. The gentleman had him by the arm again and was whispering to him urgently. The madwoman was growling to herself, clawing the floor and spitting.

Pikey stood, gripped the bars of his cell with both hands, and shouted, "I've seen your sister!"

Bartholomew froze. The gentleman spun to look at Pikey.

"I've seen her," Pikey said again, in a rush. "She's got branches for hair, don't she? And a sort of pointy face, all white and bony. I've seen her, sure as day."

Slowly, Bartholomew turned. He approached Pikey's cell. "How?"

Pikey stole a quick look down the passage to make sure the prison keeper was still at the door. "My eye," he said. "I saw it with my eye." With quick fingers, he undid the sock that hid the empty gray eye.

Bartholomew stared at Pikey, his gaze dark and unreadable. Pikey stared back. *It'll be safe,* he thought. The pale boy was a changeling after all, half faery. That was a heap worse than being just a bit touched by one. But then, Pikey was a gutter boy, too. He imagined his ugly clouded eye and how he was no better now than a filthy cobble spryte, really, squeezing through the mud under the streets. He shuffled and looked down at his feet.

"What did you see?" Bartholomew said slowly.

He doesn't believe me. Pikey knew it. And the gentleman was pulling at the boy's sleeve again, murmuring something.

Well, if Pikey were going to get out of London in anything but chains, he was going to have to *make* them believe. He looked up again.

"Just past Glockner's Inn," he said firmly. "She was in the street, but she was also in a forest. It don't make much sense, but there was a snowy forest *in* the street, all grown with black trees, and this girl, she reached out her hand to me. That's all I seen, but I know it's her."

Of course, he *didn't* know. He had no idea. There must be hundreds of changelings in England, hundreds of little girls with branch hair and sharp faces.

"A snowy forest," Bartholomew said. A faraway look had come into his eyes. He was peering past Pikey, through him, as if he were made of glass. He began to pace. "A snowy forest and black trees. A cottage in the distance with a light burning in its window. Mr. Jelliby—" He whirled on the gentleman. "Mr. Jelliby, he's seen her. He's seen my sister."

"Bartholomew, you don't know that." The man spoke gently, a little wearily, as if he'd had to say the same thing a hundred times before. "He might have heard it somewhere. News got out all over the world after the door opened. So many stories . . ."

"It was years ago," Bartholomew said, and his voice was sharp with pain. He turned back to Pikey. "How old are you? Do you remember the Lickerish Plot? Nine dead changelings and an airship over London?"

Pikey glanced from the gentleman to the changeling and back. He sensed a trap, but he couldn't see its teeth. "I— Well, I *heard* about it. But it was an awful long time ago. I'm twelve years of age, sir. Leastwise I think I am."

"Twelve," Bartholomew repeated. "Mr. Jelliby, we need to get him out. He can help us!"

The gentleman sighed. "But you don't *know*. You can't know if the boy is telling the truth, and even if he is, he—"

"I *am* telling the truth!" Pikey said desperately. "I saw her! Sure as day through this 'ere eye! You have to believe me! She has a sort of tattoo all up her arm, too, don't she? All red like she kicked a cat and it scratched her? Is that your sister? *Is it?*"

Now the gentleman was looking at him as well.

"And she has these enormous black eyes, so big you could drown in 'em. I saw her, I tell you, I saw her!"

Bartholomew stared at Pikey a moment longer. Then, very slowly, he brought his head up close to the bars. "And can you see her again? Could you tell me where she is and what she's doing?"

"I— Yes. I could, sir. I will, if you'll get me out."

Bartholomew did not hesitate. "Good. You'll get out. You'll come with us. You'll tell us everything you know and everything you've seen. But if you're lying . . ." His voice went very low. "Well, you know what sort of people are out there and what they do to people like us. Just don't lie to me. Ever."

Pikey wanted to growl at the boy, tell him he was nothing but an ugly Peculiar and in no better position than Pikey, but that wouldn't have helped him at all. He was getting out. That was what mattered. "Yes, sir," he said.

The gentleman sighed one last time and spun on his heel. "Prison keeper!" he shouted, his voice echoing in the dank corridor. "Prison keeper, we're taking this one! Get your keys! As the Earl of Watership, knight to Her Majesty, the Queen, and member of the House of Lords, I *command* you to let him go."

The prison keeper lurched down the corridor, looking somewhat startled. "Aye, m'lord," he said, bowing and ducking. "Of course, m'lord." He unlocked the cell with a toothy key. The bolt clanked back. And the instant it did, Pikey leaped out.

"Thank you, sirs. I'll help you. I swear I will, I'll help you find her." He was almost sure the air smelled better out here. Really, it was just as foul and putrid as the fumes in his cell, but to him it was as pure as pump water.

The gentleman raised his eyebrows and stared straight ahead. Bartholomew gave him a sideways look.

Pikey took that as a sign of friendship and rushed to his side, lifting his shirtfront to rub the grime from his face. "I will, I'll—"

They were walking away. He hurried to catch

up. But just as he was passing the madwoman's cell, a veined and wrinkled hand shot out and wrapped itself around his wrist. The madwoman. She had pressed herself to the bars, gasping and muttering, her head bowed.

"Good luck, boy," she said, fingers wriggling up his skin. "Good luck from Johnny and Lucy and Black Jack Pudding. Don't let the Sly King see, they say. Don't let him see."

And then she raised her head, and Pikey saw that one of her eyes was just like his, gray and empty, staring on and on into nothing.

CHAPTER X
The Hour of Melancholy

AN old grandfather clock stood outside Hettie's sleeping closet, and it always told her when it was time to run.

It was almost like a regular grandfather clock. It had a pendulum, and two spiny hands, and carvings all around it made to look like thorns. Inside, a small spryte pedaled endlessly to keep the wheels turning, and there were many creaking gears and wooden pistons. But it wasn't *entirely* like a regular clock. It did not tell time in hours or minutes. It told it in moods. Instead of numbers on its burnished cheeks, it had four small brass faces. The first was grinning, the

second sad, the third savage, and the last face Hettie
had never quite understood, but she supposed it was
asleep. Its eyes were closed and its mouth was pinched
into a pinhole. The hands had never pointed to it,
though, so she had never had reason to wonder on it
further.

That night, one in a string of long, lonely nights
in Piscaltine's house, the grandfather clock was
striking the Hour of Melancholy. Both spiny hands
snapped into place under the sad face. A deep, sad
bell sounded in the clock's belly. And the instant
Hettie heard it, she leaped from her little bed and
began fiddling frantically with the locks and bolts on
the peeling wooden door. Piscaltine did not like her
to be late.

Hettie poked her head into the passage. She looked
first up it, then down it. Then she slipped out and
broke into a run. The sleeping closet she had found
for herself (after several nights spent in window seats
and rope heaps and on a dusty sofa sewn from pea-
cock feathers) was on one of the uppermost stories,
close under the roof. It was one of the few parts of

the house that was solid and didn't move about, but it was no safer. The attics were known to be prowled by pity-faeries.

Run, run, run. Her feet barely touched the ground as she flew toward the end of the passage. Pity-faeries had long limbs and small, evil faces, and they bounded on all fours like great corpse-white dogs. They were called pity-faeries because they had none. If one came at her now, she would never be able to outrun it. And if one appeared in front of her—

She skidded around the corner and down a steep flight of steps. One of the treads was held up by nothing but a bent old nail and would plunge anyone who stepped on it to a swampy death in the house's basement far below. Hettie skipped the step handily and ran on, twisting down and down. *Don't slow,* she thought. *Don't slow. You can catch your breath once you're safe.*

She had never seen a pity-faery up close before, but she had glimpsed one once through the crack in her door, a blur of bony limbs and snapping teeth. It had been leaping after a tiny goblin woman, and Hettie had heard her shrieking, feet pattering down the passage, the sound almost swallowed by the hammering gait of the pity-faery. Not very long after, the shrieking had stopped.

Piscaltine kept the pity-faeries in cages usually, in her dining room in the Glass Wing, but sometimes, especially when the clock struck the Hour of Wrath, the faery lady would let them out with a toothy key and they would tear up the stairs and eat things. Goblins, mostly, and gnomes, and the weak little servant faeries who did not have the necessary spells to disguise themselves as candlesticks or tapestries. Piscaltine called it "weeding the house," and Hettie suspected she enjoyed it. Sometimes she let them out during the Hour of Mirth. She had never let them out during the Hour of Melancholy before, but she might do it now.

Hettie came to the last step and began climbing down a ladder. The ladder was impossibly tall, disappearing into blackness. It creaked and wobbled under her. She never faltered. Below, she glimpsed the orange lamps of the reconstructionists, some bobbing solitary in the dark, others gathered like fireflies where rooms were being built. The rooms would be sad, she knew, purples and blues to match Piscaltine's mood. Piscaltine had been sad for nights now.

"Why did you spit it out?" the faery lady had screamed when she had found Hettie again, hiding in the dusty dark on top of one of the rooms. Piscaltine had strapped herself into a reconstructionist harness and had looked utterly ridiculous. *"Don't you* want *to be my friend?* Don't *you?"*

Hettie hadn't said anything, and she hadn't needed to. Piscaltine's face had seemed to freeze, perfect and pretty. Her black-pool eyes had glistened. Then she had swooped away, and later Hettie had woken to the *scritch-scritch* sound of hands, and the swish of clothes, and had peered over the edge of the room to see Florence La Bellina and four other Belusites crawling up the walls and the reconstruction chains, searching the tops of the rooms below her, searching as if they were certain they would find someone there. The next day Hettie had gone to Piscaltine and had sat down at her feet.

Stupid faery, Hettie thought angrily, climbing down

rung after rung into the dark. But Piscaltine wasn't stupid. Piscaltine had told on Hettie. It meant she knew Hettie was a Peculiar, and it meant she also knew that Florence La Bellina wanted Hettie for something, and it meant Piscaltine was going to use that knowledge for whatever pleased her, and there was nothing Hettie could do about it. She couldn't leave. She had tried, and each time the corridors had led in odd directions, or a panel had dropped out from under her and she had tumbled into a snarl of ropes or a kettle of faery washing. In the end Hettie and Piscaltine had settled into a sort of play-act: Hettie was Piscaltine's friend and Piscaltine was her benevolent mistress, and whenever she could be she was horrible to Hettie.

Hettie arrived at the head of the huge, crimson-carpeted staircase, which she had heard was called the Innard Stairs, after the giant who had supposedly been murdered on it and was responsible for its sumptuous coloring. She hurried down. Her feet echoed in the vast, silent space. Dust rose in plumes from the carpet under her feet. For all the servants and reconstructionists bustling in the darkness, the house was strangely dead and lonely.

Halfway to the bottom, she passed a gray, long-limbed faery with moth wings. It was going up. She waved. She didn't think she had been at Piscaltine's house very long, but she already knew that faery. Its name was Snell, and it was very quiet. It had gray eyes and gray skin and gray heather growing from its head. Usually Hettie didn't like the quiet faeries—they were far more dangerous than loud ones—but Snell never did anything to anyone. Snell never even spoke and so Hettie didn't know if its name was actually Snell, but she had decided it was a good name for it. It always looked so unbearably sad whenever she saw it. Granted, she rarely ventured out of the attics except during the Hour of Melancholy, and in that hour everyone *had* to look sad. But at least Snell didn't look like it would eat her.

At last Hettie arrived at the door to Piscaltine's chair room. She paused. She took a lungful of the cold, damp air. Then she pushed through the door and into the room.

It stretched out in front of her, dark and opulent. Cobwebs hung from the ceiling. Hettie hadn't noticed before, but the paintings were cracked and old now, barely paintings at all. Piscaltine sat in the high-backed chair, eating red berries with a silver spoon.

"Hello, Maud," she called out as Hettie approached.

"Hello, Piscaltine." Hettie slowed, wary. This was not normally how the faery lady sounded. Not during the Hour of Melancholy. She usually sounded sullen and wistful, and she would have Hettie play at her feet, or hold her hand and tell her nonsense about England and how the people there hung stones from their ears and built birds out of metal. But not today. Today the faery lady looked fearsome-pretty and pale, and there was something in the curve of her lips that made Hettie afraid.

Piscaltine fixed her eyes on Hettie and poked at the berries with the tip of her spoon. "You will never guess what glorious news I have just received," she said.

Hettie went to the footstool and sat down at Piscaltine's feet. It was Hettie's own footstool. She had been made to embroider it with strands of kelpy hair, and since she hadn't known how to embroider, she'd had to learn, picking out the stitches over and over again until Piscaltine was pleased.

"Well," Hettie began. She thought for a second. "The reconstructionists have been in the Mildew Wing for ages putting up a hall. I suppose there's going to be a masquerade."

"Wrong. There is going to be a masquerade. Isn't that delightful?" Piscaltine rapped the spoon sharply against the edge of the dish. It made a little *ting*.

Hettie flinched. "Oh, it sounds lovely."

"It *is* lovely. It will be a very great event. And to think it was I who was picked to host it. Ah . . ." She sighed, and looked very self-satisfied for a moment. Then she fixed her gaze on Hettie. "And since I am so wonderful and forgiving, I have a surprise for you. On top of that."

Hettie's heart did a horrible, squirming leap. The way Piscaltine said it. Not really like a surprise at all. More like a challenge. Whatever the surprise was, it would be bad.

"See this mask?" Piscaltine set the silver dish in her lap and held up a glistening black half mask. It was edged with feathers of the deepest, most vivid blue. Black silk ribbons dangled from its corners. "It is for you. For the masquerade." The mask's eyes curved upward, mirroring the faery lady's own expression.

"For—for me?" Hettie frowned. "But I'm not—I'm not *going*, am I?"

The faery blinked at her and said nothing.

Hettie tried again. "I didn't think Whatnots were invited to masquerades." Her hands were shaking. She hid them under her nightgown. It was the same nightgown she had worn when she had first come to the Old Country. Patched and re-patched and stitched and lengthened, but the old, gray fabric was still underneath. Piscaltine had said she was far too naughty to get new clothes.

"That depends on whose Whatnot it is," said Piscaltine. "For example, *you* could never go. At least not the way you are. But you see, once you put on this mask no one will know who you are. They couldn't possibly. It is a fleshling mask. It makes you look like the creature that is your soul. Takes it from the inside and puts it on the out. I got it from the King of Coal when he asked me to marry him. He decided not to marry me in the end. . . ." Her eyes took on a faraway look. Then she smiled an angry little smile and pushed the mask into Hettie's hands. "Come now. Try it on. I'm perishing to see how your soul looks. I suspect it will be quite horrific. Twice as ugly as you are now. Perhaps an octopus or a particularly bristly boar." She lifted another spoonful of berries to her mouth and chewed them expectantly.

Hollow head, thought Hettie. *Idiot numbskull goblin-eater.* She thought it loudly, because what Piscaltine had said hurt her and she wished it didn't. She knew Piscaltine was just being awful, but somehow it didn't make it any better.

I *don't think I'm ugly,* Hettie thought. She would go to the masquerade looking like a bristly boar for all she cared. Everyone would laugh, and Piscaltine could feel very good about herself, but it wouldn't matter. Not really.

"All right," Hettie said, and set the mask on her face.

She wiggled it so that she could see through the holes. They were much too far apart, made for faery eyes, but she could still see through them. She tied the ribbons behind her head. Then she dropped her hands and made a face. It didn't fit properly. It was made for delicate Sidhe faces, not her lumpy changeling skull.

She looked down. Her feet were still there, at least. No tentacles, or feelers, or anything else disagreeable. That was good. She looked at her hands. They were the same, too, ten fingers, ten nails. And the red tattoos . . . The lines were duller now than they had been, but they were still there, looping over her arms.

"My soul looks like me, I suppose." She shrugged and returned to the footstool. "I can't go. Everyone will recognize me."

But Piscaltine had stopped eating. She was staring at Hettie, silver spoon poised, one bloodred drop of juice suspended, quivering, from its tip. Her mouth had formed a perfect *O*.

Hettie glanced at her uncertainly. Then she hurried to one of the gilt mirrors that were nailed to the wall. What she saw there made her heart fairly die within her.

A tall, beautiful figure looked back at her from the glass. She was dressed in black, buttoned all the way up the neck. Her face was narrow, but her mouth was firm, and her hair was a tumble of copper-bright curls. There were no tattoos on her arms, no branches for hair or ugly black-pool eyes. This creature was proud and strong, and Hettie was almost afraid to look at her.

Hettie blinked, peering down at herself. She saw her hands again, her old nightgown. None of it looked any different. She swished back and forth, whirled. Then she lifted one finger and poked at her nose. The lady in the mirror did the same.

The beautiful creature in the mirror was her.

"Maud," breathed Piscaltine. "Oh, Maud . . ."

And then the faery hurled the dish of berries to the floor and flew at Hettie, snatching the mask from her face. "Give that to me. Give it to me at *once*."

Piscaltine inspected the mask, glaring. She spun it quickly in her hands. Her eyes snapped to Hettie. They were so black, so horribly black, like cold, dark stars.

Don't say anything, Hettie hissed to herself. *You'll just make it worse.* She put her chin up and folded her hands behind her back, because it was the only thing she could think to do right then.

"Very well," Piscaltine said. She was standing perfectly still, but somehow she seemed to be moving, trembling and crashing like waves. "Very well. Now look at *me*." The mask was on her face. She tied the silk ribbons behind her head. When it was in place, a long shiver passed down her from the top of her head to the tips of her shoes. And then she had changed. She was made of wire now, like a dressmaker's mannequin. Inside was only air, and where her heart should have been there was a red cushion on which sat a monstrous ugly toad. There were tiny contraptions around it, bellows and pipes that shot bursts of water to keep it wet, and a padded mechanical hand that would pat it from time to time. But it had so many warts. And such droopy, mournful eyes. It opened its mouth and let out a croak.

The faery lady stared at herself a moment, wire eyelids snapping up and down. Then her metal lips parted and she began to wail. The toad croaked again, louder. Piscaltine tore at the mask. It came away from her face, dropped from her fingers. And all at once the wires and the toad and the bellows vanished, and she was a faery lady again, in a fish-bone dress.

"Maud," she said, her back to Hettie. She sounded as if she was smiling. "So special is my little Whatnot. So special to everyone." And then she spun on Hettie and shrieked, *"I hate you!* I hate you. You are nothing, do you understand me? You are nothing at all." She fled then, and the doors to the chair room crashed shut behind her.

Hettie stood frozen, rooted to the floor. *No. No, no, no.* This was not how things were supposed to go. Her tongue was still attached. Her head was still on her shoulders. But for how long?

You are nothing at all.

CHAPTER XI
The Scarborough Faery Prison

"SHE looks worried," Pikey said. He held one hand over his good eye and stared out with the other. He was in a chilly room, on a bed under low, sloping eaves. Bartholomew sat across from him. A small window looked out onto a narrow London street and the curling signboard of an inn. Laid out on the floor was an array of slim metal instruments, compasses, knives, glass tubes, and a lot of little bottles.

Pikey frowned, concentrating. "She's saying something. I don't know what, but she's frightened by something. Her eyes are real big, and she's just staring down at me . . . whispering."

Bartholomew's skin was even paler than usual and there was a little spasm in the hollow of his cheek. "Is anyone near her?" His voice was so soft Pikey could barely hear it. "Can you see anyone?"

"I—I don't reckon so. She's alone, far as I can tell. But she's in a right swish spot. In this great, long hallway with carpets and curtains and a proper glass window behind her head. It's like a mansion! Like the sort lords live in, or the Queen!"

Bartholomew rose abruptly from his stool. He closed his eyes. When he spoke again, his voice shivered. "They've found her. Heaven help us, they've found her."

Pikey switched hands, now covering his faery eye and looking at Bartholomew with his good one. "What? Who found her?"

"Oh no. No, they couldn't have, she was in the woods, in the snow, and they—"

"Who is 'they'?" Pikey asked, swinging his legs off the bed.

"It was a cottage we saw in the distance, not a mansion. A *cottage*."

Pikey stomped his foot on the floor. The glass bottles jumped and one began to roll. *"Who are you talking about?"*

Bartholomew started. He looked at Pikey as if seeing him for the first time. "What? The Sidhe, of course! Lords of the Old Country! Faery royalty! They've found her. We have to go." He fell to one knee and began gathering up the instruments on the floor.

"Well, if *I* was stuck in the Old Country, I wouldn't much mind being with these Sidhe folk. With carpets and windows and such. It looks marvelous."

"You don't know what you're talking about," Bartholomew practically sobbed. "Their houses are deathtraps. Every word my sister says, everything she does, could get her killed. She would've been better off in the wilds. . . ." He stood. "We have to go. Now."

"Yeh, you said that."

"As in, this *instant*." Bartholomew shouldered his pack and banged open the door. "She could die there. Any second, those horrid faeries could eat her alive, and I'm here and can't do anything to stop it, and wouldn't know until—until—"

"But she's *not* dead," Pikey said, hopping off the bed and hurrying after him. "I just saw her. And anyway, if she survived such a long time, it goes to figurin' she'll survive a bit longer. Leastways by my figurin'."

But Bartholomew had already pulled up his hood and was pounding down the stairs into the belly of the inn.

They went up York Road hurriedly, heads down against a brisk winter's wind. Bartholomew said they were disguised as vagabonds, but Pikey was reasonably sure he didn't look much different from usual. His sock patch was tied securely over his clouded eye. He wore his same old trousers and bean-sieve jacket, and while Bartholomew had rubbed dirt and grease into the silver feather buckles of *his* boots, Pikey's were cleaner than any he had ever worn. The day before, the curly-haired gentleman had come by and, after speaking to Bartholomew in hushed and urgent tones, had procured for Pikey a thick woolen cloak and a pair of boots so new you could smell the waterproofing oil. He had also said that he was not a pirate and thus could not be expected to know where one got eye patches. Pikey had no idea what that meant, but he had been pleased with the boots.

Bartholomew strode purposefully ahead, a wiry black shape against the ice and snowdrifts of London. His pack was on his back, bottles and metal devices clinking softly. His cloak flapped behind him. Pikey had glimpsed the inside of that cloak the other day. It was full of little pockets and pouches and mysterious bulges. Long black gloves hid Bartholomew's arms to the elbows. His hood was pulled low over his face.

No one even glanced their way. Luckily. They saw leadfaces and the black-goggled agents of the Faery Bureau swarming the streets, dragging gnomes out of cellars, pulling the wildly kicking and bucking *Virduger* out of drain holes. On Hatfield Street, a giant had disguised himself as an oak tree and had simply stayed very, very still. The leadfaces had discovered him when someone had tried to chop the tree down for musket stocks and now they were dragging him off, too. The last of the faeries were clinging to the city.

Bartholomew and Pikey came to the river. A crowd had gathered. They pushed into it. People began to squeeze and jostle, the smell of unwashed humans battering Pikey, and then everyone was shouting insults, and he saw they were yelling at a huddle of ragged piskies being herded from under the supports of Blackfriars Bridge. A turnip flew. Then a stone. Bartholomew pulled Pikey onto the bridge.

The shouting echoed away behind them. When they were in the silent alleys of Holborn, Pikey said, "So. Where're we going? I mean, today. We can't walk to Faeryland." He could easily keep up with the other boy. He was taller, even though he was sure Bartholomew was older. The thought made him puff up a bit and put back his shoulders.

They were almost at Ludgate Hill again, almost to the—

Pikey slowed. "We're not going back to the prison,

are we?" His heart squeezed. Hadn't he been enough help? Was Bartholomew bringing him back because he hadn't seen enough? Pikey wasn't going to be locked up there again. Not in the dark and the cold, with nowhere to go. He would punch Bartholomew and run fast as anything before that happened.

But Bartholomew shook his head. "No. We're not going back there. I thought about it. I thought about setting up nets and bells and all that and *making* the faeries talk, but I don't have time. I didn't even know whether Hettie was alive a few days ago, and now that I do it's as if she's in greater danger than ever. We need to get into the Old Country, and we need to get in soon."

They turned a corner, onto a long, wide road. They were high up in the city now. The houses here were scrubbed and clean and stood in neat rows like the spines of books. The ash from the chimneys drifted down with the snow, gray and white and feather soft. The light through the draped windows glowed a gentle orange. Pikey spotted a large-wheeled bicycle propped against a fence and wondered what sort of people lived here. He wondered what they sounded like, and whether they ate plums and pies, and laughed a lot.

"All right," he said, a little absently, still staring at the bicycle. "But where are we going *now*?" He shook himself, and said more loudly, "I mean, how'll we get into the Old Country, when you said you'd been searching for ages?"

Bartholomew sighed. "The faery world and England, they're not really that far apart. Sometimes people just slip in when they least want to. It's only when you're looking for it you can't find it. There are two scientific ways, as far as I know. There's the changeling door. It's complicated and destructive, and it has to be engineered with spells and blood and magic. You need a live changeling to open it, and a binding potion, and approximately seven hundred penumbral sylphs within a range of fifteen miles."

"Well, makes it easy, don't it? You're a changeling. You could just be your own door."

"Don't you think I've tried that?"

Pikey shrugged. Bartholomew had an odd way

of snapping. His voice was never very loud, but you could always tell when he wanted to twist your neck twice around.

"I've done everything. I have the lines. . . ." He pulled down one glove, exposing a web of red threads almost exactly like the ones on the arms of the branch-haired girl. "I got the potion. I found a place in Wales where the sylphs roost." Bartholomew stared dully into the distance. "It wouldn't work. Not for me. Someone told me once that I was too much a human and too little a fay, and I suppose he was right. You have to be equal parts to be a door. It wouldn't open for me."

"Well, there are other Peculiars. I mean, it'll be hard now with 'em all being dragged to the lockups, but—"

"No," Bartholomew said softly. "That's what John Lickerish did. Tried them one by one until one of them worked. Nine died before he got his door. Nine children like Hettie. I can't do that. I won't do that."

"Oh." Pikey didn't entirely understand. If *he* had a sister lost in the Old Country, he thought he might do a bad thing or nine to get her back. But he wasn't going to press the subject. "And the other sort of door? What's the second kind?"

"Natural doors," said Bartholomew. They were almost out of the city now. Pikey saw fields ahead. No alleys or factories. Just fields.

Bartholomew continued. "I've been looking for them the longest, for years and years. I went to Dartmoor and Yorkshire and all the way to France and the forests of Germany. I found cairns and abandoned faery hills and saw lots of awful things. But none of them led me to the Old Country."

How old was this boy? Fifteen? Sixteen? Pikey wondered what it was like, searching for so long, doing and hoping and thinking about just one thing for such a long, long time. All Pikey ever thought about were hot stoves and caramel apples and how to not die. He felt a little bit pointless suddenly.

"I haven't found either sort of door, but I think I've found something else," said Bartholomew. "I've got a chance now. A real one. The English armies are gathering in Yorkshire. The faeries are already there. Mr. Jelliby has connections with the Faery Bureau and rumors are spreading in the prisons that there is a leader in the North, a Sidhe, come specially from the Old Country to lead them into battle. That Sidhe had to get here somehow. I don't know how, but if there was a way for him, there's a way for me. We're going north."

And with that Bartholomew swept under an archway, and suddenly Pikey was surrounded by white, pure white snow as far as he could see, as far as he had ever seen before. He was free.

That night they slept under the stars. They found a stretch of grass, sheltered over by trees and guarded from the wind by a low hill, and laid down their cloaks. Bartholomew had somehow managed to buy meat pies at an inn outside the city without attracting attention, and Pikey wasn't expecting another meal that day, but he became rather hopeful when Bartholomew set to gathering sticks. He lit the pile with a tinderbox and three drops of something black from a bottle in the depths of his cloak, and then the heap began to crackle, smoke curling from the frozen wood. It was not a cook fire, though. It wasn't even a fire for warmth.

Bartholomew kept poking at it, hurrying to the trees, tearing off branches, coming back, throwing on more and more wood until the fire had grown into a great, angry blaze. Then he came to Pikey, and said, "All right. Can you see Hettie? Is she safe?"

Pikey untied the sock and looked out through his clouded eye, but he already knew what he'd see. Nothing. Only blackness, with the occasional fleck of light, like a snowflake against his eye. "I— Well, I don't see things all the time. Sometimes it's like it's blocked, or—or under something."

Bartholomew blinked at him. "You can't see anything."

"No?" Pikey said cautiously. He looked over at Bartholomew.

"Give the sock to me," said Bartholomew. Pikey held it out. Bartholomew grasped it, and before Pikey could say a word the sock had flown into the flames.

"You won't need that anymore," said Bartholomew

sharply. "You'll try, and try always, to see my sister, and when you do, you'll tell me. Everything. Every detail. I need to know she's safe."

Pikey let out an angry cry, but the sock was already burning. "You could've just given me the sock to *wear*, you know!" he shouted, wheeling on Bartholomew. "D'you think I have lots of those? We don't all have fancy people buyin' us boots and cloaks whenever we want! We're not all rich stupid toffs!"

"I'm not a toff," Bartholomew snapped. "I was just as poor as you once. But I—I—"

"You *what*?" Pikey demanded. "Who d'you think you are?"

They sat glaring at each other. The sock burned away to nothing. Then Bartholomew went to the other side of the fire. Pikey glared at him a while longer. He began to doze. The ground was hard, and the cold pricked at his cheeks, turning them red. Finally he huddled into his cloak and tried to sleep.

It must have been hours later when he opened his eyes. The fire had shrunk to a few red coals. Bartholomew still sat by it. His back was toward Pikey. His shoulders slouched. But he wasn't sleeping. He was saying something.

Pikey raised himself up on his elbows, silently. Bartholomew was whispering, repeating four words, over and over again. He was holding something. Then he bowed his head and began to cry. Pikey could hear the tears in his voice, the words coming ragged and weak.

"I'll bring you home," Bartholomew said, and the sound of it drove into Pikey like a thorn. "I'll bring you home."

Pikey lay down again, but he did not try to sleep. He watched Bartholomew until the other boy had dozed off. And when he had, Pikey saw the thing that was in his hands. It was a handkerchief, checkered green and black. It had parts knotted into it, arms and a head and something like a skirt. Almost like a little doll.

Pikey woke the next morning to Bartholomew shaking him urgently by the shoulder.

"Wake up! Wake up, there's a faery prison just over the rise. It'll be upon us in moments."

"What?" Pikey's mind was foggy with sleep. *It'll be upon us?*

"Now, *get up!*" Bartholomew's voice held a distinct edge now; not of fear exactly, but something very close.

Pikey propped himself up on his elbows. "What are you talking about?" He glanced about. "It's not even daylight yet." The sky was still dark blue. The fire was out, the ashes stamped into the ground.

Bartholomew dragged Pikey to his feet and practically threw him toward the thicket of brambles and stunted trees that grew along the edge of the rise. Pikey just managed to snatch up his cloak, and then he was plunged into the branches, and the frosty prickers were snagging on his clothes.

Not a moment too soon.

A deep, bellowing horn sounded from the other side of the hill. Then the faery prison mounted the ridge, and Pikey's breath came out in a cough.

The prison was an iron globe, a cage three hundred

feet high, barbs and spikes radiating out from it like a monstrous metal thistle. Brimstone bulbs pierced the early morning darkness. The globe heaved itself to the top of the hill, amid screams and the cracking of whips, hovered for a moment on the edge, and then began to roll, thundering down toward them. Trees snapped under it. In a few seconds the grass where Bartholomew and Pikey had been sleeping would be nothing but a huge gash of dirt.

Pikey looked at Bartholomew. He seemed to be counting under his breath, *four, three, two...* And then he grabbed Pikey's arm, and before Pikey knew what was happening they were out in the open, running full tilt into the faery prison's path.

"What are you doing?" Pikey screamed. The roar of the prison filled his ears. The huge metal bands were gouging tracks into the hillside, crushing trees, slinging mud.

Bartholomew ran faster. Pikey tried to pull away, but Bartholomew's grip was like a pincer. The globe loomed above them. Pikey caught glimpses of tiny figures inside, of houses and alleys and thin metal chimneys and flickering lights. Then the globe came crashing down, and he was enveloped in blackness.

Pikey heard himself yelling. He felt Bartholomew's hand, still around his wrist, pulling him desperately up onto a metal beam. Then he didn't feel it anymore, and he was sliding and falling and sliding some more, and red lights whirled past, and when he looked down, he saw that he was three hundred feet above the ground, and the arch of the cage was tipping down, down toward the snow and the tiny trees, and the earth was rushing up to meet him.

He screamed. He was pinned to the metal beam like an insect. Nothing was holding him. Nothing but the force of that great iron globe, spinning. His stomach squirmed.

"Bartholomew!" he tried to shout, but his voice cracked, lodging like a splinter in his throat. He swooped up again into the sky. His hands scrabbled for something to cling to, found nothing. He began to slip. And then he saw a shape, crawling toward him along the beam, slowly, painfully. It wasn't Bartholomew. Pikey couldn't tell what it was for all the black grime that covered it, but he saw that its limbs were barely bones, and it dragged a chain behind it, made of iron. The creature let out a sickly, gurgling wail. It had almost reached him. "Help me," it coughed, and a wave of black sludge slid from its mouth. "Help us all. Take us away from here—" And then the globe slowed, and Pikey was tumbling through empty air.

His chest slammed against a railing. He clung to it with all his might. A hand reached down to grip him, and Bartholomew pulled him over onto a walkway. Pikey dropped like a sack to the grating. All at once, the rushing in his ears stopped. The creaking and the cries and the darkness clattered away. Pikey lay still, dizzy and gasping.

Owww . . . he thought, and then, *If that bleemin' Peculiar pulls another trick like that, I'm leaving, I don't care what happens,* and then he noticed the ground wasn't swaying. At least, not badly. He pushed himself onto his elbows. Somehow the faery prison's insides didn't move with the rest of it. Somehow it had been constructed so that its core remained flat even as the outside whirled across the countryside. It was probably a marvel of science, but Pikey took one look at the sky and the ground spinning outside and pinched his eyes shut so that he wouldn't be sick.

He would have liked to stay like that, but Bartholomew was stooping over him, nudging him to his feet.

"Up," Bartholomew whispered. "Come on, we can't stop here."

Pikey opened his eyes and stood shakily. They were on a long curving walkway. Everything was dimly lit, tinted red. Above, going up for hundreds of feet, he could see protruding black metal and ladders and air vents and the endless ruddy flicker of the brimstone bulbs. And below, over the railing, was a seething mass of limbs and faces. A thousand, thousand faeries. They were chained to the skeletal rim of the globe— goblins, sprytes, tiny water piskies, beautiful nymphs and merefolk, all dying on the cold iron. They were pushing the great prison, on and on, collapsing as they swooped overhead, then pushing again as it they spun down and it was their turn. Whenever a faery went limp, a guard in goggles and a gas mask would lean off the walkways and ladders and prod it with an extendable black pike, poking until the creature was up. The globe never stopped.

A shout sounded nearby. Pikey whirled. He had stared a moment too long.

One of the guards was coming along the walkway, pike raised. It had seen them. It broke into a run. A crackling, metallic shriek came from the air filter on its mask. Another guard materialized at the other end of the walkway. Pikey and Bartholomew went back-to-back, eyes jerking about for a way to escape. Both the guards were running now, boots clanging against the metal walkway. Pikey could see his own terrified reflection in the mirrored lenses of the goggles.

"Climb!" shouted Bartholomew. *"Climb!"* And then he leaped onto the railing and clawed his way up a chain.

Pikey scrambled after him. Just in time. Below, he heard the two guards collide, clockwork and black rubber crashing together.

Pikey and Bartholomew struggled upward, up ladders and snaking passageways that were little more than pipes.

It was so strange being in this dark metal jungle, when minutes ago they had been in an English field, with nothing but snow and silence. Pikey still felt half asleep, in a daze.

Bartholomew helped him up onto a ledge. "I'm sorry I burned your sock," he said.

"Sorry I couldn't see your sister yesterday," Pikey mumbled.

They climbed on. Steam hissed into their faces. Sometimes the metal under their hands was scalding hot, sometimes icy cold. Pikey's cloak snagged on a bolt and got a tear right up to the knee, which made him want to scream. At last they pushed up through an air vent and burst onto something broad and solid.

They were on a dismal, bustling thoroughfare, and a faun was about to stomp on them.

Pikey stood bolt upright. Bartholomew rolled into a crouch. Faeries were trudging past on all sides, wandering the gloomy street. They were dressed in rags, tattered waistcoats, and broken hats. Branches and wings poked this way and that. Whole families were here, huddles of sprytes and tired-eyed goblin mothers, their many tiny children clutching at their skirts and crying. None of them seemed to notice the intruders.

The ground was sheet metal. A layer of cauterized black grease coated it like mud. The houses on either side were built of slag and sooty bricks. Gasoliers burned, weighting the air with fumes. Above, the great arc of the globe cage rolled on. There was a constant wind, a constant thundering, but the houses stayed steady, only creaking gently now and then, sending flakes of rust falling to the street.

"Why'd you have us jump aboard *this* place?" Pikey whispered. "We could've been killed or squashed into jell*mph*—"

Bartholomew clamped a hand over Pikey's mouth and pulled him backward into an alleyway.

"Shh," he said. "Faery prisons travel north. All of them. Away from London and Parliament and any chance of treachery, or so Parliament hopes." Pikey tried to wriggle away, but Bartholomew was stronger than he looked and he continued to speak in a quick, low voice. "Trains don't go north. Not with passengers. Not with anything but war goods nowadays. And you'll not get a carriage to take you as fast as this. Look at the sky. Look at the clouds passing. We're moving at forty miles an hour, and nothing goes that fast that's not a train. We'll lay low until it gets us past Leeds and then we'll jump off again. I don't know how long Hettie'll be alive. A day here could be a year in the Old Country, a hundred years. I don't know how long we have, but I'll not take any chances by dillydallying."

Pikey stared at Bartholomew dumbly. Then he nodded, eyes wide.

"Good," Bartholomew said. He dropped his hand from Pikey's mouth. "Now. This place will be swarming with leadfaces soon. Let's try to—"

But Bartholomew never finished his sentence, because just then a booming, crackling voice blared from above, echoing through the entire prison.

"Attention, Detainment Unit Inhabitants. Attention, wardens of the Scarborough Faery Prison."

"Oh, now we did it," Pikey said under his breath.

"There are two intruders aboard our peaceful facility. They are hooded and cloaked, of diminutive stature, and without doubt in league with the enemy. Do not give them aid. Do not speak to them. Any faery found fraternizing with them will be assigned to the Pushing Pits. Permanently. All sightings are to be reported to the Royal Officer at the head of this facility."

Pikey glanced into the street. The faun with the chipped hooves had galloped back to the air vent where Pikey and Bartholomew had emerged and was scratching about, head lowered. It had a sharp, pale face. Even from a distance Pikey could see that its eyes were dead-black.

"Attention, Detainment Unit Inhabitants. There are two intruders aboard our peaceful facility."

Bartholomew pulled Pikey behind a fat, steam-belching pipe that curved up out of the ground.

Pikey spat. "Good luck hiding now. Now they're looking for us. How are we supposed to lay low when everyone in the prison wants to *find* us?" He looked down the alley. It ended in a high wall studded with rivets and popped sheets of metal. Dead end. Not even a door. Ignoring Bartholomew's grip on his arm, he peeked around the pipe.

The faun had disappeared, but the other faeries in the street were looking about now, too, squinting from under hat brims and mossy eyebrows. The thoroughfare seemed to be emptying, the gasoliers dimming. Ragged creatures disappeared into alleys and doorways.

"They are hooded and cloaked, of diminutive stature . . ." the voice droned on. *"Do not give them aid. Do not speak to them. . . ."*

"We'll survive," Bartholomew said. "But not if you keep popping your head out like a jack-in-the-box. Stay hidden!" Again he jerked Pikey back.

"Any faery found fraternizing with them will be assigned to the Pushing Pits. Permanently."

And then the faun cricked its neck around the pipe and stared at them, black eyes glinting.

"Found you."

Bartholomew's hand went to his side. A knife

appeared, narrow as a blade of grass. He spun it in his hand, letting the point stop at the creature's throat.

The faun crouched back and put up its hands, making a ch-ch-ch sound as if to calm them. "Now, now, my pretties, hush. Hush! I won't tell. You come from the Sly King, yes? He has sent you to us, yes, in the hour of our desolation?"

Pikey and Bartholomew exchanged glances. Or rather, Bartholomew looked in bewilderment at Pikey, and Pikey looked suddenly very frightened.

A tower of blood, a tower of bone, a tower of ash and a tower of stone, he heard the madwoman singing again, the tune slithering through his head. *Don't let the Sly King see. Not the Sly King.* Pikey didn't know what it meant, but somehow hearing the name uttered here, in this strange iron cage, by this strange faun as if it were real, as if there really *was* a Sly King, made Pikey go cold.

"What?" Bartholomew managed at last. And then, hurriedly, "Oh, the—the Sly King. Of course." His voice steadied. "Yes, we are from the Sly King. In fact, we have just delivered a message to one of Uà Sathir's spies and now we must get to the Old Country.

Is there a way in that you know of? Even just a rumor?"

The faun tilted its head. It did not look as if it had understood him. There was a strange smell coming off it, a horrid tincture of rot and graveyards and decay. And that was when Pikey saw the thing clutching the back of the creature's scalp, the sagging, wrinkled little faery, all teeth and warts and eyes like the eyes of insects. *It* was the one doing the speaking. Not the faun. The faun was dead.

The leech-faery squirmed. "The Sly King is coming to rescue us, yes? All of us. And you are his emissaries. His envoys. His flag-bearers." It was not a question. The faun slid itself over the ground, inching closer. "We've all been waiting for you. We all knew it would be soon."

Bartholomew was beginning to frown. "Yes, but did you hear me? We need to get in. The Sly King is still in the Old Country and we—"

"*What?*" The leech-faery's many eyes widened. "Still in the Old Country?"

Oh no, thought Pikey. *Wrong thing to say, Barth.*

"But I heard he had come! Come to the North with a great army, come to lead the free faeries. To fight!"

"Well— He will!" said Bartholomew. "I'm sure he will, but only once we've—"

A commotion cut him off, a din out on the thoroughfare. Pikey could no longer hear the rustle of the faeries. All he could hear was the *snap-snap-snap* of something large coming across the metal plates. Several things. And shouting.

Slowly he inched around the pipe. Six leadfaces were in the street, standing on great, jointed stilts, iron blunderbusses against their shoulders. They were turning circles, scanning the rooftops, peering into blackened windows. A dozen goggled guards swirled below them, pointing and gesturing with their pikes. Pointing toward the alley.

Pikey rapped Bartholomew's shoulder. "They've found us, Barth. We've got to go."

"Just tell us the way," Bartholomew hissed at the faun, gesturing Pikey to wait. "We'll help you! We'll get you out, but we *need* to know where a door is!"

The guards were moving, straight toward them.

The leech-faery blinked. "A door? A door in? I—"

The leadfaces burst into the alley. Their voices echoed, their stilts throwing grotesque shadows up the walls.

"Barth?" Pikey whispered.

Bartholomew stayed deathly calm. The leadfaces had almost reached the pipe. They spotted the faun. In the last instant Bartholomew raised his hand and a plume of blue powder flew from it. It enveloped them. And then Bartholomew pinned Pikey against the wall, his arm like iron. They crouched, very, very still.

The faun shrieked and began scrabbling away, its hooves scratching sparks. It tried to pull itself up the rivets in the wall at the end of the alley, but the leadfaces leaped off their stilts, right onto the faun, smashing it to the ground. It let out a tortured wail and twisted away, crawling back to where Pikey and Bartholomew hid. But it couldn't see them. They had turned to air.

The faun searched, eyes dark and desperate. Pikey sat stock-still, hardly daring to breathe. The faun's face was right in front of his. He could smell its rotting organs, see every line in its dead white skin.

"Edith Hutcherson," it whispered, as the guards swarmed around it and gripped it. "Find Edith Hutcherson. She knows the way to the Sly King. *She's been there.*"

And then the guards were dragging it off, and its hooves were sliding in the grease, and its eyes were fixed on them until it had disappeared into the thoroughfare.

CHAPTER XII
The Masquerade

Aᴧᴛᴇʀ the incident in Piscaltine's chair room, all the clocks in the house pointed their hands to the Hour of Wrath, and that was where they stayed for the next twelve nights.

Hettie hardly dared leave her closet anymore. Pity-faeries prowled the upstairs almost always now. She heard them howling and snuffling along the passageways, sometimes right in front of her door. She heard the shrieks of the servants, the chittering of the reconstructionists as they swung away in their harnesses. But the pity-faeries were the least of her troubles. Florence La Bellina hadn't left

Yearn-by-the-Woods with the other Belusites. She was still in the house. And she was following Hettie. Every time Hettie stole down the ladders and pulleys into the lower house, she spotted them. Sometimes it was the pale half, sometimes the dark one, sometimes both together. Hettie would be on her way back from the lavatory, or from the kitchens with a mushy fistful of cake, and then she would glimpse Florence, and Florence would glimpse her, and in an instant the Belusite would be after her. She would slide out of the dark and follow, gliding fast as anything. Hettie would have to climb and crawl and run with all her might to lose her, but every time Florence came a little closer, a little closer to Hettie's hiding place in the attic.

Hettie sat on her bed and stared at the door. It was bolted with its flimsy bolt and then wedged closed with a chair. She had barred it with several locks, too, that she had built for herself out of spoons and cooking utensils. They wouldn't stop anyone, but they made her feel a little better.

A whirring sounded from the hall. Then a *click.*

Then the grandfather clock's bell echoed along the walls. Hettie waited, listening. *Two strikes for the Hour of Mirth, three for the Hour of Wrath.* She waited. The sound faded away. The hallway became silent again. *One strike for the Hour of Melancholy. Oh no. . . .*

She got up, sat back down, patting her hands nervously on her knees. The clock rang according to Piscaltine's mood, so that the reconstructionists and all the other servants could prepare the house to suit her. The Hour of Melancholy always, always meant Piscaltine wanted Hettie. But Hettie didn't want to see the faery lady again. She never did, ever again. Perhaps she could just ignore it. Perhaps Piscaltine didn't *really* want to see her, and the clock was simply ringing, and Piscaltine was being melancholy without any desire for Hettie's presence at all.

Bong went the clock again.

Hettie leaped to her feet. The bell reverberated in the passage, long and solemn, and all over the house the other grandfather clocks answered. There could be no mistake. Piscaltine was waiting.

Hettie slipped out of her room. No pity-faeries,

but there were other sorts about, more than she had ever seen this high up in the house. They darted in front of her, in doors, out other doors farther down, carrying pails of dust and jugs of water and armfuls of paint shavings. The masquerade must be nearing.

Hettie pushed past a wart-faced goblin carrying a birdcage full of small blue eggs, and started down the stairs. *Five steps, skip one, onward.* The wood creaked noisily.

She came to the ladder, began to descend. What did Piscaltine *want*? The faery lady wouldn't have forgiven Hettie. She would still be sulking, and she would want to pinch Hettie and call her names. Hettie gritted her teeth. She hated Piscaltine. She hated that Piscaltine could keep her locked up even though the faery was nothing but a weakling and a bully.

She reached the bottom of the ladder and glanced about. The ladder ended in the Dragonfly Wing tonight, the part of the house that looked like the palace of that French king who, Barthy had told her once, had gotten his head chopped off by anarchists.

The reconstructionists were forgetting about not letting her near the outside. A long, window-lined gallery extended into the gloom, real windows, facing out. She rushed down the gallery. She passed Snell, the moth-winged faery, but she didn't wave at it this time, or even look at it. And then she caught sight of something through one of the panes. Something outside. Something that had not been there before.

She skidded to a halt. The window looked onto the field and the wet green woods. A mist lay over the grass, just as it had when Hettie had first emerged with Piscaltine's riding party. The sky was the color of dishwater, the trees dense and drooping, weighted under their foliage. The whole world outside looked damp and lush and distinctly unpleasant. But there was something else, too.

She leaned forward, squinting through the thick, water-streaked panes.

A solitary statue stood just inside the shadow of the trees. It was carved of gray stone. A hood hid its face. It was too far away for Hettie to see any other details, and yet she felt sure its eyes were fixed on the house.

Watching. She shivered and turned away. She had passed that same window once before, very shortly after she had arrived. She remembered looking out at the trees and wondering how far they stretched and whether the horse-people's tracks were still there for her to follow. There hadn't been a statue standing at the forest's edge.

She started down the gallery again. The statue might have been put up for the masquerade. Perhaps the faeries had built it to greet the guests as they arrived. But then why was it facing the house? And why did it look so dreary?

She crossed to the other side of the gallery, away from the row of windows. Best not think about it. She had been here years, she felt. So, so long. She had seen worse things.

She came to the end of the gallery and swung down a rope onto the Innard Stairs.

"Maud, my sweetkin," Piscaltine said as Hettie hurried into the chair room. Hettie's insides went cold at the sight of her, but she did not slow down.

Don't be afraid, she thought. *Don't let her see.*

The faery looked frightful. Her face was powdered and painted. Her lips were a ruby heart, and she had put on a vast gown and curled wig. In her hands was the mask. "Come to me, sweetkin. Quickly."

Hettie bobbed a curtsey, not meeting Piscaltine's gaze.

"I won't need you for long. I simply want you to do something for me," she said, and her voice was sweet and dark as blackberry wine.

"What is it?" Hettie asked, and curtseyed again. Curtsying wasn't something faeries did, but Piscaltine had laughed when she had done it the first time, so she did it all the time now. When faeries laughed they were less inclined to kill her.

But Piscaltine did not laugh today. She did not even wave Hettie to the footstool the way she usually did and pretend to dote on her and stroke her branches while tearing off the little nodes on the end of the twigs until Hettie cried. She gazed at Hettie coldly, and said, "The masquerade begins at moondown. It will be a glorious masquerade with dancing and feasting and phantasm shows. And a gentleman. At my masquerade there is going to be a gentleman. He will be wearing a sea-green suit and a mask like a tortoise. I want you to steal something from him."

Hettie's heart lurched into her throat. She felt her skin prickling, going cold. She tried to stammer something, but the faery lady raised a hand, cutting her off.

"Now, now. Don't fret. This gentleman is of no consequence. A lowly noble I once slapped during a game of cards. Only it was a most unsatisfactory slap, not nearly hard enough for the occasion, and so I'm going to have you steal something from him to . . . how shall we say it . . . even the odds. All you must do is bring me the thing hanging around his neck." The faery lady tapped a finger against the mask in her hands. "I will even give you this to wear again. Since it makes you so very, very beautiful." Piscaltine tittered. "No one will recognize you. No one will even suspect. And if you can do it, if you can steal this one thing for me, I will let you go. I will let you leave my house if that is what you want. I will let you go home."

Hettie gasped. She wanted to cry and laugh, both at once. *Home.* Piscaltine would let her go. Let her be free again. She could go back to the cottage, and Bartholomew would be waiting for her there, and maybe Mother, too.

Piscaltine held out her hand, the mask dangling from one silk ribbon.

Hettie took it quickly. "I'll do it," she said. "I'll do anything if you'll let me leave. I'll—I'll do anything."

The faery lady looked at Hettie curiously from beneath her wig. "You know . . ." she said, very softly. "All I wanted was that you would be my friend. That isn't very much to ask, is it? Doesn't everyone in the Smoke Lands have a friend? Doesn't everyone have someone?" She smiled pitifully and looked away. "I wanted a little person who would be mine, because no one else is. Life is so lonely when one lives as long as we do, in such a horrible, horrible house. But you never wanted to be my friend. You never, ever did."

Neither of them moved. The silence felt huge and hollow in the great room.

Then Hettie said, "I have to go home, Piscaltine.

I can't be your friend. But someone else might be. Someone else, later."

The faery's face emptied like a bucket. She sat up straight. "Until this evening, my sweetkin," she said. "I will be on pins and needles to see you."

Hettie's fingers tightened around the mask.

"Yes, milady." She began to back away. "Until this evening."

Hettie watched the guests arrive from a little window above a lavatory on the third floor of the Dragonfly Wing. They came out of the woods in twos and threes, an endless long line of faeries. Some rode sharp-faced horse-people, some went on foot, and all of them held little white lamps in their hands, like a drop of starlight. They made a glowing worm, uncurling out of the dark of the woods. Eventually a coach appeared, black and ornately wrought, flanked by four vicious, green-plated grasshoppers. After that the line went on unbroken.

Hettie watched until only a few stragglers were left coming across the field with their white lights. Then she wiped her eyes on the hem of her nightgown and climbed down from the window. She didn't know why she had been crying. She had been thinking of Old Crow Alley again. She had been thinking of Mother and Bartholomew. She hadn't thought of home in forever.

She stole out of the lavatory. The house was dark and still. Even the reconstruction faeries were silent behind the walls. The masquerade would be starting soon. Perhaps it already had.

She hurried down a narrow, wood-lined corridor. *Be brave now,* she told herself, clutching the mask to her chest. *No one will recognize you. No one will see who you really are.*

She passed a clock. The hands had moved some-time while she had been hiding. They pointed to the Hour of Mirth now, the grinning face. It looked suddenly horrible to her, fat-lipped and hungry. She ran on. She did not look out the windows as she passed them, but if she had, she would have seen that there were two statues now, standing just inside the woods, watching the house. Two statues where before there had only been one.

At a mirror she paused and took the pendant from inside her nightgown. It was warm, as always. She paused a moment, just holding it. She took a deep breath. Then she let go and held up the mask. The blue feathers around its edge glimmered. She set the mask on her nose and tied the ribbons behind her head.

No sound preceded Florence La Bellina's arrival. Hettie felt a presence in the corridor, a weight in the air. And then the doll-woman swished past behind her. Hettie whirled, heart hammering. The Belusite did not stop. She glided on down the corridor, her skirts a vivid tear in the darkness.

Hadn't she seen? Hettie stared after her. *Hadn't she even noticed?*

As if in response, Florence turned slightly, looking back over her shoulder. Her black-and-white face gleamed, hard and smooth. She stared at Hettie a moment, those empty, empty eyes like two drain holes. Then she swept on, peering up staircases and into doorways.

She's looking for me, Hettie thought. She turned back

to the mirror. And gasped again at the beautiful apparition in the glass. Florence *had* seen. But not Hettie. The figure in the mirror stood so tall, its copper curls glinting, its black gown buttoned all the way up its neck. Its cheekbones high and perfect. Its eyes were like storm clouds.

No one would recognize her. Not in a hundred years. And all at once the woods and the cottage and the road home were so close she could feel them. Even if the guests did catch her stealing from the faery gentleman, she could simply take off the mask and hide and no one would even suspect her. They would be looking for an exquisite beauty with copper curls. Not her. Not the ugly little Whatnot. She would find the gentleman and steal his treasure. . . . And Piscaltine would let her go.

Hettie set off toward the Mildew Wing. It was the part of the house that looked like a huge old fortress, and it was where the masquerade was going to be held. Her gown whispered along the edges of the corridor as she went. The clocks grinned at her from the walls. The mirrors showed a tall lady, all in black.

Oh, she thought. *I'll show you, Piscaltine. I'll show you what I can do.*

She passed into the Glass Wing, where everything was lit and glittering like ice. The floor was strewn with ivy vines and hawthorn branches, making a pathway toward the Mildew Wing. Banners in peach and blue and gold hung from the ceiling. She followed them until she came to a high, pitted black door.

The masquerade was being held in the Hall of Crepuscular Hankerings. Hettie had only seen it once before, its huge wall panels propped up in storage. The panels had looked unremarkable then, old stone with strange grooves in them, like pieces of a jigsaw puzzle all out of order.

The doors opened in front of her, untouched by faery hands, and what she saw snatched her breath right out of her. The hall was vast. Hundreds upon hundreds of white lamps floated up into its heights, carried by tiny, winged faeries, like dragonflies. The walls were sculpted with sinuous beasts and faery knights, all in gray, and the gently drifting lamplight turned the darkness even deeper and made the beasts and knights look as though they were stirring. The floor below was thick with shadow. Faery ladies and gentlemen wandered here and there, dressed in the colors of rain and winter fields, all with masks on their faces. Spriggans with ten-foot-long limbs leaped and slithered among the guests, doing tricks, pulling grimaces. Jugglers whirled glass globes full of wasps and fish and pin tacks. High above, hanging among the ropes and chains, thin, bony reconstructionists watched, beady-eyed.

Hettie realized she was standing in the doorway, gaping, and swept into the hall. Servants dropped their gaze when they saw her. High faeries nodded to her, or bowed, and she nodded back, very slightly. She felt so proud and cold all of a sudden, as if she were wrapped in spikes and armor. Nothing could touch her like this. No one could hurt her. She started to smile, hid it behind a raised hand. It was rather lovely, really. She began to wonder if she would ever want to take the mask off.

She moved to the center of the floor and glanced

about. A great table had been set up along one wall, its benches already filled. Piscaltine sat at the head, wearing the mask of a fish as befitted her station as the Duchess of Yearn-by-the-Woods and Daughter of the Ponds, etcetera, etcetera. Snell was there, too, and Florence La Bellina, and the lady with the hollow back, and a great many other Belusites and Sidhe. The lady with the curtained window-eyes sat to the right of Piscaltine, her mouth open, the red bird extended out of it. The chair to the left of Piscaltine was empty.

Dishes and tureens filled the table, platters of spotted mushrooms, huge tumbles of grapes, berries, and cakes and strange, charred-looking animals. Everything was impeccably arranged, but no one was eating. Heads were together. Faeries were whispering, some were sitting very straight watching the Sidhe and performers on the floor, but the food remained untouched, as though it was all only glass and plaster, as though it wasn't meant for eating. It was a very silent masquerade. Hettie wondered if this was what the balls had been like in the old days, if this was what Piscaltine had been missing.

In the far corner of the hall, three pale faery musicians started a slow dirge. As one, the guests rose from the benches and drifted toward the center of the hall. It was time to dance.

Hettie flowed along with them. She passed Piscaltine's chair. The faery lady looked up, saw her. Hettie held her gaze, still moving. The faery lady nodded ever so slightly. The corner of her mouth twitched. "Go on, my sweetkin," she whispered. And then Hettie was among the dancers, searching for a faery in green with the mask of a tortoise.

The dance began before she found him. The faeries glided across the stone space. They formed a line, then an archway, a corridor of slender white arms that the couples darted down two at a time. When the last one had gone through, the dancers swirled into a star. The star became a flower that bloomed and wilted in one smooth motion. Up among the ropes, the sprytes and winged faeries hooted and whistled softly.

Hettie walked the length of the hall, slipping

along the edges, watching, sharp-eyed. She passed back on the other side. *There.* A sliver of green. He was dancing.

She waited until the fiddle and pipes had died away and the lonely sad drum had stopped banging. Then she moved into the assembly of faeries. The ladies and gentlemen were circling one another, preparing for the next dance. He was standing with his back to her. His coattails were pronged, faultlessly ironed and sewn.

He started to turn. Hettie didn't see it, but behind her at the table, Piscaltine rose a fraction out of her chair. Hettie reached the faery gentleman's side and laid a hand on his sleeve. He faced her. The green tiles of his mask glinted in the lamplight.

Hettie inclined her head. *Simply go to him and take the thing that is hanging around his neck,* Piscaltine had said. But there were many things around his neck. Dozens of them, clinking quietly. Hettie drew her breath in sharply. *Necklaces.* Necklaces just like the one she had under her nightgown, under the illusion of beauty and black velvet. So many eyes, brown and green and robin's-egg blue, looking at her from their metal fixtures. What were they? And where had he gotten them?

"Hello, my lord," Hettie said, and almost flinched at the sound of her voice. It was deep and dark, like coal and chocolate.

"Hello, my lady," the gentleman said. "How lovely you look. I do not believe I have had the pleasure of seeing you before." He was tall and thin, with long, elegant hands. The tortoise mask had slitted eye holes, and through them she saw only black.

"Oh, I hope not," she said. She tried not to stare at the pendants hanging between the lapels of his coat. *Which one am I supposed to steal? Does Piscaltine know there are so many?*

She had to do something. In a second the silence would have gone on too long. The faery gentleman would drift away.

"Do you want to dance?" she asked hurriedly. She didn't know how to dance. But it was either that, or her snatching a necklace and running off with it, and somehow that did not seem wise at all.

The faery regarded her, not speaking. Then he said, "Of course," and held out a hand. Hettie took it. It was cold as stone. She gripped it tighter. They moved into the center of the floor. Out of the corner of her eye, she saw the other faeries slowing, watching them.

The fiddle picked up, playing a sad little tune. Hettie and the gentleman began to dance. They swooped left, then right. They bowed, spun, three steps, four. He was a very good dancer. He swept Hettie along, and she didn't even notice how clumsy her own feet were.

The music became louder. The pipes joined in, growling a deep, rolling countermelody that fought against the sound of the fiddle. Then the drum began to beat, one-*two-three,* one-*two-three.* They sailed across the hall. The music flew up and so did their arms, pointing toward the rafters. None of the other faeries were dancing anymore. Everyone stood, rows of faces, whispering to one another behind raised fans.

Hettie's feet began to hurt, but she did not want

to stop. Her head spun with the joy of it. The music became faster and wilder, and suddenly she was filled with a sort of lightness that made her want to fly, made her want to sprout wings and feathers and swoop away in her beautiful, haughty form. No one could match her. Not Florence La Bellina, nor the beautiful girl from Brightest Summer, and certainly not Piscaltine.

"What are those things around your neck?" she gasped as they spun yet again across the floor. "Why do you wear them? Will you give me one? Give one to me?" She reached out. Her fingers closed around metal and she pulled, snapping the chain against the faery's neck. Then she whirled away, a laugh of triumph on her lips.

But the faery gentleman was not laughing. The music screeched on a wrong note and stopped. The entire hall went utterly, horribly still.

Hettie half-turned, breathless. She saw Florence La Bellina, moth-winged Snell, all the Sidhe in the room just staring at her, their black eyes filled with a sort of dread she had never seen before in faery faces.

Only Piscaltine was smiling, a wicked, wicked smile.

The faery in the tortoise mask stepped toward Hettie. His mouth curved up.

Hettie's heart lurched. "Who are you?" she whispered, and even from her great lady's throat, her voice sounded thin as smoke. "Who are you, really?"

"I am the Sly King," the gentleman said, and then he began to laugh.

CHAPTER XIII
The Ghosts of Siltpool

Pikey and Bartholomew escaped the prison outside a dreary town named Siltpool, just as a gray rain started to fall.

The globe had groaned to a halt for an inspection by officers of Lord Gristlewood's Black-Hat Brigade, and Pikey and Bartholomew had slipped off into the heather and run wind-quick for the brush.

The effects of the blue powder had all but worn off by the time they had made their escape. In fact, they had barely been invisible at all, and not a few guards and decrepit faeries had stared in bewilderment at the dark smudges racing away along the beams. But escape Pikey and Bartholomew did. They found a stony, muddy road and a sign on rusty clockwork spider legs that read, *Siltpool: that way. Population: 4X0 87,* and set off toward the town where they had heard the English army was encamped.

The faery prison rolled past them a short while later. Pikey expected it to be gone for good, but then he and Bartholomew trudged over a hill, and he saw something that snatched the breath right out of his lungs: spread out below him for leagues and leagues were vast barren fields, the ground torn to filthy swaths. In the distance were the sharp rooftops of a town. And congregated about it were twelve iron globes, so huge it looked as if metal moons had dropped out of the sky.

Pikey and Bartholomew stood frozen at the top of the hill. There were so many. Each packed with faeries. Tens of thousands of faeries, locked up in iron, dying.

"Are they—are they just going to leave them there?" Pikey asked at last. "Are they just going to leave them in those cages until the war's over?"

"If the war is ever over," said Bartholomew, slipping and stumbling down the other side of the hill. "And even then, who's to tell? Parliament might think it better just to keep them there. The English will be furious when the war is done. They'll want the faeries to pay. So why not just keep them locked up, everyone will say. Why not leave them there to rot? I don't know if it matters, to be honest. It's not so different from how the faeries lived before."

Pikey frowned and plucked at a pussy willow that had grown out into the road. He looked again toward the great globes, now silent, looming against the dark day. He felt a stab of pity for all the creatures inside. He could just as well be in there himself, locked in some dungeon. And all anyone would say was, *Well, you might get out when the war's over. Or not. I don't know if it matters.* And that would be the end of Pikey Thomas.

They smelled the town of Siltpool long before they got a good look at it. The smell was something between dung and mildew and mushy gray roots, and it whispered up along the road and into their noses.

A short while later, Pikey began to *hear* Siltpool, too. Rain drumming on canvas, harnesses clinking, a general shuffling, rattling sound of busyness. Then he followed Bartholomew over a hill and saw it.

The army's tent city dwarfed the little town. It spilled out of the huddle of low stone houses like intestines from a goat's belly, tents and shacks and wagons spreading across the grass for almost a mile. Toward the center of the town, the tents were large and important looking, flags hanging limp and damp. Farther away, the tents became progressively sloppier and more mud-spattered, and at the very edge of the camp there were only a few broken wagons and some wild-looking peasants washing in a stream.

Everywhere there were soldiers.

"You got some more of that stuff?" Pikey whispered, casting a worried glance up the road. It was empty, but the town was seething with people even in the rain. "Could you make us invisible again? It would be mighty handy right around now. . . ."

Bartholomew put a finger to his lips. "We'll be all right." They were almost at the first tents now. Voices rang out, dull in the rain. "Pull your hood down low and keep your eyes on the ground," he said, and threw his own cloak over his pack so that it looked like he might be carrying a bundle of sticks. "The soldiers have other things to worry about than a few children gathering wood."

They passed into the tent city. Soldiers sat under dripping awnings or huddled over cookstoves. Some played cards. Others just stared into the downpour. A line of horses stood soaked and miserable, tied to a peeled log. A food tent vented greasy smoke. A few soldiers glanced at Pikey and Bartholomew as they went by, but none of them spoke. Their uniforms were sodden and their mustaches drooped. They looked glum, their eyes glazed. *Like cows,* Pikey thought. *Like leadfaces.*

Pikey and Bartholomew plodded on. They came to the solid, stone part of town. The houses on either side of the main road were silent, the windows cold. But they *were* lived in. Smoke coughed from some of the chimneys. Donkeys looked sullenly over the tops of fences. Pikey saw sows in the muck. No geese, though, neither in the yards nor in the street.

"So?" Pikey whispered, when he felt it was safe. "What now? Who's Edith Hutcherson and how do we find her?" He was tired and very wet. He wanted to go to sleep.

Bartholomew didn't look at him. His eyes were on the ground, and Pikey noticed he took small shuffling steps, just like a little boy would. "We don't. Edith Hutcherson could be anyone. She might be a hundred years dead. Or the faery might have been lying. We don't know. We'll stay with the original plan."

"Which *is*? Walk over to the faeries and ask their toffer if he won't just let us through his doorway because we're ever so sad and put-upon? Yeh, it'll work out smashingly."

"What?" Bartholomew glanced at him, and Pikey saw irritation on the other boy's face. "When you have a better idea you can tell me," Bartholomew said. "And when you see my sister, tell me that, too. It's been three days."

That shut Pikey up. It *had* been three days. Three

days since he'd seen Hettie, and it was the only thing he was here for. He wondered what would happen if he never saw her again. He wondered if Bartholomew would just leave him somewhere, and Pikey would wake up one morning in this strange part of England all alone and with nowhere to go. The thought made him afraid. He wished a little bit that Hettie was his sister, too, and that he had just as much right to search for her as Bartholomew did. But of course that was stupid. He wasn't Hettie's brother. He wasn't anybody's brother.

They were almost on the other side of Siltpool, when Bartholomew sidled into an alley between two ancient houses. Pikey followed. No windows looked into the alley and it ended in a stick fence, low enough to escape over if need be. The alley was filled with mud and puddles, and there was a crick in it so that its back half could not be seen from the road. When they were almost at its end, Bartholomew pulled Pikey into a crouch and said, "Here. We'll set up camp here."

"We're going to sleep here?" Pikey wrinkled his nose. "The roofs don't go over more 'n an inch. I saw a better place a ways back, with a roof that went over at least a foot and a—"

"We're not sleeping. We have work to do. You'll be listening. You are going to infiltrate the English camp."

"What?"

"You're going to—"

"Yeh, but *me*? Why don't you do it?"

"I have other things to do." Bartholomew reached into one of the many pockets in his cloak and took out a pinch of the blue powder. "Here's the last of it. I only had a thimbleful to begin with and it cost a fortune. It was meant for later, when things are worse. Well, now it's gone, so don't waste it."

And with that, Bartholomew extended his fingertips toward Pikey and blew. The powder swirled into Pikey's face. Bartholomew whispered a word. Then the muddy alley seemed to flicker and Pikey vanished.

He didn't feel any different. *He* still saw himself, though he felt lighter somehow, hazier. A slight needling was in his shins, but otherwise all was the same.

"Now," Bartholomew said, and Pikey smiled a little at the way the other boy looked straight past him at the wall behind his back. "Don't be gone more than an hour. That was a smaller dose than the last one and the effects wear off over time. Right now you're air. In twenty minutes you'll be a shadow. In forty you'll look like a breath of ash. In an hour you'll be almost solid again. Before then you've got to learn things. I want details of the English plans. Where the faery armies are located. When the English are marching. When the battles are expected to be fought. I'll not have us stumbling into the middle of a firefight and getting shot." And with that he gave Pikey a push, which went straight into his face because he couldn't see him at all, and off Pikey went, splashing into the street.

"I have other things to do," Pikey thought sourly. *Oh, do you? So you send me off into the middle of the English army all by my lonesome. If I come back and you're sleeping, I'll leave you behind.*

He went to Siltpool's tavern first. Taverns were where the talking happened, and if he could gather all that information Bartholomew wanted while staying warm and dry, it would be a whole lot better for him. He was already reasonably sure he needn't worry about anyone seeing him. In the Scarborough Faery Prison he had walked right between the stilts of the leadfaces and they hadn't noticed a thing. Still, Pikey went cautiously. He made sure not to kick up the mud as he walked, or tip anything over. He tried to keep his feet from making splashing noises. Luckily for him the rain was coming down hard and the wind was howling, and no one even noticed the little trickle of footsteps twisting along the road.

A group of soldiers was playing cards under the tavern's eaves. The cards were damp and dog-eared, their painted figures sinister in the half dark. The men were silent. They said nothing of interest, only grunting from time to time and frowning at one another over the tops of their hands. The tavern's windows were cold and dark. The place had been locked up. Pikey pulled his cloak closer around him and hurried on.

He had better luck in the tent city. He listened through canvases and at tent entrances. He listened to soldiers and sergeants and the colonels in their soiled sashes and tarnished gold epaulettes. No one saw him. Pikey half-suspected they wouldn't have bothered with him even if they had. They were afraid of other things.

The troops did not want to be here. Their gunpowder was damp and their boots had holes in them. They had lost three days on their way up from Bristol after some faery magic had made the road lead into a bog and wild swamp goblins had dragged an entire division of men into the reeds. And on the way to Doncaster, the troops had come upon a young man in tattered military garb, standing in the middle of an empty road. He was standing very still, simply staring at them mournfully, and something about him made everyone afraid to come close. No one dared walk by him, not even the generals. Then everyone had heard a sound like distant guns, and the young man had dropped with bullet holes in his chest. When they rushed forward to help him he was no longer there.

That story made Pikey shiver. He wondered if it was just a fib to give everyone a bit of a chill, but when he saw the black looks the men were giving one another, and the way they dug themselves deeper into their coats, he didn't think so anymore. They were afraid. Afraid of the faeries, like Pikey had never thought an English soldier could be.

After a while he came to an overturned wagon. Three soldiers sat huddled under it, sodden and miserable, rain spouting off their hats. One of them, grizzled and older than the rest, was missing an eye, an empty socket where it should have been. Pikey heard him speaking and stole behind the wagon to listen.

"Lousy rain," he grumbled. "Lousy mud, lousy town, lousy war."

"Aye," said another, a boy of barely sixteen. "And lousy bread, too. I was told they'd feed us better 'n the Prime Minister if we just signed up. White bread as soft as clouds, they said. Feh. There's more mold than meal in our bread and it's as hard as rocks."

"It'll be over soon enough," said the third soldier philosophically. "A few more days and we'll all be going back to where we came from."

"Oh, you do seem sure o' that," the older man snapped. "Upon my gone-away eye, we've no idea what's going to happen."

The third soldier chuckled. "Your gone-away eye . . . That's a pretty way of putting it. How *did* you lose that eye, eh, Glivers? Mistook a cat for your spectacles?"

"No. I pulled it out. With my own hands."

The two other soldiers turned to look at him. Pikey shivered.

"It went bad somehow," the man named Glivers said. "I was seeing the strangest things through it, a tower, and a staircase, twisting up, up, up. And I didn't want to get into trouble with the leadfaces over anything. So I thought it best to do away with the offending object."

It went bad somehow. He'd had it, too. Glivers'd had a clouded eye. Pikey started to back away. He didn't want to hear any more. Not from this lot, anyway. *Find out when,* Bartholomew had said.

Pikey hurried around the wagon. And barreled straight into a soldier. Pikey bounced off his chest, sprawled into the muck. The soldier let out a grunt of surprise. Pikey looked up, panic-stricken. He was right out in the open, only inches from the worn leather boots of the men under the wagon. In a heartbeat Pikey was up, slopping through the mud.

The boy-soldier jerked to his feet, staring. "Is it a ghost? Was that a ghost just now?"

"Might've been," Glivers said, barely looking up at all. "There ain't a place left that's not been touched by the blasted faeries. Siltpool's bound to have ghosts if it's any sort of self-respecting."

"Lousy ghosts, probably," the third soldier said, but by then Pikey was long gone.

Flecks of black were already beginning to speckle his invisible arms by the time he came to the general's tent. But it was raining hard. He didn't see. The tent stood by a well and an old stone church. Flags flew overhead. Herbs and iron had been laid out in a ring around it, and several guards were there as well, leaning on blunderbusses and brutal-looking pikes. Pikey flickered past them and peeked in through the tent's flap.

The sharp, hot smell of paraffin and wet wool filled his nose. Three men stood around a wooden table, their faces deeply lined in the light from a lantern. A map was spread in front of them. Small wrought iron figurines had been set here and there across its surface, and the officers were frowning at them, occasionally twirling them, but never moving any.

"The faeries will be waiting for an attack," one of the officers said. He was a dark, angry-looking fellow, and not very tall. "But they will not strike first, not outright. We have fought them long enough to know that. They will stay in their woods beyond Tar Hill, where they are safe and hidden, and they will wait. So we shall flush them out. Gas into the trees, out they come, and we will be herding them to the prisons before they know what's happened."

Pikey pricked up his ears, straining to hear every word. He didn't dare move any farther into the tent, but at the same time he was terrified someone would come from behind and bump into him. He kept glancing back over his shoulder, into the rain. The square was still. The sentinels sagged against their weapons, half asleep. He turned back to the tent.

The second officer was nodding, his brows low over his eyes. "Yes, but only if they do not escape around the hill or into the fields. My troops will come from the left flank, yours"—he nodded toward the third officer—"from the right. We will create a bottleneck, with the main force coming over the hill. They will have nowhere to go."

The tall one, the one with the most medals on his chest and the largest plumes in his hat, nodded.

"Indeed. Haddock, to the east; I, to the west. Braillmouth? Up the hill. You will set off earlier than the rest of us. The fay will be strongest at night. We shall strike them in early morning while they are still dull and sluggish. I have scheduled the gas insects for a quarter to seven. You will set off at the same time. Haddock, you and I leave with our regiments at seven o'clock sharp. And one more thing, Haddock." The general nodded at the small, angry-looking officer. "It is of the utmost importance that you secure the hill before the faeries come out of the trees. We *must* not let them gain the high ground. There will be skirmishes likely. The faeries will be in a fighting panic. Spare none that raise weapons against you. Remember these are traitors, the cold and heartless beings who fight our Queen and spit on their rights as Englishmen. They do not deserve our mercy."

Pikey looked down at his hand. It was not solid yet, but the dark veins were seeping across it, slowly forming knuckles, fingers. Soft as air, he left the tent flap and returned to the muddy alley.

Bartholomew was waiting for him.

Pikey reported everything: the general's plans; the soldiers' stories; how everyone was so drenched and weary and afraid.

"Gas," Bartholomew murmured when Pikey had finished. They were sitting by a tiny fire they had built at the very end of the alley. Fires were not allowed in the camp. None but the ones in lanterns and stoves. A few weeks ago, a faery had crept into the town and told the flames to run and play among the canvasing. Forty tents had been devoured before the men had even fastened their suspenders.

Bartholomew flexed his fingers over the warmth, his face thoughtful in the orange glow. "Gas to bring out the faeries. Well, it looks like the English have just as many tricks up their sleeves as the fay now."

"Yeh," said Pikey, watching Bartholomew and then flexing his own fingers over the flames. "The faeries'll never know what hit 'em. The English'll win, looks like. "

"The English *have* to win," said Bartholomew, so fiercely that Pikey flinched. "The woods are crawling with faeries. We'll never get in unless someone forces them out."

Pikey stared at him. "Is that where you were? In the faery wood?"

"Not inside. But as close as I dared."

"What did you see?" Pikey asked, eyes wide.

"I didn't see anything. But I heard things. Pipes and voices and scratching sounds in the branches. They're there. I know they're there, and their leader is there, and the door will be there, too, even after they've left."

Pikey and Bartholomew sat in silence for a while. Pikey watched the struggling fire, spitting and snapping in the wet. Bartholomew sat across from him, the smoke turning his face ghostly. After a time, Bartholomew drew his boots in under his cloak and asked, "I don't suppose you've seen Hettie?"

Fear slithered through Pikey. "I—I tried. I did, honest, but— Well, the last thing I saw were the fingers and a bit of light and what looked like some nice shiny wood and red carpet. And I already told you about that," he added quietly.

Bartholomew nodded. Pikey hoped he wouldn't say anything more about it, and he didn't. Instead he looked at Pikey over the tops of his knees, and asked, "How did you lose your eye?"

"What?" *Blood. Blood welling between the stones.* He blinked, hard. "Oh. Something took it."

Bartholomew looked at him curiously. "You don't have to tell me if you don't want to. I don't tell you everything."

You don't tell me nothing, Pikey thought, but he said, "No, it's—it's all right. It's just, it's not a big thing. It's a long time ago now, and just an eye. Not a sister or anything."

Pikey hoped Bartholomew would smile, but his face was grave and serious. "It's a big thing for you," he said. "I don't think you like faeries very much. I don't think you like having their eyes."

"I get by." Pikey nudged the embers with the toe of his boot. "It's having it in my head that's the worst." He paused. It made him feel cramped and uncomfortable talking about it, as if all his clothes were too tight. But at the same time he didn't want to stop. No one had ever wanted to listen before.

"I was sleeping when it happened," he said. "It was winter like it is now, and I was dreaming about plums and apples and— Well, I was dreaming. And then I heard this sound. I didn't think nothing of it. Just a sound, I thought. But it kept coming, right up to my hole under the chemist's shop. And I see these two feet. One's all nasty and really gray. And I'm awake then, all the way. A face leans down, this horrid, peeling one with eyes like red lanterns.

"'Hello,' it says to me. And then something in a language I don't understand. And then something about an Englisher. And then it puts its fingers over my eyes and starts mumbling. I tried to fight it. I did. I tried to shout and punch and call Rinshi to bite its gimpy leg off, but no one came. Rinshi was dead, see. They were all dead, old Marty and his work-boy and everyone."

Pikey looked up. He half-expected to see Bartholomew curling into his cloak, going to sleep. Because why would he care? Why would anyone care what had happened to Pikey? But Bartholomew was still listening. Pikey peered at him sharply a second. Then he went on, his words coming faster.

"There was this terrible hurting, like a ripping *in* my eye. And it's pulling it, the faery is. Not really the eye, but something in it. The faery takes it and bounces it in its palm, like it's a shilling. And then the faery just turns and limps away into the night. I never saw it after that."

Bartholomew was silent. For a long while the

two of them sat, staring into the dying fire. Finally Bartholomew said, "What d'you suppose the faery did? Why can you see the Old Country through it?"

"I dunno. Might be some sort of disease. Something the Sidhe boiled up to scare us. Just like that ghost in the road, and the fire in the camp, and all those things. It's a stupid sort of game is what I think. I hate it."

"I hate it, too," Bartholomew said. Somewhere in the distance, the scream of a crow. "But it's good, too, isn't it? A little? I mean, not good exactly, but—I wouldn't even know Hettie was alive if not for your eye." He gave an apologetic smile. "So thanks, Pikey. We'll get Hettie back. And when we do, we'll all go to Bath, all three of us, and nobody will mind if you have a faery eye there. Nobody will mind at all." Then Bartholomew hunched into his cloak and closed his eyes.

Pikey didn't move. He sat a long while, feeling warmer than he had in months. It was true what Bartholomew had said. It *was* a little bit good. He never would have gone on this adventure without that awful gray eye. He never would have even started. For the first time in his life he was going somewhere, somewhere important, and it was all because a faery had stolen his eye, and a leadface had chased him, and a cobble spryte had tripped him in Bluebottle Street, and a boy in a brass-buttoned coat had punched his stomach in, and a sylph had stolen a boatload of gems, and Pikey had gone to prison. It was all because of that.

For the first time in his life Pikey felt lucky.

CHAPTER XIV
The Fourth Face

THE Sly King stared at Hettie through the slitted eyes of his mask and his laugh went on and on, howling up out of the hall.

No one was laughing with him. The faeries had all gone still as statues. Piscaltine was still smiling, her lips pulled back across her teeth. One hand picking feverishly at her frock.

You knew, Hettie thought. *You knew all along who the Sly King was. You didn't want me to succeed. You were never going to let me go.*

Hettie whirled, searching for the door. Her head was still spinning from the dance and the frantic wailing of the pipes. *Think, Hettie. You have to think.* Any second the Sly King would stop laughing. The faeries would snap from whatever enchantment they were under. They would come for her, and they must not catch her.

She backed away. The Sly King stopped laughing. The smile fell from his face. "Oh," he said. "Don't go. We were having such a wonderful time."

His necklace dropped from her hand and clanged against the floor, impossibly loud. "I'm sorry," she whispered, "I did it because I had to, I—"

"The mask," said Piscaltine from the edge of the crowd, and she practically shook with wicked glee. "Take off her mask, *Mi Sathir.* She stole that, too."

The Sly King turned to Piscaltine. Slowly he looked back at Hettie. His eyes glittered. "She is a liar, is she not? Such a little liar. I will deal with her. But you . . . You would not do such a thing, would you? You would not pretend to be something you never were." He smiled again. "Englisher." And then he reached out and snatched the blue-feathered mask from her face.

Hettie froze. The black gown withered around her like a dying flower. Her copper hair twisted into branches. She shrank and turned, and a second later she was nothing but an ugly little Peculiar in the middle of a great, shadowy hall. All around her, the faeries' eyes widened. Their mouths fell open. They saw her branch-hair, the red lines all over her arms like threads of blood.

"Milkblood," a faery whispered.

"*Valentu,*" said another.

"Oh dear," said Piscaltine.

The Sly King spun on them. "You are all traitors and liars here," he said, and his voice slashed through the hall like a gale. "That is why you were invited. A valuable creature was hiding under your very noses, and you never said. You *kept* her from me. To thwart me. Well." He giggled. "I will not need you in the world ahead. None of you will leave this house alive."

And then a great many things happened at once. Piscaltine's hands went to her mouth, and she looked suddenly as if she had made a terrible mistake. Snell, the moth-winged faery, began to run at Hettie full tilt. Florence La Bellina split in two, a pale figure, and a dark one. And Hettie took a deep breath and lunged toward the door.

The Sly King did not move. He simply raised his hand and said, "Catch her."

The guests drew back in fear as Hettie pelted toward them. No one stopped her; no one dared. The door loomed. She had almost reached it. Then the last of the faeries parted and Hettie saw that the pale Belusite was standing directly in front of her and the dark one was gliding at Hettie's side.

"Come with us," Florence La Bellina said as one. The dark twin reached for her. There was a knife in her hand. Hettie saw its glimmer, heard the ring of steel. She didn't stop. Out of the corner of her eye she saw Snell burst from among the faeries and fling itself at the pale Belusite. Her twin whirled in surprise. In a flash, Hettie was through the door, kicking up ivy and branches as she fled down the hall.

Behind her she heard shrieks and desperate weeping. The music began again, a frenzy of scratching chords and whistling pipes. She came to the Glass

Wing, flew through it. Everything was hollow and deserted, the night and fog pressing against the glass walls. Ahead were the Innard Stairs. She started up them. A sharp pain was stitching into her side, but she didn't slow down. Behind, she heard footsteps, hundreds of them, echoing through the great house, and shouts and cries.

She came to the top of the Innard Stairs and limped down the long window-lined gallery. A clock was bonging, over and over again. She did not stop to look at it or count its strikes. She didn't care what Piscaltine's mood was anymore.

Then Hettie glanced out the window and stopped.

Five statues now. Under the shadow of the trees, staring at the house, five stone-hooded statues. She spun away from the glass. But she had waited a moment too long.

Florence La Bellina stood at the end of the gallery, her face all pale. At the other end, the dark half. They had appeared without a sound.

No! Hettie thought. She started walking. *No, I didn't do anything, it was Piscaltine who told me to.* She started to run, desperately, barreling straight toward the dark twin. It didn't move. It stared at her, its expression blank and malevolent. Hettie started to cry. Her lungs hurt very badly. *Go. Go, leave me alone,* she wanted to scream, but she didn't have the air. The dark twin spread out her arms, like a cross, and opened her mouth. She began to speak, a word, half-formed. Then the moth-winged faery slammed into her back and she tipped straight forward, as if made of stone. Her head struck the floor with a solid *crack.* Snell leaped over her, gripped Hettie, and dragged her out of the gallery. Behind them, the pale twin shrieked. Hettie looked back over her shoulder. The pale one's arms were outspread, too, her mouth open. A tongue the color of old milk darted out. And then Hettie was scrambling up the ladders toward the attics, close at Snell's heels.

"Who are you?" Hettie sobbed as the moth-winged faery dragged her onto a landing. "Are you the Sly King's? Are you going to take me back to him?"

She could barely keep herself moving. Every joint and muscle ached. They came to the attics and turned down a strange little passageway Hettie didn't think she had ever seen before. They hurried this way and that, up steps, under gables, and at last Snell stopped and turned on her. It didn't look so gentle anymore. Its face was the same, drooping and gloomy, but its eyes were a deep, angry black. It touched a hand to its face. A ribbon appeared in its fingers, seemingly coming out of the back of its head. And suddenly it began to change, its skin bubbling and warping. The moth wings fell away. It became gaunt and hunched, and its eyes slanted up. And there, in front of Hettie, stood the faery butler, a mask in his hands and bruises and half-healed cuts all up his neck and around his mouth.

"Do not look so pleased to see me," he growled, and Hettie almost collapsed on the spot.

No. No, he was dead. He had died all that time ago in the snow in front of the cottage. And yet here he stood. He was just a shadow of the tall, ghoulish butler she had known in London. He looked as if he had been chased with scissors and then dragged through a bog and then put into the chimney of a steam engine. The brass clockwork that wrapped around one side of his face hung useless and broken. His green eye was dark.

He gripped her shoulder. "We are leaving. Now."

"What?" Hettie felt dizzy. She tried to pull away, but he dragged her around, back toward the Innard Stairs and all the frightened, angry Sidhe.

"No, *stop*. I'm not going with you!"

"Be still. They're after you. All of them. Piscaltine and the Sly King and that abomination of a red woman."

Hettie stopped struggling. "Are you rescuing me?" She practically sobbed with relief. "Are you bringing me back to the cottage? Is that why you came?"

The faery butler looked down at her. Hettie looked up, and for a second she thought she saw something behind that slanted eye. But it was gone again as soon as it had come.

"No," he said, and his voice was hard. "I have been hunted and harried for a hundred moons because of a petty killing, because I was protecting *you*. You will be my pardon. A Whatnot for a Whatnot. You are the London Door. The first changeling in a hundred years to be such a great and perfect gateway. If the King doesn't forgive me out of gratitude, I shall sprout a new head."

Hettie's face went dark. "You can't kidnap me again," she said. She had stopped crying. She was done with that. Again she tried to wrench away. "You can't, I won't *let* you!"

The faery butler didn't even blink. "We go to Hezripal," he said, his hand squeezing and his face leaning down, tilted, eyes sharp. "The City of Black Laughter. Capital of the Old Country. This house is doomed. Piscaltine is disgraced. If we stay, I will die with the rest. I will get you away just long enough for them to fear you are gone for good, and then I will deliver you to the King and be done with you once and for all."

Hettie writhed, hissed, scratched at the faery butler, but he only shrugged her off and, slipping a cord around her wrist, set to pulling her along the upper passageway like some sort of unruly goat.

Below them in the house, the music was still wailing. The hall they traveled down was silent, but the distant footsteps still pounded, causing the pictures to shiver in their frames.

"I can't leave," Hettie said. She spoke it calmly, but her stomach was tying itself into knots. "I've been trying every day since I got here, but I can't. I've eaten faery food." Her voice turned savage. "You and your stupid plans. Piscaltine will have to be dead before I can leave this house."

The faery butler said nothing. He dragged her down another flight of stairs. They were in the window-lined gallery again. Florence La Bellina was gone. At the place where her dark half had struck her head, the floor had splintered in a perfect circle.

The faery butler hurried them down the gallery, Hettie fighting against his long, long strides. And then she stopped dead in her tracks, and not even the faery butler's yanks could get her walking again.

"What *is it*, you little—?" he started, and wheeled around. Then he saw it, too.

The statues were everywhere, all along the edge of the wood, looking out at the house. Hundreds of them.

The Fourth Face

The grandfather clock gave a whirr. Hettie spun to look at it. The hands were moving again, past the grinning face and the sad face, past the Hour of Wrath. With a sharp *clack* they locked onto the fourth face, the flat, cold face with its eyes shut tight and its mouth pinched into a pin hole.

Not sleep, Hettie thought. *Death.*

Outside, the statues stepped toward the house.

CHAPTER XV
Tar Hill

Pikey and Bartholomew woke early on the day of battle and walked a short way out of town. It was hours before dawn and the fields were silent, sheathed in frost. Pikey looked around him, his boots crunching on the stony road. He saw the landscape he had glimpsed on the generals' map, but it looked very different now. On the map it was as if you were a bird, flying high overhead, but on the ground everything was huge and dark and far-away. Trees grew in black tufts here and there, until they formed a dark mass of woods in the distance. The twelve iron prisons encircled the town. About a half mile away, between the town and the forest, a high hill arched out of the sweeping fields, bare and round as a knucklebone.

"Tar Hill," Bartholomew said softly, as if it was special somehow.

Pikey squinted at it. "Tar Hill's a silly name for a hill."

Bartholomew laughed. "It is. It doesn't even look like tar. But it's famous. A battle was fought on it, ages ago. It was between the faeries and the English. Just like now."

"Oh. We won then, I s'pose."

"We?" Bartholomew frowned. "The English did, if that's what you mean. They slaughtered the fighting faeries and took the rest to the factories. People called it a great victory for the Empire. Better than defeating the Scots and the French and the Americans put together."

Pikey shrugged. "I'd heard that." He hadn't. No one had ever told him. He changed the subject. "The forest on the other side—that's where they are, yeh? But the English aren't marching yet, so we should have slept longer. The faeries'll eat us alive if we go in now."

Bartholomew ignored this bit of reasoning. "We have an hour until the soldiers march for Tar Hill. We'll go to the other side of the hill, to the western flanks of the wood, away from the battle, but a safe distance from the trees, too, in case there are any stray faeries about. Then we wait. The English will gas the woods, the faeries'll leave, and in three hours no one will spot us going in."

They came to the base of the hill and started walking around it. It went up in a smooth, steep line, so smooth Pikey thought it looked as if a giant had set his bowl upside down and then forgotten about it for a hundred years until it was covered with dirt and plants. The grass at the bottom was tall and wet, soaking his cloak. He wished it weren't so cold. It was not snowing, at least, and there were no drifts like there had been in London, but his teeth still chattered as the water seeped into his cloak. Worse yet, the hill was much larger than it looked. It took almost half an hour to get around it.

Once they were, things became trickier.

The fields stretched away in front of them, empty but for the clumps of trees, all the way to the faery wood in the distance.

"They'll have posted lookouts," Bartholomew said, stopping Pikey with a warning hand. "We'll move from tree to tree. *Don't* go until I tell you." He took a small clockwork device from one of his many pockets and held it to his eye, scanning the dark woods.

"What d'you see?" Pikey asked. He wanted to look through the device as well, but he didn't know if Bartholomew would want him to, so he didn't say anything.

"Nothing yet. Nothing's moving, besides the— Wait." Bartholomew went stock-still.

"Besides what?" Pikey's hands clutched at the sides of his cloak. "Faeries? Are faeries coming?"

"No. But something's wrong. Something's wrong with the trees. The branches, they're . . ."

Pikey shivered.

"I can't see," Bartholomew said. "We need to move closer. Run." And before Pikey could protest they were off, sprinting toward a trio of dead witch hazels that twisted out of the field a few dozen strides away. They flattened themselves to the trunks, gasping the icy air. Bartholomew pulled out the device again and peered through it.

"What is it?" Pikey asked. "Can you see now?" He strained to see the woods himself, but they were so far away. He squinted as hard as he could. There *was* something strange about the trees. The leaves were almost black and they stirred though there was no wind, sometimes swirling away in bursts of darkness, as if picked up on a gust.

"Closer," Bartholomew hissed again, and again they ran. The next tree they took refuge behind was a birch, white and leafless, a skeletal hand clawing out of the earth. Bartholomew put the clockwork lens to his eye. Pikey waited, peeking around the trunk.

"Can you see it now?" he asked, gripping the bark with both hands. Above, the branches swayed, empty, silent. Pikey froze. *Leaves. Leaves in the trees, even though it was winter.* There were only a few trees in London, but he knew how they looked in summer and he knew how they looked after the frosts. The branches should be bare now, the leaves all gone. He turned to Bartholomew.

Bartholomew had seen it, too. The device dropped from his hand. He looked at Pikey, his eyes wide.

"Oh no," he breathed. "They're going to be slaughtered."

The soldiers set off from Siltpool at precisely a quarter to seven, as was scheduled. They moved across the fields in straight lines, guns to their shoulders, heads held high. General Braillmouth rode at their front upon a proud steed as black as death. Above, the clouds hung low and ominous.

At the same time, four steam-powered beetles skittered out of town on pointy metal legs. Thick glass canisters full of carefully engineered gas were bolted to their backs. The beetles slipped into the grass, only a shiver of movement marking their paths as they streaked toward the faery wood.

It was seven o'clock sharp.

General Braillmouth reached the foot of the hill.

He gave the signal to break rank. The soldiers' pace quickened. They started up the steep slopes, six hundred seventy-two men, swarming up the hill like so many ants.

No one heard the cries from the other side. No one saw the two small figures racing across the fields, away from the faery wood. *"Run!"* they screamed. *"Run, turn round, turn round!"* But no one heard, and no one saw.

Braillmouth's soldiers scrambled and crawled up the hill, their bayonets lowered. Rain began to fall suddenly, pouring down their faces and spouting off their hats, spattering their uniforms. Drums beat, but the rain was louder, and the noise of boots. And then the soldiers heard another sound. A hissing, shivering sound. It grew stronger, stronger, until it was not a hiss but a roar, like a waterfall.

Pikey and Bartholomew had reached the base of the hill. They waved their arms and shouted, but the soldiers did not see. They did not hear. The soldiers mounted the top of the hill and pooled for a moment, scurrying every which way, setting up aether cannons. The roaring became deafening. A shadow passed overhead, a cloud darker than the storm. As one, the soldiers looked to the sky. Their guns fell from their hands. They tried to turn back, but soldiers were behind them, soldiers were everywhere, and the officers were shouting, and the drums were beating, and the troops were trampling one another trying to get away.

The sky was filled with birds. A hundred thousand birds. Blackbirds of Dartmoor, jackdaws of London, ravens and crows from Cumberland, Dunne, and Yorkshire. They swirled above the army, a great black vortex of shrieks and flapping wings. And then they dove, straight down onto the troops, and for a short while the hill became as black as tar.

CHAPTER XVI
A Shade of Envy

THE Innard Stairs were blocked.

Hettie and the faery butler skidded to a halt and stared in horror at the pandemonium below. *Faeries.* Hundreds of faeries swarmed up the steps in a glistening swath of gowns and masks. They slipped, fell, wriggling over one another in their attempt to flee the lower stories. Jackets and skin hung in shreds. Some of the faeries bled, slow strings of black gore.

"There *is* no way out," said the faery butler. The cord that bound Hettie's wrist dropped from his hand. He stood perfectly still, watching the guests boil up the steps. Below in the house, a jarring crash sounded.

The Glass Wing.

"There is now," Hettie whispered, and this time she was the one pulling the faery butler, down, down into the writhing mass of Sidhe.

The faery butler let out a shout. Hettie thought she might have screeched a little bit, too. Then they smashed into the oncoming faeries, into a wall of silk and muscle. At first the panic was too great. Legs and arms and masked faces were everywhere, and the pushing threatened to wash Hettie and the faery butler back up the steps. But Hettie wasn't going up there again. She hooked her foot into the boot of a faery gentleman and clawed her way up his waistcoat and began leaping across the top of the throng, from shoulder to head, hurtling down the staircase. Faeries were tumbling everywhere, over the banister, flipping into the dark. They shrieked at Hettie, but she didn't stop. She had to get to the bottom. She could already see the lower hall. Then a hole opened up in front of her and she dropped. Shoes pounded down around her.

She began to crawl on hands and knees, step after

step after step. A sharp red block heel came peril-
ously close to mangling her hand. Then a lady in the
mask of a wolf pulled her to her feet and shook her.
"He will kill us," she whimpered, not really at Hettie,
though her fingers dug into her arms. "Kill us all
for coming. Oh, Piscaltine, you fool, what have you
done, what have you *done*?"

Hettie tried to pull away, but the faery wouldn't
let go. Hettie was being pushed up the stairs again.
The lady clung to her, screaming, her fingers bruis-
ing. Then the faery butler was at Hettie's side. He
snatched her away from the lady. Hettie was swooped
up into the air. And he practically hurled her down
the remaining steps. She felt so high up, so high she
would break every bone in her body when she landed.
The last of the madness flew away beneath her. She
fell with a thud in the lower hall and rolled over the
floor.

A second later she was up on one knee, head
pounding. The hall was almost empty now. Only a
few stragglers were rushing down the trampled pathway of leaves and branches. *Wrong way,* Hettie thought

as she passed them. *There's no way out up there. You'll all be trapped.* For a brief instant, Hettie thought now might be the time to slip away and lose the faery butler. But then he landed next to her and she was running with him, though she wasn't sure she wanted to be.

They came to the place where the guests had been received, where the path of ivy led away toward the Wings of Glass and Mildew.

Boom. Another crash, some ways ahead. They turned a corner. Above, Piscaltine's flags and banners flickered in a gust of wind. They went down three steps. *Boom.* Around one more corner and into a hallway made of green and pale blue glass.

Boom. The crashes were coming closer.

Boom, boom, boom, louder and faster, and then the hallway shattered and three statues stood before them, taller than the faery butler, their heads bowed under stone hoods. One of them stepped forward, a long silver blade in its hand.

The faery butler flew at the statue, and even in his decrepit state he was faster than anything. Just as the statue swung its sword, the faery slid onto his knees, head back, eyes looking up at the ceiling. The blade hissed over him. In an instant the butler was back on his feet, whirling, smashing his own knife into the statue's head.

The knife snapped with sharp *ping.* The statue didn't even flinch. It turned, slowly, and brought up its sword again. The faery butler scrambled to his feet. Hettie didn't see the rest, because just then the other two statues stepped toward her. Their swords swung. She dropped to the floor and twisted onto her back. She saw the blades descending, descending. For an instant she glimpsed under their hoods, saw stone faces and stone lips. Then she slid to the side and the blades cracked down beside her. She was on her feet in a blink. The broken walls of the Glass Wing were so close. She leaped. Cold air slapped at her and grass crushed under her. She rolled out into the field beyond.

The faery butler followed a second later, already running.

"What are they?" Hettie screamed, leaping to her feet and flying after him. She could barely keep him in

sight. The fog was so thick and the faery butler went so fast, sometimes dropping onto all fours like a dog. *Like a pity-faery,* Hettie thought.

"I don't know!" he screeched back over his shoulder. "The Sly King's, most like. He is angry about something. You. You, and Piscaltine for keeping you. The Duchess of Yearn-by-the-Woods has fallen from favor, methinks. And her head from her shoulders."

Behind her in the fog, Hettie heard shouts and the ring of metal coming after them. She strained to see something in the whiteness, but there was nothing. The fog swirled on all sides, endless and blinding. Only the patch of grass she moved over was visible, as if the fog were afraid of her and hung back.

"But I didn't steal his stupid necklace!" she shouted. "I—I left it, or dropped it somewhere—" She couldn't even remember anymore. The other one was still with her though, knocking inside her night-gown as she ran.

"It's not *about* the necklace." The faery butler appeared, grabbing her hand. "I told you, you're the Door. Red lines. Branch hair. You're so obviously a

Door. And the lady Piscaltine keeps you locked up and hidden, as if you were nothing at all, as if you were a nobody. The Sly King will be furious with her for not delivering you to him."

Behind them, Hettie could hear footsteps now, beating the grass. *How close are they?* She couldn't tell. And then there was the rattle of a harness, and the footsteps became hooves, galloping.

"They're after us!" the faery butler shouted. They sped into the fog.

Hettie's side ached terribly. It was all she could do to keep her legs moving. Somewhere she heard a horn, low and groaning. And a river? Was that water rushing nearby?

"Where'll we go?" she gasped. "We might be going in circles and you wouldn't even be able to *tell!*"

The river sound was coming closer though, a gurgling, somewhere up ahead. So were the hooves. Then, without warning, the field dipped down a steep grassy bank and there was a waterway, black and deep.

The faery butler let go of her hand and hurried

along its edge, sniffing, waving his long fingers over the water. He went a few paces, peered about, went a few more. The horn sounded again, and all at once the fog was filled with terrible cries. They were not even that far away from Piscaltine's house. In the fog, what seemed like miles might not have been more than a few hundred feet.

"Here we are," the faery butler said, his voice low and urgent. Hettie followed his gaze. A boat was moored to the bank of the river. Or grown to it. Like a great white caterpillar, it clutched the grassy slope, pale tendrils hugging the dirt. The faery butler herded Hettie onto its deck.

"*Hartik,*" he said. "*Mahevol Kir.*"

The boat seemed to shrivel, the wooden tentacles drawing in around its belly. A second later the boat was picked up by the currents and pulled into the middle of the river.

Not a moment too soon. Florence La Bellina bloomed out of the fog like a bloody flower. Her horse looked like her, black coat, white mane, eyes like pits. It skidded to a halt on the bank, and Florence stared at Hettie, her shiny doll's face a mask of rage. Hettie stared back, breathless and aching, watching her until she was swallowed again by the fog.

The boat was very strange. It sliced through the water without a sound. Its sail was silver, glimmering in the mist, and it had two eyes in its prow, half-lidded and very haughty looking. A trapdoor was in its deck, though there were only shadows and squeezing, glistening tubes underneath. Sometimes the pale tendrils that twisted along the boat's sides would skim over the waves like the legs of a sea creature.

But when Hettie looked over the railing at the boat's reflection it was even stranger. It was as if a different boat were attached to the bottom of this boat, upside-down in the water. The mirror-boat was moss green. The mast was broken and the sides were full of gaping holes, the tendrils dragging, limp in the waves. Even Hettie's reflection looked worse. It was difficult to see because the ripples in the water kept cutting the image into ribbons, but it seemed to Hettie that her reflection was wrinkled and stooped, as if it were a hundred years old. Its hands clutched the railing like claws.

They had been on the boat for what felt like an age, Hettie and the faery butler, sailing on black water through white fog. The only sound was their breathing, close and muffled, and the hoofbeats. Florence's horse, following them along the river's edge. Hettie tried not to hear that part. She walked the boat prow to keel so many times she could picture every twist in the railing. She squinted at the eyes in the prow. Now she was occupying herself by staring at the figure in the water. The figure stared back.

It did everything she did. Hettie waved at it. It waved back. She smiled, wondering if it would smile, too. It did. It curled back its lips and opened its mouth, but there were bugs in its smile, black beetles and thousand-footed centipedes scuttling across its old, dead teeth.

Hettie gagged and snapped her mouth shut, half-expecting to feel the insects wriggling over her tongue.

"A Shade of Envy," the faery butler said. Hettie started. "That's what it's called. The boat. It was Lady Piscaltine's. Very fitting."

Hettie turned away from his voice. She thought about ignoring him. "It's horrid," she said finally. "Your whole Country is horrid. It doesn't have anything nice in it."

The faery butler sat against the mast, very still. "It does. I'm sure it does. Perhaps we just haven't found it yet."

Hettie made a face, but she went to the mast and sat down on the other side of it, so that her back was to the faery butler's back. "Well, I'm sick of looking," she said, resting her chin in her hands.

She thought that would be the end of the matter, but the faery butler snorted. "You? You never looked. You wouldn't see anything pretty if it were sitting under your nose."

"I would too!" Hettie turned a little, insulted. "And I looked all over the place. There's just nothing here. It's all dead."

"You aren't dead."

"That doesn't have anything to do with anything," she said under her breath.

She heard the faery butler shift against the mast. "Yes, it does. You are a little fool."

"No, you are. Everything keeps getting worse and worse, and I don't know where I'm going, and I don't know what's going to happen."

She listened for a sound from the faery butler. For a long while there was nothing. Then, "Do you want to know how I survived the *Virduger* in Deepest Winter? You thought they had finished me, didn't you? But they hadn't. Piscaltine never had them kill me. She ordered them to wound me so that no one could tell the Belusites and the Sly King that I had gone unpunished, but if anything, she was pleased I had gotten rid of another of his servants. I did not know that then. I did not know that until many moons later when I stumbled half-dead up to her house. And now I'm here, on my way to someplace new, someplace better, I hope. Perhaps none of us know how important we are. Perhaps some of us never find out, because we simply lie down and die."

Hettie peered around the mast at him. She saw that his green eye was glowing again, dully and very faintly.

"I didn't say I was going to die. I—I just said I didn't like it here."

"What is this *liking*? If you *liked* everything that happened to you, you would be quite the most feeble person. A thousand things will happen to you, and some of it will be good and some of it will be bad and some of it will be utterly dreadful, but they all . . ." The faery butler paused. "They all lead somewhere."

"Where?" Hettie inched a little closer. "Home?"

The faery butler's head was tilted up. He was looking into the distance, into the endless, still fog. "I don't know," he said. "Perhaps if we make them to."

Another pause. On the shore, the hooves pounded. Trees poked out of the whiteness, skeletons in a cotton sea. "When the Sly King has you, and I am gone, try to escape," the faery butler said. "Try to get away."

Hettie gaped at him. Slowly his eye went out again. He slumped against the mast as if he'd never spoken.

And then, suddenly, the fog lifted. For the briefest instant Hettie saw the river, curling away in front of her, and the moon shone down, and the river became a silver ribbon, a silver road. Hettie gasped. Then the fog closed again, and they were plunged into murk.

She woke up at some point in the night and tried to think. She felt like she should be plotting, scheming a way to escape, but her mind was empty. So many strange and powerful creatures were snapping at her heels, and she didn't understand what any of them wanted. In London, Mr. Lickerish had tried to make a Door of her and so she had been special and dangerous, but she couldn't imagine Florence La Bellina would care about that, or the Sly King. It was such a hollow-headed thing the faery butler had suggested. Doors were for escaping, for the faeries to *leave* the smoke and factories of England and go home. But these faeries already were home. They were already in the Old Country. It had to be something else they wanted. It had to be— Her fingers tightened around the pendant under her nightgown. The warmth spread up her hand. *Like it's alive,* she thought, for the hundredth time.

The Sly King had had so many of those necklaces, hanging inside his coat. And he was a king. They were important, then. Perhaps they were magic. She thought of how hers always made her feel braver and better when she held it, and how it never went cold, even in the winter wood and the painted halls of Piscaltine's house. Perhaps the Sly King really did want her for a Door, and perhaps Piscaltine hadn't known about any of it and had simply kept Hettie as a pet as she had always supposed. But if it *was* the necklace they wanted . . .

Hettie slipped the chain from around her neck and hurried to the side of the boat. If it was what they wanted, then they could have it. She could live without it. She could live without a lot of things if it meant she could escape this place. She leaned over the railing and dangled the necklace above the green-black waters.

The ugly old Hettie stared up from the waves, from a broken, mossy boat. Something dark and hairy swayed from her hands. Hettie ignored it. She looked toward the river's edge. The Belusite was riding, her head turned toward Hettie at an unnatural angle. Their eyes met. Hettie took a deep breath. Then she let the necklace fall. It tumbled toward the water. It struck with barely a sound and sank beneath the waves.

CHAPTER XVII
Puppets and Circus Masters

PIKEY fell flat on his stomach, and the birds shrieked overhead in a deafening gale. He clapped his hands to his ears, but the shrieking only seemed to get louder. The wings flapped on and on. Any second he expected to feel talons sliding into his cloak, beaks pulling his skin.

Something gripped his arm. He cried out. He tried to wrench away, but it was only Bartholomew, dragging him to his feet and shouting, "Come on! Back to the woods! There's nothing we can do here!"

Pikey stumbled, almost fell again. *The woods? The faery woods?*

Bartholomew was already running, back across the fields the way they had come. The birds were no longer overhead. Behind him, Pikey heard a horrible, desperate wail. He looked back over his shoulder.

The birds were on the hill. They covered it now in a black swarm, glistening in the early winter light. He couldn't see the soldiers anymore. But he heard them.

"Barth!" Pikey screamed, setting off after him. "Barth, the soldiers! *They're being killed!*"

Bartholomew didn't slow down. "We can still get through!" he shouted back. "The gas will have gone off. The faeries will all be asleep, or fleeing. We can still make it!"

But then Pikey heard another sound, beyond the wailing and the flap of wings—a heavy beat, echoing in the earth. *Marching.*

"Barth!"

To the left, he saw soldiers, row upon row of them, tramping across the field toward them. To the right, hundreds more. The regiments from Siltpool were creating their bottleneck, setting the trap for the faeries.

Only nothing was leaving the woods.

"Bartholomew!"

Bartholomew was twenty strides ahead, feet flying. The trees stood silent in the distance, the shadows between the trunks deep as oceans. *What's in there?* Pikey thought. *What's in those shadows?*

The gap between Bartholomew and the trees was narrowing swiftly. *Five hundred strides.* Pikey had almost caught up with Bartholomew. *Four hundred fifty.* The forest loomed. Was something moving in there? Was that a thin shape he saw, drifting back into the dark?

And then Pikey's foot caught on something hard and sharp and he fell face-first into the grass.

Bartholomew spun. He ran back.

"Get up! Get up, Pikey, it's so close. We can still make it if we—"

Bartholomew froze. The sound of marching came closer, boots crunching in frosty grass. He remained motionless, staring at the thing Pikey had tripped over.

Half-hidden in the winter grass was a clockwork beetle. It lay on its back, spiked feet pointing toward the sky. Its belly had been torn out. A tangle of gears and sparking wires spilled onto the ground. And bolted to the insect's back were two glass canisters, pale green gas still pressing against the walls. The canisters were full.

Bartholomew let out a pained little cry. "No," he said, turning to Pikey, as if Pikey could do something about it. "No, no, it's not. The gas, it couldn't have—"

"It never made it," Pikey said. "The faeries are still in the woods. They're all awake."

The troops were only a hundred strides away now, on either side of the hill. The first rows shouldered their muskets, eyes trained down the barrels. Pikey looked to the woods, then back at the approaching soldiers.

"We have to go, Barth," he said.

General Haddock was riding out across the field toward them, his horse throwing up clods of frozen earth. Bartholomew didn't move.

"Who goes there?" the general bellowed. "Friend or fay?"

"Barth?" Pikey spun on Bartholomew. "Barth, we have to *go*!"

But they didn't go. Pikey and Bartholomew stood in the field beside the beetle's gutted carapace, and General Haddock bore down on them, his horse letting off shots of steam in the cold air. A handful of soldiers rushed forward to surround them.

For a second there was distraction: the birds were whirling off the hill, into the sky in a great black plume. They flew overhead, and the soldiers pointed their guns to the skies in a panic. But they needn't have bothered. The birds passed over and settled again in the branches of the faery wood. The fields were silent. The hill was very, very silent.

General Haddock leaped off his horse and stormed over to Pikey and Bartholomew. His boots were deafeningly loud in the sudden stillness. Pikey pulled his hood down low and hoped the general wouldn't notice his bad eye. He saw the ruined beetle at the grass by his feet. He stepped away from it abruptly, but not before the general saw it, too.

"Treachery," General Haddock said. "*Faery treachery!*"

Pikey glanced at Bartholomew. *Say something,* he

pleaded silently, but Bartholomew didn't say a word.

"We—we ain't faeries, sir," Pikey stammered. "We didn't do nuthin'."

"They knew!" General Haddock shouted, turning to the soldiers. He began to pace, striding across the grass, spinning, then back again. "They knew we were coming. The faeries in the woods, somehow they *knew*."

"It weren't us! I swear it weren't," Pikey said, but he felt so sick and desolate. The words sounded like old washing, sodden in the rain.

"*Silence!*" General Haddock roared. "Another word from you and I'll shoot you where you stand. Haversack! Lacewell! Take them to the nearest faery prison and see that they are locked up. I will deal with them later. Arvel! Surgeons and nurses to the hill this instant."

And with that the Second Battle of Tar Hill ended. The surgeons and white-bonneted nurses climbed the hill, and two boys were dragged across the fields toward the waiting iron prisons.

Pikey and Bartholomew sat slumped inside a holding cell in the Birmingham Faery Prison. Pikey was crying softly, his head against the wall. Bartholomew stared blankly into nothing. Chains were bolted around their ankles. The cell was one in a row of small iron boxes, gates at their fronts, leading onto a hanging walkway. The boxes were very high up, and the wind never quit blowing, in the barred window and out through the gate, freezing them.

Officers and soldiers were hurrying up and down the walkway outside, but none of them noticed the new prisoners. Their faces were drawn, their heads bowed in the shadow of their hats. When they spoke it was in urgent whispers.

After a while Pikey sat up and wiped his nose. "All right," he said. "No use just sitting around. How are we figurin' on getting out of here?"

Bartholomew didn't look at him. He hadn't looked at anyone since seeing the broken beetle in the grass. He hadn't spoken.

"We still can, Barth," Pikey said, sliding over to him. "We can get out and find a way into the faery wood. Even without the gas! We can!"

"No," said Bartholomew. His voice was bare. Hopeless. "No, we can't. There must be an army of faeries in those woods. The trees are full of birds. We're not going into the faery wood. We're not going anywhere."

Pikey stared at him. "We're not even going to try?"

Bartholomew turned his head to look at Pikey. His eyes were bloodshot. "I *have* tried," he said. "I've tried for so, so long. I left Mother alone in Old Crow Alley, and I spent Mr. Jelliby's money hand-over-fist with not so much as a thank-you, and it didn't hurt because I was looking for Hettie and I thought if I could get her back, all would be well again. But it isn't ever going to be well. Everything is horrid, and I don't even know if Hettie is alive."

"She is alive," Pikey said, "She is, she just *is*."

"But we don't *know*!" Bartholomew snarled, and it was so sudden and savage that Pikey jerked back. Bartholomew stared at him a second longer, his eyes huge and liquid. Then he sagged again, as if all his strength had been spent.

The cell was silent. The only sound was the moaning wind and the drum of feet, deep in the globe. Then, his voice so hoarse and quiet Pikey could hardly hear it, Bartholomew said, "When I found you in that prison, I felt I would know, finally. I felt I would know where my sister was and how she was faring and even if it took the rest of my life, it wouldn't be so bad, because I would know she *was* somewhere and I could find her. Well, I don't know anymore. Perhaps I never did."

With that, Bartholomew Kettle wrapped his fingers around his chains and did not stir until long after night had fallen and the moon hung fat and pale in the sky.

Pikey woke with a start. His faery eye hurt, stung, as if something wet were sliding against it, as if rain were splashing straight into it.

"Bartholomew!" he said, feeling about in the dark. "Bartholomew, my eye!"

He felt the panic rising in his throat. In the blackness it could be anything, or a bit of smoke, or a flea, or something bad enough to kill him.

Bartholomew mumbled from his corner of the cell, but he didn't move.

"Wake up, it's *hurting*!" Pikey put his fist to his good eye and opened his clouded one wide. What he saw made his blood run cold. He dropped his hand, gasping.

He was underwater. Everything was tinged green, eerie and slow moving in the half-dark. Bodies floated in the water. Pale ladies in gowns, men in armor holding shields and swords. They floated silently, eyes closed, lips white and sealed. Wisps of seaweed rose from the murk below and tangled with their feet and ran through their hair. Each of the bodies had a chain around its ankle, disappearing into the depths.

Pikey slapped his hands over both eyes, but even then he saw. He could not block it out. He sank past the bodies, past the still, white faces.

"Bartholomew!"

Now Bartholomew was awake. Pikey heard the slither of chains. "What? What is it?"

Pikey didn't answer. The water was becoming

darker and darker. He sank past pointed shoes, a little sharp-faced boy, clutching a knife. It looked like the boy was sleeping. The ground rose to meet Pikey. Silt and stones and a tangle of chains and weights. He saw jewels in the silt, trinkets and faded ribbons. The faery eye went black.

"What d'you see? Can you see Hettie?" Bartholomew whispered. He had pulled himself out of the corner and was crouched next to Pikey.

Pikey let his breath out slowly.

"No, I—" He tried to focus on the cell again, on England. Five days. Five days, and he hadn't seen finger or branch of her. She could have drowned, drifting with all those other bodies in the dark green deep. And if that was the case, everything *was* over. For Pikey, for Bartholomew. They would both be shot, or hanged, and if Pikey had ever been any use, it wouldn't matter, because nothing good had come of it. For a little while he had thought he might be important, not just a sniveling boy from a cracker box, not just a faery-touched.

He barely thought about what he said next.

Ignoring the ache in his eye, Pikey steadied his voice. "Yes," he said. "I saw her."

Bartholomew's eyes went so wide Pikey could see his own face in them.

"She's safe," he went on. "She's just sitting. Eating pie. I don't know why my eye started hurting. It's gone now."

Out on the hill, the nurses in their white bonnets stood very still though it was well past midnight. The surgeon's aprons were spotless, no gore or stains from tending the wounded. The night wind whistled around them.

The soldiers were on their feet as well. Their uniforms hung in tatters, and some of the men bore scratches and signs of a struggle. But they were all alive. Blood pumped in their veins. Their eyes were open, staring at nothing.

A tall, thin shape walked among the figures on the hilltop. His long fingers brushed them as he passed. "Make them dance, my friends," he said. "Make them sing."

"Mi Sathir," they answered, though not one of them opened his mouth. *"Isdestri mankero."*

Then the clouds shifted overhead and the moonlight sluiced down, showing the hill and everyone on it in stark relief. The nurses' hands were frozen to claws. Their satchels lay overturned in the grass. The soldiers' eyes were black, their faces unnaturally pale. And on the backs of every one of their heads was another face, a dark, twisted one, with sharp teeth and too many eyes.

There were no wounded on top of Tar Hill. No bodies. Only the English and their faery puppet masters.

The thin figure whispered a word.

Six hundred soldiers went sliding and jerking down the hillside toward the sleeping prisons.

The moment the lie left Pikey's lips he felt the guilt, a horrible weight, like a stone against his heart. *Just don't lie to me,* Bartholomew had said, that very first day in the prison. *Ever.*

"You saw her?" Bartholomew asked. "She's alive?"

The corner of his mouth started to wobble, and Pikey was afraid he was going to cry. But he didn't. Instead he stood up and went to the gate that separated them from the walkway, dragging his chains with him. He leaned against the bars. He pressed the lock, weighing its strength. "We'll get out," he said in his old, quiet, determined voice. "You and me, Pikey. They took everything out of my cloak, but we'll find a way. We'll get into the Old Country and we'll get Hettie back."

We. "All right," Pikey said, trying to keep his breath from shaking. "But—but we can't go through the woods. The birds and all the faeries, they're just waiting there."

Bartholomew shook his head. "We won't. It was a daft idea from the start. I thought we could do anything then. But there's still Edith Hutcherson. I know I said we'd never find her, but she's our only chance now. We'll look for Edith Hutcherson just like the faun said, and she'll tell us the way in."

And what if Hettie's dead? Pikey felt a stab of fear. *What if she's at the bottom of a river, even though I told you she was alive?*

He was so close to opening his mouth again, to telling Bartholomew he had lied and he didn't know, he didn't know anything at all. "Barth—" he started, but he never said any more.

Sounds were echoing up through the floor, out of the depths of the globe, clanks and frantic shouts. Then the unmistakable crack of gunshots. Something hammered against the door at the end of the walkway.

Pikey scrambled to his feet.

Bartholomew moved in front of him, head down, shoulders hunched like one of the pit fighters in Angel Street heading into a fight. "If something comes through, we let them unlock the gate, but we can't let them open it. We keep it between them and—"

A handful of loose bolts went rolling into a ventilation grate in the corner. Then, far, far below, a scream went up from ten thousand faery throats.

With a great, straining groan, the Birmingham Faery Prison began to move.

CHAPTER XVIII
The City of Black Laughter

ONCE, when Hettie was very small, she remembered sitting with Bartholomew under the window in the kitchen in Old Crow Alley, watching a storm brew outside. Rain was beginning to flick against the panes, and Mother hadn't come home yet. She had gone out to find supper, and Hettie was worried. So was Bartholomew, but he was pretending not to be. He said, "Het, I'm going to tell you a story, and by the time it's done Mother will be home." Hettie knew he was going to make it up and that it might not be a very good story, but she nodded anyway and burrowed into him, listening for the sound of footsteps in the alley below.

"There was once a huge castle," Bartholomew started, looking out the window. The sky was dark, the clouds heaping. "It stood in a sunny land, and the castle, oh, it was the grandest castle you ever saw. It was built of chocolate and it had rooms just full of food, just so full it dribbled out the windows."

More rain struck the glass. A wind howled up the alley. Hettie curled up in the crook of Bartholomew's arm, listening to the rain just as much as to Bartholomew.

"I'm hungry," she said.

Bartholomew ignored her. "One of the rooms," he went on, "was made out of green peppermint, and another was out of taffy, and another was of licorice, and another was rock candy, all different colors. It had rooms full of toys, too. And dolls and books and pillows."

The door to the alley banged open. Hettie tensed, straining to hear if it was Mother. It wasn't. It was a faery, shuffling up the stairs, its skin, or perhaps its clothes, rustling along the spindles like leaves. Both Hettie and Bartholomew held their breath as the heavy feet passed their door. Then Bartholomew continued, a little softer.

"There was only one way into this castle. It was a great big front door carved with . . . carved with sausages. And one day the enemies of the castle said, 'We want that castle. We want all of it.' So they sent a witch to trick the queen of the castle. The witch came up to the queen, who was very grand and wore a dress sewn out of stained glass, and the witch said, 'The enemy! The enemy is coming and they will conquer you! But I can help. I will give you a powerful magic that will protect you, and in return . . .'" A gust of wind rattled the window. "'In return I ask only one small thing from your castle, and it will be so small it will fit in this box.' And here she held up a tiny box. And the great queen thought, *Oh, it's such a small box. Not even my smallest jewel would fit in there.* So she said, 'Anything, anything! Hurry! Give me the magic.' Because by this time the enemy was already marching, and the queen could hear the footsteps tramping up the road up to her castle.

"'Very well,' said the witch, and she gave the

queen . . . gave her . . . oh, gave her a glove that would turn her into a wild, savage wolf. Then the witch went to the great front door and took one nail out of the hinge and put it in the box. The queen was shocked, but even then she didn't quite understand. She didn't really see how important the little nail was, you see. I mean, no one really likes nails. They get hit over their heads with hammers. But if they weren't there, people would be in trouble. People would know what awfully important things nails are. But the queen didn't. The queen put on the glove and turned into a wolf, and she slobbered and growled and sharpened her claws, and the enemies came up to the castle. And they walked right in because the hinge was loose on the door and it wouldn't close properly, and they shot the wolf-queen with forty-seven arrows so that she looked precisely like a pincushion.

"Now, while all this was happening, the witch was going down the path from the castle, holding her little box. But the witch didn't know everything either. Because in *fact*, the nail was the true queen who had been enchanted. Her name was Hettie, by the way . . ."

"No, it wasn't!" Hettie sat up, laughing. "What was it actually?"

"It was! Her name was Hettie, and she had the same sort of branches you have, except probably not as messy, and not now because she was a nail and—"

The door to the alley creaked open again. It was a tiny, quiet, rusty-metal sound, but both Hettie and Bartholomew heard it. "Hurry," whispered Hettie. "Finish the story."

Bartholomew sat up. "And as soon as the nail was out of the castle, Queen Hettie turned into her real self, and destroyed absolutely all her enemies, including the witch, and became queen again, and everyone was much kinder to nails after that." Then Mother slipped in, smiling and shaking the rain from her hair, and Hettie and Bartholomew helped her set the table and boil up the cabbage stew while the storm raged outside, and Hettie remembered thinking *that* was the most marvelous story anyone had ever told her.

The river was becoming wider. The water was deeper now, darker, flowing swift and silent toward some greater body. After a while the fog lifted. The grassy banks turned to stones, then ruined towns, then bleak gray fields and chalk-white trees.

Hettie watched it all with growing dread. They were so far from Piscaltine's house, so far from the woods, getting farther with every passing moon. She felt as if she were tied to England by the flimsiest of threads, and it was wearing thinner and thinner.

The Belusite still followed them. She flew along the shore on her empty-eyed steed, her red cape streaming behind her. She did not sleep. She did not slow. And every night, through the dark and the moonlight, Hettie heard the hooves pounding along the shore.

Hettie had thought Florence would give up after Hettie dropped the necklace into the river. The Belusite had seen it fall. Her eyes had widened into black moons and her mouth had opened. But she had not stopped. She galloped on along the river, and Hettie began to wonder if perhaps it wasn't the necklace she wanted after all. She began to wonder about the doorway again and what the faery butler had said. And the more Hettie wondered, the more worried and alone she felt.

She wished she had the mask again. She had felt so brave wearing it. When she strode into Piscaltine's masquerade, everything was possible. Everyone had looked at the ground as she passed, or bowed so low their noses touched their shoes. If she had the mask again, she felt sure she would know what to do now.

She wandered along the deck, imagining the wood turning to stone under her feet and walls rising up. The distant sound of pipes and a fiddle filled the air. Faeries made of shadows surrounded her, all sweeping low and whispering. She felt the cold power again, welling up inside her. *I was so beautiful, then. I was so brave.*

In her imagination, one of the shadow-faeries broke away to ask her for a dance. She ignored him, glided straight for a huge, black-pitted door. It stood open. Beyond the door was a field, then a wood, then a cottage, and beside the cottage was Barthy, waiting for her. . . .

She walked to the boat railing. She stared into the water, and the hideous Hettie was staring back at her, eyes sharp and flinty. It tilted its head. A fat black centipede slid out of its mouth and disappeared into its ear.

Hettie stumbled back, pinching her eyes shut. The reflection in the water seemed to become uglier with every passing day. Hettie had on several occasions wondered if she should leap out of the boat and escape before it went any farther. She didn't know how to swim, and Florence La Bellina was on the bank, but that was not what stopped her. It was the thing in the water, with its mouth full of bugs and its horrible, wrinkled face. Sometimes it seemed to whisper to her. She didn't really hear it, and yet somehow she always knew what it was saying. *We're too ugly,* it said, its voice in the wind and the lick of the waves. *We won't escape, not us. Ugly things are useless. Ugly things are weak. Everyone has forgotten us at home, and we'll never find the way on our own.*

"Shut up," Hettie hissed. She turned away, her

hands balled into fists. *I'm not you. Barthy's still looking for me. I'll get home one day.*

She dropped down and huddled against the mast, her back to the faery butler. She pushed away the thought of Barthy. She tried not to think of him very often. If she did, she would think of Old Crow Alley, and her cupboard bed, and she would wonder if perhaps Barthy and Mother thought she was dead. She would wonder if they were going about their day, washing clothes and cranking the wash-wringer and living their quiet, dangerous lives without her. It would make her heart want to snap in two.

After a while the river became a bay. The boat slid into it, and Hettie hurried to the stern to look back at the land. Florence La Bellina had turned along the shore and was galloping west, her horse sending up a plume of dust from the stones of an old road. Hettie looked over the desolate fields. She saw hills in the distance, round and bare like old men's heads. She glimpsed faery houses, too, little crooked dwellings with broken roofs and beams sticking up like snapped ribs. Scratches and faded lines showed where other roads and causeways had once led. They became more and more prominent, stitching ruined house to ruined farm to ruined town.

She hurried to the other side of the boat. That was when she saw it—a great city rising from the farthest part of the bay. It was all towers, stone needles pricking the sky. The clouds were low and seething overhead, purple-gray.

"The City of Black Laughter," the faery butler said, crawling up beside her. "We're almost there."

Hettie looked back to the shore, searching for the Belusite. She was a bead of crimson, riding straight for the city.

"She's going to be there soon," Hettie said. "Just as soon as us, and then what are you going to do? What if she catches us again?"

"She won't catch us." The faery butler straightened, seven feet of bony limbs uncurling into the air. "Not as long as she is alone. I will be able to keep you well away from her until I can hand you to the Sly King."

Hettie frowned, but her stomach squirmed with worry. Because she wasn't going to be handed to the Sly King. She wasn't going with these faeries. She was going to run. Before the faery butler could hand her over. Before she even saw the Sly King.

She only hoped she could run fast enough.

The boat neared the city. The towers were listing and old, and the roofs drooped like wizard hats. The windows were black specks, like flies on the walls.

Hettie's knuckles tightened around the rail. It was too quiet. Old Crow Alley had never been this quiet. Not even at night. There were no other ships in the harbor. She listened for shouts or whistles, the noises one would expect from the docks of such a great place. The water lapped against the boat, but there was nothing else.

"Doesn't anyone live here?" she asked, edging a little nearer to the faery butler. "If it's the capital, shouldn't there be faeries everywhere?"

"No." The faery butler gripped her hand. The boat approached a wharf and grew onto it, the white tentacles wriggling like roots around the stone.

"The Sly King had it emptied. The capital was for the greatest of the Sidhe, the lords and ladies of Summer and Winter and Fall and Spring and all their courts, but there aren't many great Sidhe left. They have been dwindling away. Tales have it he did away with them, sank them in rivers and ponds until all their lives were spent. The last of them were at Piscaltine's. Even the lowercase cities are empty now. He has gathered all who are left outside the city. To wait."

To wait? Hettie looked back at the bay. *To wait for what?* The shoreline extended away in a vast crescent toward the horizon. Nothing stirred. The whole country, for miles and miles, was dead and empty. The Sly King had ruined it all. But why?

They set off along the wharf. High up in one of the towers, a knotted strand of dead vine snaked out of a window, like a hand, waving gently.

"A tower of ash and a tower of stone," the faery butler said under his breath. "A tower of blood and a tower of bone."

"Stop it," Hettie whispered at him. "You're just

making everything worse." The faery butler closed his mouth.

Hettie looked about. They were on a long, wide street. Metal fixtures stuck out of the stone here and there where signboards might have hung once. Alleys opened off on all sides, doorways to slip into and galleries to flee down.

"Where are we going to go?" she asked, and at the same time gently slipped her hand out of the faery butler's.

He didn't notice. "Someplace high," he said, scanning the buildings. "We need a vantage point of a good portion of the city, but the towers are the King's, so we must not risk—"

Hettie wasn't listening. She would have to hurry once she was away from him. She had to get out of the city, and then her troubles were only starting. Florence would still be hunting her. There would be wild faeries in the countryside and the butler would not be beside her with his great, long knife. But she could follow the river again. At Piscaltine's house, she would go into the woods.

Taking a deep breath, she peered about for a suitable direction. The faery butler was several steps ahead, still speaking. Hettie slowed.

I'm sorry your plan won't work, she thought. *I hope the Sly King won't be very angry at you.*

Ahead, the street forked. To the right was an archway shaped like a curled stone tree. It led into a dark courtyard. Beyond, Hettie just glimpsed another street, twisting away. They were almost there. She tensed, preparing to run. And then Florence La Bellina strode out of the left fork, straight toward them. She was flanked by four Belusites, four creatures in dragging ball gowns and puffed breeches, all arms and claws and strange metal appendages. Her black-and-white face had arranged itself into a sharp, square smile.

"The London Door," she said. "Take her."

The Belusites fanned out behind Florence.

The faery butler shouted. His knife slid from his sleeve.

Now, Hettie thought. *Go!* She hurtled toward the archway.

"*Sathir!*" Someone screamed from behind her. "*Tir valentu! Tir hispestra!*"

Hettie looked back over her shoulder. The faery butler's knife slashed through the air, keeping the Belusites back. Florence was still grinning. Hettie looked forward again. And smacked straight into the green-embroidered waistcoat of the Sly King.

"I liked you better when you wore a mask," he said, and shoved her. She fell backward and instantly a boar-faced Belusite was on her, dragging at her. She saw two others battling the faery butler. He ducked, whirled, kicked one in the leg and the other in the side of the head. They did not flinch. They grabbed his arms and he shrieked, his knife clattering to the street.

"*Mi Sathir,*" he whimpered, going limp in their hands. "*Sathir,* do not harm me. I bring you a gift! A child who can step between worlds! Do not harm your humble servant!"

"Why, what's this?" the Sly King asked, drifting toward the faery butler. "Florence was just about to bring me such a child. One she had been investigating for many moons. Have I become so lucky that there are *two* of these children in my humble kingdom?" He laughed quietly. "Or is someone lying? Whomever shall I believe?"

He exchanged a glimmering look with Florence La Bellina.

The faery butler tried to stand. "*She* lost the girl," he snarled, jerking his head in the direction of Florence. "If it were not for me, your doorway would have been trampled to death. I saved her!"

The Sly King ignored him. Hettie struggled. The Belusite holding her clacked its yellow teeth and hauled her back.

"What are your orders, *Sathir*?" said Florence. "What shall we do with them?"

The Sly King squinted at Hettie, then at the faery butler. "The child," he said, "will go to the Tower of Blood. She will make a fine addition to my collection. Kill the faery."

The faery butler's eye snapped wide. "*What?*" he gasped, but the Belusites were already at his back, forcing him to his knees. He struggled. They struck him. One of them leaned down and picked up the knife off the ground, the faery butler's knife.

"Run!" the faery butler shouted. "Run, Hettie, don't let them catch—"

Hettie saw the blow fall. It caught the faery butler in the shoulder, and Hettie flinched as if she had been struck herself. The knife drew back, slick and dark. The faery butler's eyes fixed on her. The green one sparked. Then he tipped forward into the street.

Hettie almost screamed. She felt a pain and a horrid sadness, and the tears welling up like a flood. But she knew that if she started crying now, she would never, ever stop. She clawed the boar-face's hand and spun on the Sly King like a wild little beast.

"You'd better let me go," she spat. "My brother's coming. He is, and when he's here you'll be sorry. He'll smash you into little pieces."

"Your brother?" The Belusites were already surrounding her again, hemming her in. The Sly King smiled. "Not Bartholomew Kettle, surely? And he wouldn't be in *London*, would he? I hope not. You see, I read your country's newspapers, and I saw once that he had been all but adopted by a certain Lord Jelliby. So he probably is. In London. How very sad. . . ."

The Sly King pushed between the Belusites and leaned down by her ear. "As we speak, twelve faery prisons three hundred feet high are thundering down out of the North, their lord commanders having been infested by leech-faeries, and let me assure you, they are quite intent on pounding that wretched city into the earth." The Sly King laughed. "So you see, it is not *I* who will be smashed into little pieces."

CHAPTER XIX
Pikey in the Land of Night

*U*RGENT *Correspondence to the Privy Council, and to the Parliament and the House of Lords:*

Evacuate the city. Alert <u>all</u> military personnel remaining to you, all cannon and weaponry, coal-powered conveyances and dirigibles. The faery prisons have been overrun and speed toward London. Tar Hill is lost. Many of our bravest have been infested with leech-faeries, and some witchcraft turns them against us, makes them evil with treachery and bloodlust. They may already be among you, in your halls and drawing rooms. Be advised to set up a perimeter across the northern side of the city, trenches and troops, scouts with clockwork birds at least twenty miles outside, in position to issue warnings.

THE WHATNOT

The prisons <u>must</u> be stopped. The defenses must stand. God help us if they do not.

In utter haste,

General William Haddock, Viscount of Earswick, November 27, 1857

The Birmingham Faery Prison was speeding southward with reckless abandon. It had already leveled two small forests, a flock of sheep, and innumerable stone walls. Villages and farms had been spared up until now, but it was a close thing. Pikey doubted whoever was steering the great globe would blink an eye at smashing a few townships into the ground.

The mutiny had been over in minutes. Pikey and Bartholomew had waited, wound tight as springs, as the prison began to roll and the sounds of fighting echoed out of its depths. Boots had rung against grating. The door at the end of the walkway had been struck so hard it dented. But then the commotion had died away. No one came for them. No one brought them any news. All they heard now was the prison, thundering over the countryside.

Bartholomew went to the little barred window and stretched his hand out, sticking his fingers into the wind and squinting at the stars. "South," he said. "We're going south."

Then he dropped down and began wrenching frantically at the bolt that fastened the chains around his ankles. Pikey watched him a second, then did the same. The bolts were iron, no more than a year out of the forge. They would not give easily.

But neither would Pikey and Bartholomew. They didn't need to be told what this new direction meant. Parliament would never order so many faeries back toward the war factories, the train stations, and themselves. Some other voice had spoken the command. And as Pikey and Bartholomew twisted their fingers raw on the bolts, they both knew: the faeries had the Birmingham Prison now.

They worked into the wee hours of the night. Things scratched at the door at the end of the walkway, thin, skittering sounds like twigs or sharp fingernails. The door had a wheel at its center, like the sort in a boat, and once the wheel turned partway around, as if someone was trying to get in. Finally Bartholomew gave a quiet whoop and held up his bolt.

"Got it," he whispered, wriggling out of the chains. He helped Pikey with his bolt, which hadn't given even an inch yet, and then went straightaway to the gate. The lock wouldn't budge. Bartholomew tried whispering to it and smashing it with his boot. That only made an alarm go off—a metal pellet shot out of the keyhole and struck a peg on the other side of the walkway. The peg pulled a wire and the wire set a jumble of cogs in motion and soon brimstone bulbs were blazing all up the walkway and an alarm bell was shrilling. Pikey and Bartholomew dove to the floor, waiting, but no one came. Eventually the bell wound down.

"Well," Bartholomew said, and stood up awkwardly. He began to pace, testing the joints in the walls next. Pikey stayed on the floor.

He tried not to think of his lie. He tried not to think of anything, because right then it seemed like every option was bad. He dreaded to think what sorts of faeries would come down the walkway first. A horde of goblins maybe, or a Sidhe. And if nothing came it would be even worse. They would starve. There was a little water dripping down the walls, enough to stay alive, but there was no food. They hadn't eaten since the day before the battle of Tar Hill, and Pikey's stomach seemed to have forgotten how to be silent.

"We're coming," Bartholomew whispered in his sleep, when they finally lay down again, and Bartholomew had drifted off. "We're coming."

Pikey put his arms over his head to block out the sound.

The prison rolled all through the night, and when the first gray of morning touched the edge of the window, Pikey climbed onto Bartholomew's shoulders and looked out. The globe whirled around them, iron and slag, and beyond that, foggy England. Hills and hedgerows were flattened. A river was sent spraying a hundred feet into the air. Then the fog broke for an instant and Pikey saw three more faery globes, rolling close by, looming like dark planets out of the gloom.

Pikey leaped down off Bartholomew's shoulders. "It's not just us," he said. "It's all of them. All the prisons."

The faeries were returning to London.

The first thing to come down the hanging walkway, as it turned out, was not a Sidhe or sharp-toothed gnome, but a severely disheveled General Braillmouth. He lurched onto the narrow walk, bouncing off the guardrails. He had lost his plumed hat, and his blue coat was spattered and filthy.

Pikey scrabbled away from the bars. Bartholomew stood his ground, watching the general keenly.

The general stumbled up to the cell. "Hello, my pretties," he breathed, flopping against the gate.

Pikey's eyes widened. *Pretties?* Where had he heard that before? Where had he heard that voice?

"General Braillmouth," Bartholomew said. "I am the ward of Lord Arthur Jelliby, Earl of Watership, and—" Suddenly he drew in his breath sharply and leaped back.

"Oh, good," the general said, but his mouth did not move as he spoke. "I have been looking for you. I have been looking *everywhere*. In pots and pans and graves and suitcases. And now I've found you." His eyes were half-closed. His lips were stiff and dry.

Pikey crept forward, peering around Bartholomew's shoulder.

"Who are you?" asked Bartholomew quietly. "Who are you, and why have you come?"

"Do you not remember?" the general said softly. "Lickspindle? The Kingspringer? Or Abraham Carlton Braillmouth, if you don't know any better. But of course *you* do."

The general's eyes had slipped almost completely closed. His face was so white, his lashes like stitches, sewing up his lids. "I shall introduce myself again. Formally. I am Thimble Tom, head of *Uà Sathir*, the Sly King's Infestation Corps, at your service." He performed an ungainly bow, and as he did his head tipped forward, and Pikey saw the other face, slithering on the back of the general's scalp, the wrinkly, drooping face, beaded with warts and bulbous eyes.

The faun. The dead faun that had found them in the alley and thought them to be emissaries of the Sly King. The faun who had told them about Edith Hutcherson. This was its leech-faery.

"You . . . ?" Bartholomew gasped, and for a second he appeared at a loss. But only for a second. Then he stood ramrod-straight and said sharply, "Thank goodness you've found us. The English took us prisoner at Tar Hill. We never made it to the Old Country. You have to get us out."

The general's face remained sleepy, and yet somehow his voice sounded like a smile. Like a *grin.* "You can't leave. I know who you are. I know who both of you are. You can't leave."

"What?"

"You aren't emissaries. Little liars." The general opened one dead, veined eye and winked at them. "The Sly King is so grateful. We are all in your debt. We can't let you run off again."

"I don't know what you're talking about. It's His Majesty's orders. Get us *out of here!*"

"Liar-liar! No. You have done your work already. So well."

The general swung about and began to shamble back up the walkway. Bartholomew screamed and kicked the gate in frustration. "Get us out! Please, we can't stay here, please—"

Pikey didn't move. He was staring at the faery on the back of the general's head, the hideous, wrinkled face like a melted candle. Its eyes glinted, and it watched Pikey as Pikey watched it, until it had sunk back into the shadows.

On the third day of their imprisonment, General Braillmouth returned, carrying a load of mushrooms and moss and a small dead bird. It appeared the faery wanted them to eat.

But Bartholomew and Pikey were not hungry anymore. They were waiting.

"No word from the Sly King," the general whispered, dropping to his knees and shoving the strange items into their cell one by one. "But he will be here soon. He *promised* he would. Then all will be sorted.

We must all be understanding for just a little while longer. He has so many other things to deal with."

"Does he?" Slowly Bartholomew inched up to the bars. He was watching the general like a hawk. Pikey hovered behind him. "And what would that be?"

"Rebels." The general's swollen fingers were trying to poke the bird under the gate, but it wouldn't fit and its wire-thin talons kept snagging on his sleeve. "The faeries who don't want to leave and who don't want to fight and who don't want to obey our King. Wicked things." He forced the bird in with a vicious stab. "There are so many of them, hiding, scheming. But it will be over soon. I heard *Uà Sathir* had them all slau—"

Bartholomew threw himself at the bars. He looped a chain through, around the general's neck, and jerked him against the gate.

"*Fascinating,* but we're leaving now," Bartholomew hissed. "Thank you for coming."

Pikey darted forward. He felt over the general's coat, his hand slipping in one pocket, then another. *Buttons. Tinderbox. Where are your keys?*

The general's body thrashed, eyes bulging. "Stop!"

the leech-faery shrieked. "*Stop*, it is the King's orders! His *orders!*"

Pikey's hand touched cold metal. A long, old key lay in his palm, the teeth shaped like a leaf. It was so complicated. He had seen keys like this before. Keys that fit into every lock, likely every lock in the prison.

He whirled away and jammed the key into its hole. He twisted, once, twice. The bolt clanked back. Then Bartholomew hurled himself at the gate and it swung all the way around, slamming the general into the outer wall of the cell.

The general crumpled to the ground, and the leech-faery clinging to his head closed its eyes and let out a high, anguished wail. "Why are you so *cruel*, my pretties? Why are you so wicked? Do you want to end up like the others? All dead in Yearn-by-the-Woods. All killed. That is what happens to those who fight him. That is what happens to all who defy him."

Bartholomew dropped down next to the corpse. "Who is Edith Hutcherson?" he whispered. "You said she knew the way into the Old Country, so where is she? Where do we find her?"

The leech-faery looked up at them, its many eyes bright black like a spider's. "She was his favorite," it said. "Long ago. She knew the ways in and she knew the ways out, but she was not careful. They caught her. They put her in an iron carriage, locked her in a cell in London. Lunatic, they call her now. *Madwoman.*"

Pikey gripped Bartholomew's arm. "It's her," he said. "It's her! It's the batty lady! The old batty lady in the lockup in Newgate!"

"What?" Bartholomew stared at him. Then at the leech-faery. "No. No, she was right there! Right there for us to speak to!"

"You were going the wrong way," said the leech-faery, with a bitter, gurgling laughing. "All this time going the wrong way. And you still are."

Bartholomew stood. "Let's go," he said, but Pikey didn't know what to think. London was the last place he wanted to be. He didn't want to see Spitalfields again. He didn't want to be in those muddy, snowy streets again, and he didn't want to see the madwoman either, even if her name *was*

Edith Hutcherson. *Faery-fed,* the prison keeper had said. Pikey hadn't believed him then. He did now.

All at once, the globe gave a skull-shivering jerk, and Pikey and Bartholomew were thrown against the guardrail. The general went rolling and sliding over the walkway, limp as a puppet. The cell gate swung wildly on its hinges.

"Out!" Bartholomew shouted, pulling himself to his feet. "Run, Pikey!"

"No!" the general screeched. "The Sly King does not want you to go! Do not disobey him!"

Pikey and Bartholomew leaped over the general's body and pelted down the walkway. At its end was the metal door, battered and dented. Bartholomew gripped its wheel and wrenched it about. Pikey joined in, pushing with all his strength. And then there was a distant, echoing clang, like something huge and solid, snapping . . . And everything began to tip. The walkway tilted down like a slow trapdoor. The general slid under the guardrail and plummeted into the dark. Pikey and Bartholomew held on to the wheel for dear life.

"It's stopped!" Bartholomew yelled. "The prison's stopped!"

Pikey's foot found the guardrail under him and he stood. Gritting his teeth, he gave the wheel one last turn. The door slammed open, and Pikey and Bartholomew clambered onto it, into a stairwell. The globe lurched again. Pikey tumbled into the wall and fell. Everything was on its side now. The walls were the floor and ceiling, and the steps went up sideways.

"We need to get to the ground!" Bartholomew shouted as a huge iron cog came bouncing and crashing past them. "Get on the railing and climb. Move!"

They found a hatch in the floor and climbed down, down into the depths of the prison. They passed pipes and machinery and dim flickering brimstone bulbs. And then they were in the pushing pits and the faeries were swarming around them. Piskies buzzed. Goblins shrieked, clacking their teeth. They had been worked into a frenzy. They were sliding everywhere, trying to escape. They carried weapons. Extendable pikes and blunderbusses. English weapons. None of them paid any heed to the two cloaked figures hurrying among them.

Pikey and Bartholomew scrambled over spikes and iron garters, swept along in the tide of faeries. They launched themselves off a beam, down onto mud and crushed grass. And then they were out from under the globe, climbing up out of some great ditch. When they got to the top, all they could do was stop and stare.

The Birmingham Faery Prison was stuck in a huge slash in the earth, a ditch forty feet deep and five hundred feet long. Great, steam-driven shovel machines stood at the ditch's edge, silent and deserted, their engines dashed to pieces. In the distance, London was a smudge against the snowy sky. Three other globes had fallen into the ditch as well, Pikey saw. Eight more caught in trenches farther back. Regiments of red-and-blue-coated troops dashed everywhere, shooting, fighting. Guns bombarded the globes, but they might as well have been firing flowers. The bullets pinged off the metal, harmless. Faeries poured out of the prisons. English soldiers walked among them, black-eyed, with leech-faeries clinging to their heads. They carried spades, plates, anything to dig with.

Pikey turned to Bartholomew, but neither of them said anything. The faeries were going to dig the prisons out. It would take days. The globes would have to ease up the slope of the ditch little by little. But eventually they would be free. And when they were, London was done for.

"Let's go!" Bartholomew shouted above the din, and they set off across the wintry fields, leaving twelve globes and one hundred thousand faeries clawing their way out of the mud behind them.

"Now, my little Whatnot," the Sly King said, pulling Hettie into a doorway and up a winding stair. "Now we send you home."

"You don't know where my home is," Hettie said. "You don't know anything about me."

"My dear, I know everything about you. Your home is England, Bath, Old Crow Alley, and there's a face in the front door, and a round window in the roof, and your mother gathers washing in a green-painted wheelbarrow. You have a checkered handkerchief that you carry around with you, and you speak to it as if it can hear you."

Up, up they went, the spiral so tight it made Hettie dizzy. Before they had begun the climb, the Sly King had snapped his fingers and her eyelids had fallen shut, as if there were lead weights hanging from them. She still couldn't open them. She couldn't see where she was, or where she was being dragged. All she knew was that she was in a tower and the steps were wet under her feet.

"You're lying," she snapped, trying to wriggle out of his grasp. "You're *lying!*"

It was a trick. It had to be a trick. Why would he send her home? All faeries ever wanted was to keep her and lock her up and tell her she was useless.

"Oh, I'm not lying. In fact, I've not said so many truthful things in a row in some time." He laughed again, a soft, hissing laugh. He seemed always to be smiling or laughing, as if everything were funny.

Hettie tripped on the slick steps, pulled herself up again.

"You are the London Door," the Sly King went on. "Our great success. Or almost. Mr. Lickerish very nearly had you work all those years ago, in Wapping. Until *someone* had to ruin everything."

Hettie saw it all again, snipped in black-and-white behind her eyelids. *Wings like shreds of night, wind, and a shrieking fit to tear the world in two. A door opening around her, swirling, destroying. Barthy shouting, yelling for her to jump. His hand stretched toward her. Couldn't reach. Couldn't reach his fingers, and the tears in her eyes, and the wind in her face, and the faery butler's hand on her shoulder, pulling her away, away into the Old Country. . . .*

"Ah well. It was for the best, I think," said the King. "Now is the proper time. Now when there is war, and England is truly ready to fall. You will be the end of one age and the beginning of another."

And then there were no more steps under Hettie's feet, and the Sly King tossed her to the ground like a little soggy bundle.

"When you next open your eyes, you will be in London, and her river will be running through your toes, and her houses will be lying at your feet in

shatters and shards. And everyone will be screaming and weeping at you, saying, 'Oh, Hettie, Hettie,
look what you have done. Look what devastation you
have wrought.'" The Sly King laughed. "What a sight
it will be. What a new and wonderful sight."

Once inside the city, Bartholomew and Pikey took a
smoke-spewing trolley down Farringdon Road, past
Holborn, and on toward the prisons at Newgate.
No one else was on the trolley. No pilot sat behind
the gears and dials up front. The little paint-and-
iron contraption simply went, traveling its rounds
through the frozen, desolate city though there was
no one left to use it.

London was deserted. The streets were empty,
newspapers flitting like ghosts over the snow.
Shutters were bolted, doors shut tight, and in the
poorer neighborhoods there were signs of looting.
Shopfronts had been smashed in. Streetlamps had
been sawed down. On one long brick wall, someone
had written in huge dripping letters: *Fly far from here, ye
wicked birds. Death Comes.*

THE WHATNOT

At Newgate, Pikey and Bartholomew leaped off the trolley and hurried up the street toward the prison. The trolley trundled on and was lost around the bend. A cold wind flew in Pikey's face. It smelled dreadful. *Rotting fish, that is,* he thought. *Rotting everything.*

The prison was not at all the way Pikey remembered it. It was nothing but a leaning old house with bars over the windows. He didn't know why he had ever been afraid of it. It was nothing compared to wars and faery prisons and a million birds.

They hammered on the door. It was bolted, but not locked, and it slipped off its hook under their fists. They stepped in and went down a short flight of steps into the sunken passageway.

The prison keeper sat sprawled on his chair, seemingly fast asleep.

"Let's just take the keys," Pikey whispered. "Let's not wake him." He dashed forward, but Bartholomew caught him and pulled him back. *Wait,* Bartholomew mouthed, and pointed a finger at the prison keeper's open eyes. "He's not asleep. He's ill."

Sure enough, the prison keeper's cheeks were

growing with a strange sort of fungus, and his eyes were dull, the whites gone yellow as old paper. He looked at them blankly as they approached.

"Sir?" Bartholomew said, leaning down a bit. "Sir, thank goodness we've found you. We were here several weeks ago with Lord Arthur Jelliby and we need to speak to one of your inmates again. Edith Hutcherson is her name. It's very urgent."

"Hm? What?" The prison keeper stirred, snorting, and sat up in his chair. "What's that noise?"

"Edith Hutcherson!" Bartholomew said, louder this time. "We need to speak to her."

The prison keeper started to stand, his fists grinding at his eyes. He was unshaven and stank like a sewer. Bartholomew took a step back. Pikey didn't bother, and he didn't need to because the prison keeper collapsed again a second later, so hard the iron nibs on the bottom of the chair's legs squealed against the floor.

"Edith . . ." he said. "Who is Edith . . . ?"

"The madwoman!" Pikey practically shouted. "The one who was being fed by the faeries! Is she still here?"

"Madwoman." The prison keeper seemed already falling back into his stupor. "Faery-fed." His eyes blinked open.

"Look, just give us the keys and we'll leave you alone."

"She's not here." His voice was soft, his gaze faraway. "She's not been here a while. They took her to the Magdalene Hospital, they did. . . . Weeks ago."

"To the hospital?" Bartholomew gripped the man's arm. "Why to the hospital? *Tell us!*"

The prison keeper's head drooped. His eyes slid shut. "She was starving," he said.

Pikey and Bartholomew stood before the great wooden desk of the Sister Orderly in the Hospital of the Holy Magdalene on Dowd Street, shuffling and fidgeting.

She eyed them sharply over the top of her spectacles. "Family, you say?" She had the clipped, high voice of an aristocrat, and it echoed up the walls and slithered across the ceiling. Night was falling outside. Only one lamp was lit, a tiny island in the darkness, casting shadows up onto the Sister Orderly's face. Whitewashed halls and glimmering floors led away into pits of blackness.

"Yes," said Bartholomew from inside his hood. "Nephews. On her husband's side. It's really awfully important. She's still here, isn't she? She hasn't—she hasn't died?" The last part was spoken in a whisper.

The Sister Orderly blinked. "No. No, she hasn't. But Edith Hutcherson is in a strange and unnatural state. You may speak to her, but do not expect her to answer. She has had no human company for far too long. It seems she has forgotten what human voices sound like."

"Thank you, ma'am," Bartholomew said. "Thank you, we'll be very quick."

"Room three hundred and four. And no need to be quick. Everyone has left who wants to live."

Pikey stared at her, but Bartholomew was already hurrying down a hall.

"The faeries will be here before the morning, they say," the Sister Orderly went on matter-of-factly. "The hospital's empty. The patients are all gone home, those that have one. I'll be here to the end."

Pikey gaped at her a second longer. Then he turned and raced after Bartholomew. The Sister Orderly's voice seemed to fill the hall behind him. *I'll be here to the end. To the end, end, end . . .*

They found Room 304. The door was already ajar. All the doors in the hall were. The Sisters must have opened them before they fled.

The room was dark. Only the faintest squares of blue light fell through the window, illuminating a washstand and an iron bedstead. The madwoman lay on the bed, covered by a single sheet. Her limbs were thin as sticks. Her face was haggard and her eyes had sunk deep inside her skull.

"Edith Hutcherson?" Bartholomew stepped toward the bed. "Can you hear me?"

She did not turn her head. "Mr. Pudding." Her voice was just a rasp, creeping out of her throat. "Dear Jack Pudding, is that you?" Strands of hair puffed away from her mouth as she spoke.

"No, it's Bartholomew Kettle. I need your help." Somewhere outside, a siren began to wail. Any other night it would have been answered by the clanging of a fire-carriage bell, the squeak of rubber on cobbles, but not tonight. The siren turned off. The city was silent again.

"Help," the madwoman said. Still she did not look at them. Her eyes, one sky-blue, one cloud-gray, were fixed on the ceiling. "Help's all gone. They left, my little friends. They left me to starve."

"I'm very sorry," said Bartholomew, kneeling down next to the bed. "I was— Well, we were told you know the way in. Into the Old Country. We were told you had been there. Please tell us? Please?"

"The way. The way to gray roads and black woods and death."

"Yes, how do we get in? Is there a door? A door in London?"

"The boy knows," she whispered, and then, without even looking at Pikey, she pointed a thin, trembling finger at him.

Pikey flinched. "What?"

"Ask him," she said, somewhat louder. "Ask him, he knows."

Bartholomew turned to Pikey. "What is she talking about?" His voice was a little bit flat.

"I don't know! She's mad!" Pikey said. "She's mad as a hatter, I—"

But then an image formed in his mind. *A tall, thin figure standing in the shadows of a storeroom. A cold hand. Flying through the city on a winter wind. Where did we land? Where were we?* He felt himself walking backward through the passageways of his brain. *Where, where, where?* And then he saw it, looming in front of him as if he were there right now. *A tree. A tree in Spitalfields called the Gallows Tree.*

He looked at Bartholomew. His eyes were wide, like a rabbit in a snare.

"What? Pikey, if you know something, tell me. Tell me how to get to my sister!"

"I'd forgot," Pikey stammered. "I didn't remember, I'm sorry—"

"What?" Bartholomew almost shouted. "What did you forget?"

Pikey looked away sharply. "A tree," he said. "There's a tree in Spitalfields, and it opens."

Bartholomew practically flew from the room.

Pikey heard his feet pelting away down the hallway. He hurried after him. At the door, he looked back at Edith Hutcherson, one last time. She still lay like a stone under the sheet. But she had turned her head, turned it to watch them go. "Run," she said. "Run, Pikey Thomas."

They found the tree within the hour. It was a huge, black, gnarled thing, standing in a ring of cobbles in a small court behind a butcher's. The tree was dead. Its whole trunk was hollow, eaten out by insects. There was a hole at the tree's base, very small, worming into the roots. Only a child could ever fit in it. Or a Peculiar.

"He said something," Pikey mumbled as they circled it. "He said a word to make it open, I don't remember what. . . ."

Bartholomew wasn't listening to him. He dropped to his knees and stuck his head into the hole. Pikey shut up. He'd had the answer all along. He could have been a hundred times more important than he had been, a million times. And now they had found the way, and it was too late to make everything right. Hettie might be dead. Bartholomew would hate Pikey forever, because he was a filthy liar. Or Hettie might be alive. She would have her brother back, and they would be happy, but they wouldn't need Pikey. Pikey would be alone again.

Bartholomew's head was all the way in now, then his neck and his shoulders. A second later his silver-buckled boots had disappeared down the hole.

Pikey glanced about. The court was so quiet.

"Bartholomew?" he called. *Perhaps it's just a hole,* he thought. *Perhaps it doesn't go anywhere, and only that tall faery can open it.* Bartholomew might still be under the roots, still in England.

"Bartholomew?" he called again. No answer. Above him the branches creaked.

Panic seized Pikey. He dropped to the ground and wriggled in. It was pitch-dark. Roots pressed around him—*too narrow, too narrow*—no air. Nothing but blackness and moldy wood, and the whole great tree above him, swallowing him up. Roots were in front of him, roots were behind him. He struggled on, but it only seemed to make the passage smaller, tightening around him. And then he felt something. Wind. A fresh, swift wind, full of salt and the sharpness of the sea. He stretched out his hands, clawing. The wind brushed his fingertips. And then his hands came down on rocks. The wind was full in his face. He heard the crash of waves. Sky was above him, endless black sky.

Pikey pushed back dirt and pebbles and stepped out into the Old Country.

CHAPTER XX
Lies

HETTIE'S eyes split open. She was alone. The Sly King's footsteps were echoing on the stairs, down into the dark.

She looked about, spinning, trying to see where she was. She was in a small, shadowy room, smooth as an egg. The room at the top of a tower.

It was very cold. There was no furniture, though the marks on the floors said there had been once. The beams overhead went up in a point under the roof, and there were things hanging from them, what looked like huge dripping bundles of grapes. Dark liquid flowed down the walls. Wind gusted through a narrow, unglazed window. The window looked out into the night and a sky full of towers.

The next sight you'll see is London, and her river will run through your toes, and her houses will lie at your feet in shatters and shards.... But this wasn't London. And she could see well enough, stupid faery. She hurried to the head of stairs and peered down.

The Sly King's footsteps still pattered in the depths of the tower. He would hear her if she began to descend. She went to the window and pulled herself onto the sill.

Her stomach fell. She was so high up. Perhaps a thousand feet. Wisps of cloud floated below her. The tower was a dull, rusty red. Across from her was another tower, ash-gray, the window almost level with hers.

Can I jump? It was only a few feet. Fifteen, maybe twenty. Her fingers gripped the sill. She imagined herself leaping, arms spread. Even in her imagination she only got a little ways and then dropped like a stone. She went back to the stairs and peered into the dark.

All was silent now. The stairs wound away into shadow. She began to descend, quickly, hopping down the steep steps two at a time.

Her hand slid along the wall to keep herself from falling. The stones were wet. Everything was wet. She tried to wipe it off. It clung to her skin in ropes. Then, far below, she heard footsteps, coming up.

Hettie spun. She began racing up again, but whoever it was was coming quickly, impossibly fast. She heard a laugh, as if this were some horrible game. Her feet slapped the stone, splashing wet all up her nightgown. She didn't care. *Back. Back to the top.*

And then she was in the little room again. She took three gasping breaths so that it wouldn't look like she had been running and dropped into a heap on the floor.

"Not trying to escape, are we?" the Sly King's voice floated up the stairs.

Hettie let out a little cough.

"*Are* we, my dear?" He had reached the top. He was in the room.

She sat up a bit, trying to keep her lungs from

heaving. "No," she said. Her head pounding from lack of air.

The Sly King took something out of his pocket and stepped toward her. "Of course we aren't . . ." he said, a little light igniting next to his ear and floating there like a star. And then Hettie's breath burst out of her and she was gasping again, swallowing the air in great gulps. Because in the Sly King's hands was a round glass bottle filled with a liquid dark as violets and midnight, and all over Hettie's feet and her hands, and smeared and tracked across the floor, was blood.

A tower of blood and a tower of bone, the wind seemed to sing. *Who's at the top, who's in the dark, who climbs the stair without leaving a mark. . . .*

The Sly King wasn't smiling anymore.

Bartholomew practically flew along the cliffs. In the distance, a pale castle stood, leaning over a shadowy sea.

"We did it, Pikey! We did it!" he shouted over his shoulder, and ran on, his hood billowing from his shoulders.

Pikey skidded to a halt. His voice was so light, not old and solemn anymore, but a boy's voice. Pikey had never heard him sound like that, not once in all their adventures.

"What're we going to do?" Pikey yelled after him. He began to run again, his feet jarring against the rocks. "We can't just— Barth, I don't know where she is!"

"You said you saw her in a Sidhe house!" Bartholomew shouted back.

She might be dead. She might be dead, dead, dead. . . .

"You said there were carpets and windows!" Bartholomew leaped a little brook that gurgled between the boulders. "So then that's where we'll look! She'll be somewhere in a great house, and there's one so close. What luck, don't you think?" He laughed, tripped on a spar of rock and kept going, still laughing.

Pikey caught up. He hurtled along at Bartholomew's side, blinking away the ocean spray and something else. Above, the night sky was speckled with stars. *Luck? It's not luck, it's nonsense. It won't be this house. It won't be this house or any house.*

Bartholomew slowed a little. "Have you seen her lately?" he asked, breathless. "Hettie. Have you seen her since the prison?"

No, Pikey thought. "Yes," he said. "She's still just sitting." *No!* he wanted to scream. *All I see is blackness and black water over my eye.*

Bartholomew stopped, looking at the castle in the distance and smiling. "Well, that's good, then. Can you see any details? Anything would help. Can you see out the window? Can you see what sort of land is outside?"

Pikey pretended to concentrate, but it was a halfhearted show, and he felt so foolish and horrible. "Trees," he mumbled. "It's not here. No rocks. Trees."

But Bartholomew was already running again, and Pikey followed, on toward the castle by the sea. *Oh, Pikey,* he thought. *What are you doing, you dunderhead?*

"This is what you will do," said the Sly King.

He stood in the center of the tower room, like a

pillar, like an iron thorn, polishing the bottle in the palm of his hand. "When you are in London, you will walk. Walk as fast as you can, and make for the river. The globes will be coming at the city like bowling balls, and—" He started laughing, stopped himself. "And I would not want my Whatnot harmed. Cross the river. Do not stop. Do not stop until you are at the very farthest edge of the city. There wait until your door has grown as large as the sky."

Hettie sat on the floor, barely listening, trying frantically to wipe the blood from her hands, her feet, her nightgown.

"Pay attention, Hettie," he said. His voice was soft, lilting.

Hettie started. She looked up at him.

"My subjects are ready." He slipped something from his pocket, a piece of glass, like a lens. "The City of Black Laughter is empty, the great houses that have been obedient to me have been evacuated. They will all pass through you, into their new home."

Their home? Hettie stood, taking a step toward the King. "It's—it's not their home. It's *my* home. Oh, they won't like it." Her heart was squeezing itself into her throat, choking her. "The faeries that are already there are so miserable and unhappy, and there's smoke in the air, and the bells ring every five minutes, and there's iron and gin, and—"

"They are miserable and unhappy because the English are despots," the Sly King interrupted, smiling. "And yet your world is so new, so fast and fleeting and always different. I come to rule. I come to build a new world for the faeries, with the English under *us*. Anyway, what do we care of bells and foreign things? Have you not noticed how we all speak English? And wear waistcoats and frocks and ride with bells on our harnesses? I have made everyone immune. I want your world, you see. I have wanted it for so long." He began to circle her slowly, like a great, sinuous cat. "The door that opened in Bath was not an accident. It was an *experiment*. An outpost. A foothold. But we slipped. We failed that time. No one was aware of his role, neither the high faeries nor the low, and they were unprepared for your wretched factories and your clockwork and coal. Things are different now. I am wiser. And I am hungrier. I will win this time."

So that was it, Hettie thought. Piscaltine had been jealous and petty, but she had been more than that, too. She had been hiding Hettie, keeping her locked away in Yearn-by-the-Woods to keep her from the enemy. To keep her from being a pawn for the Sly King. If only Piscaltine hadn't been such a fool. . . .

"I won't do it," Hettie spat. "I'm the Door, and I *won't.* I know the trick. I've done it before. Stay on the line and the door stays, go into the Old Country and it closes, go into England and it grows. Well, I'll close it. I'll close the door and there won't be anything you can do about it."

The Sly King stared at her, his eyes very round and very dark. Hettie stared back, shaking a little.

Then a hiss sounded from the stairs, like a spray of sparks. *"Mi Sathir."*

A Belusite stood in the archway. Hettie had not heard her come up. Hundreds and hundreds of steps, and she hadn't heard a sound. The Belusite wore black silk, the skirts ballooning below the wasp-thin waist. She had a battered pewter teakettle where her head should have been, and her hands were pewter cups.

"*Mi Sathir,* Englishers. At the House of Sorrows. They came through the hole in Spitalfields, through the secret way. We are watching them. Shall we add them to your collection?"

The Sly King turned, staring at the Belusite intently. His fingers went to the necklaces under his jacket. "What sort of Englishers?"

"A boy. A boy and a Milkblood."

"Bartholomew." It was out before Hettie could stop herself.

The Sly King spun on her. "You don't know that," he snapped. There was not even a ghost of laughter in his voice anymore. He turned back to the waiting Belusite. "Kill them."

"*No!*" Hettie shrieked. She leaped at the Sly King, beating his waistcoat. "No, you *can't!*"

"Oh, I can and I will." His voice was low and savage, and he grabbed her by the wrist, pinching. "Kill them, Yandere, and bring their bodies here."

Hettie stopped struggling. "It might not be him," she sobbed. "It probably isn't. Barthy's cleverer than you are, and it's not him, and I don't really care."

But it was too late for lying. The Sly King laughed again, a sharp laugh like splintering glass. "If it's not him, what of it, and if it is, perhaps his death will teach you some obedience."

Again he looked to the Belusite, standing silent at the stairs.

"What are you waiting for, Yandere? Go do something ghastly."

They came to the castle and hurried around it, searching for a door in its sheer chalky sides. They didn't see one. The stones were smooth, without gaps or footholds. Higher up Pikey saw leaded windows and arrow slits and curving towers like the necks of swans, but not on the ground. Nothing until far above his head.

"She's not here," he said. "There are trees outside. Trees outside the window, I told you."

"There might be trees inside. There might be a courtyard. We won't know for sure until we've—"

Bartholomew froze. He had just gone around the corner of the castle, the side hidden from the sea and the cliffs. He stared a second at something high up on the wall. Then he turned, hands raised to keep Pikey back. Too late. Pikey rounded the corner. He saw it, too.

The goblins dangled against the wall of the castle, trussed up with ropes. One was pointy, one short. One wore a patchwork hat, one a red leather jerkin with copper bottles along the belt. Their heads were inside wire cages, and each cage had a sharp-toothed piskie inside it, scurrying over their faces, gnawing. Pikey stood staring up at them, solemn.

"Don't," Bartholomew said gently, taking him by the arm. "Don't look. Let's go to the other side." He began hurrying Pikey around the next corner.

Pikey kept staring at the goblins over his shoulder. "Barth, let's go," he said. "Let's go, she's not here, I know she's not."

Bartholomew didn't stop. "We have to try, Pikey. We'll be all right. We'll search this place and then we'll be on our way."

But just as they were rounding the final corner of the castle, there was a hissing and a snapping, and suddenly a lady with a teakettle for a head appeared. She stood several paces away, very still, and stared at them. Or she would have been staring, but Pikey could not tell where her eyes were, and where her mouth was, so she appeared strangely blank and sinister. Slowly she raised one hand. It was shaped like a pewter teacup.

"Barth?" Pikey edged a little closer to him. "Is it a faery? What is it?"

Another hiss, hollow and metallic.

Bartholomew pushed Pikey behind him. "I don't know," he said. "Stay back."

There was something dripping out of the spout of her teakettle, *drip-drip-drip.* Pikey squinted. He couldn't see what it was, and by the time he saw the three ladies slip from behind boulders it was too late, too late to run. Long knives whispered from their gowns. They flicked their points toward Pikey and Bartholomew and began to converge.

❥ ❥ ❥

"Please," Hettie whispered. "Please don't let her kill my brother."

The Sly King looked down his long, sharp nose at her and said nothing.

Hettie wanted to hit him again. She wanted to push him out the window. "Barthy can't die now. He's been looking all this time, and—and he *can't!*" She broke off into a series of hiccuping sobs.

The Sly King sighed. "You know, it is so simple. If you don't want your brother to die, you only have to do as you are told. You have to be a proper, obedient servant, and when your King tells you to open a doorway for his people, you will do so! Then all will be well. You will be such a wonderful Belusite. One of my greatest. Perhaps you will even replace Florence one day."

Hettie stared up at him. She didn't want to replace Florence. She didn't want to be a doorway and she didn't want to let this mad king and his faeries into England. But she already knew what she had to do. She could cry and scream all she liked. It wouldn't help her escape the tower. It wouldn't save her brother.

She wiped her face and stood. "All right," she said. "I'll walk when the door's open. I'll do it, but you can't let anyone hurt him. You can't let them kill my brother."

The Sly King held the bottle out to her.

She took it.

"Drink," he said.

Hettie drank. The Sly King's eyes became slits again. He smiled. Far, far away, soft, but getting louder, Hettie heard the sound of wings.

"There," the Sly King laughed. "Good-bye." And then he was gone, and the tower shuddered, as if being slammed with some great force.

"Bartholomew!" Hettie screamed.

There was another shudder.

Kill them. Kill them. Kill them. Perhaps it will teach you some obedience.

Black wings whirled through the window, slashing around her. The tower shattered like a glass spindle.

And then Hettie was falling, down, down into the City of Black Laughter.

><

"No . . ." Bartholomew's hand went to his side, but his own knife was long gone. "No, stop, we're not your enemies! We're here to find my sister! Please!"

The blades kept coming. The tips glinted in the starlight, closer, closer.

"*Hsthil?*" Bartholomew tried in the faery language. "*Makevinia pak. Mak tur hendru!*"

No use. The three ladies wore long, beaked masks and the eyes behind them glinted, fixed on Pikey and Bartholomew.

Oh, crikey, they'll run us right through, Pikey thought desperately. *They'll run us through and they won't even blink.* A blade slipped into his cloak. He felt the cold metal on his skin, biting.

And then someone laughed. "Now, now," a voice said, as if it were scolding a naughty child.

The ladies whirled toward the speaker, but their swords remained, just pricking Pikey's and Bartholomew's skin.

A tall, thin figure was coming toward them along the cliffs. He wore a fine coat and waistcoat, and many necklaces that jangled against it. "Do not kill, my dears. Not yet. I need these two a little longer."

He stepped nearer, his coat swishing softly in the wind. Pikey's heart lurched. *A slender figure. A hand unfurling out of the shadows. "Don't do anything stupid," he had said.*

"Hello, Pikey Thomas," the faery said, stopping directly in front of him and smiling a wide, white smile. "What a good and useful boy you've been."

Pikey gaped at him.

"Who could have known? The boy from the cracker box. Such a valuable specimen. Such a help."

"I don't know what you're talking about." Pikey tried to growl, but his voice was shaking, and his hands were, too, and his legs. "I don't know you."

"Don't lie, Pikey Thomas."

"I'm not lying." Pikey dropped his eyes. "I don't know you."

The Sly King's smile never wavered. "Let me prod your memory. A boy in a brass-button coat, punching the air from your lungs. A lady with a fly hat, walking into a bright, bright house. A metal beetle, belly-up in the grass."

Pikey's skin went icy. "You didn't see those things.

I saw them, you couldn't have—"

The Sly King said nothing.

"You couldn't have *seen them*!"

"Oh, but I see everything," the Sly King said. One long white finger reached down and tapped Pikey's clouded eye. "I see everything you see. My little spy."

CHAPTER XXI
Truths

LITTLE pale faces flickered between the wings. Their mouths were moving, their whispers filling Hettie's ears. She saw the door growing around her as she fell, not the flimsy little thing it had been in London, but a great storm cloud of wings, vast as the sky.

A piece of roof tumbled past, almost smashing into her. The tower was going to bury her. It was going to fall on top of her and make a hill. She flipped in the air, saw the ground rushing up. And suddenly small, bony hands grasped her. She was dragged to a halt, her nose inches above the gravel. Then she was swept onto her feet, and there was a deafening shriek. She staggered, clamping her hands to her ears. And when she had regained enough sense to look around her, the tower was gone. Everything was gone. The City of Black Laughter, with all its streets and buildings, had been blown to bits, and all that was left were stones and jagged archways and feathers falling like snow.

Hettie dropped her hands from her ears. She turned a full circle. She stood at the center of the door. It was a gigantic ring, hundreds of feet high, hundreds of feet across. And it had flattened everything. She could see from the sea all the way to the fields beyond the edge of the destruction, to the low hills and the deserted farms.

Her heart thudded.

Something was in the fields. Many things, moving swiftly through the dead grass. Banners and flags sliced toward her, snapping in the wind.

Faeries. Thousands of faeries, emerging onto the rubble of the city. Goblins and satyrs and piskies and sprytes, advancing row upon row, like an army.

My people are ready, she heard the Sly King's voice. *Ready for their new home.*

⌣ ⁄ ⌣

"You were not my best spy," said the Sly King. His eyes were very bright, as if he were telling the funniest joke. The beaked ladies made a velvet wall around Pikey and Bartholomew, blades only a hairsbreadth from skewering them.

"In fact, I never thought you would amount to anything. You are not the sharpest needle in the haystack, and the chances that you would see anything useful were very low. I mean, really, that sentimental sylph brings you a gem and you strut straight off to a Mayfair jeweler. Of course everyone would think you stole it. You ought to look in a mirror sometime and see just what a pitiful little creature you are. I saved you because you happened to witness a fetching angle of the fall of Wyndhammer House, but then you went and got yourself caught *again*, and went to *prison*, and stared at people's boots for days on end. I simply couldn't be bothered to save you a second time."

The Sly King winked at Pikey. "I'm so glad I didn't. You, meeting the infamous Bartholomew Kettle. You, and the three naughty, naughty faeries in prison, and my poor, dear Edith, and all of them trying to warn you of your purpose. You, a little shadow at the general's tent in Siltpool, gathering information, a little boy at the foot of Tar Hill, watching the soldiers hurrying up the slopes. It all worked together so perfectly."

Pikey wasn't looking at him. He was staring at the stones between his boots. He could feel Bartholomew's eyes on him. He could feel the Sly King's eyes on him.

All those troops. All dead because of me. "Don't let him see," Edith Hutcherson had said. "Not the Sly King." But Pikey had seen. He had seen everything, and so the Sly King had, too.

He looked up. "You stole it," he said. "My eye. You made me hurt folk and—and I never wanted to hurt them."

"Yes, but it makes no difference what *you* want. *I* wanted it. I sent my Belusites into your streets and alleys, into English drawing rooms and houses to steal eyes, and then I watched!" He lifted a small glass object, like a telescope lens or an oblong marble. For a second Pikey glimpsed tiny, tiny scenes flickering inside it, one after another, landscapes and rooms and faces. Then the Sly King put the glass to his eye.

"Right now, in Buntingford, a little girl is looking out a window, watching a great big prison roll past," he announced. "Yandere stole her eye in 1854. Everyone said it was polio. But it wasn't, and now I know that the prisons are thirty minutes from London." He returned the lens to his pocket and sighed. "Isn't that practical? The plan is not flawless, of course. The English eyes must be kept sound in the Old Country. They continue to function and to be the window to your soul, and sometimes my spies can see backward, into this world." He brushed his hand over the chains around his neck and the many eyes that dangled there stared, deep and watchful.

English eyes, Pikey thought. Edith Hutcherson's, and the soldier in Siltpool who had pulled his out with his own hand, and so many others. *And all of them spies.*

"But it is a small price to pay," the Sly King finished. "Very small indeed. Florence?"

A tall woman, her doll's face black as a chess piece,

emerged out of the dark and moved to stand beside the faery king. Her skirts were a rich, deep red like cherry skins. She slipped her arm through his and stared at the two boys inside the circle of blades.

"My dear?" the Sly King said. "Are you watching?"

"Yes," she answered. "I am watching."

They began to whisper to each other, heads bowed, in a language Pikey could not understand.

Suddenly Bartholomew spoke. "My sister," he said.

The Sly King and Florence looked up.

"My sister was lost here years ago." The faeries' eyes were full of disdain, but Bartholomew's voice was steady. "Her name is Henrietta Kettle, and I need to find her. I don't care about your wars and your schemes, and Pikey didn't know about them, so no one can blame him for anything. Please, have you seen her here? Has anyone seen her?"

The Sly King stared at Bartholomew an instant longer. Then he began to turn toward Pikey, slowly, so slowly, and Pikey saw that his face was pulled into a savage, hungry grin.

"Your sister is dead," he said to Bartholomew,

though his gaze was fixed firmly on Pikey. "What, did my little spy forget to tell you? She drowned in a river."

Hettie could see London. It lay only a half mile distant, a hedgehog of snowy roofs and chimneys against the ink-blue sky. The fields were pure and white. Black smoke rose in chains toward the clouds, as if to fasten them to the ground.

Above her, the wings boiled and shrieked. Feathers flew in gales around her. She stood on an invisible line, and behind her was the Old Country and ahead was England. Home. Where the houses didn't move, and trees didn't swallow people, and dolls never spoke unless you wanted them to. Where Bath was, and where Old Crow Alley was, and where Mother was.

But Hettie didn't feel happy. She felt like a rabbit in a thorn bush, caught and tangled. She wanted to scream at the door, at the sky, at nothing in particular, that she was too small to do this.

She looked back over her shoulder. The ruin

of the City of Black Laughter stretched toward the Old Country's star-spattered horizon. The faeries marched across it, their feet kicking stone dust into the air. Somewhere in that place was Bartholomew. Hettie imagined going back for him, running straight into the faeries, crashing past shields and spears, the door closing behind her, running and running until she found her brother.

But then a sliver of red caught her eye. On the English side of the door, only a few steps away, stood a huddle of barren apple trees. A face was in the branches, a pale doll's face. It was Florence La Bellina. She was watching Hettie, her skirts swishing silently in the wind. Their eyes met. Slowly the Belusite lifted a dagger, the tip pinched between her fingers. She began to wave it, back and forth, back and forth.

Hettie faced London, all pretty and new under its blanket of snow. She began to walk.

"What?" Bartholomew's voice was barely audible. He looked suddenly insubstantial, as if he were made of paper and ash and the slightest wind would send him spinning away. "She what?"

Pikey wanted to disappear. He wanted the waves to come over the cliffs and pull him into the sea.

"She drowned," the Sly King said again, enunciating each word so that it drove like a spike. "In a river."

Bartholomew looked at Pikey. His eyes were watery, red. "Pikey?" he said. "You lied to me?" His voice was so full of hurt.

"I had to, Barth, I—"

"Did you ever see her?" Bartholomew was crying now. "Did you see her even *once*?"

"Yes!" Pikey shouted. "I saw her loads of times, right up until we left London! I swear I did, and she *is* alive. She—she just *is*."

"Don't lie to the poor boy, Pikey," said the Sly King. "Don't lie anymore. She is dead and there is nothing for you here. Nothing for any of us."

Hettie hurried out across the snowy field, a tiny, twig-headed figure in a great white sea. The wings followed her, spreading like a great storm. The Old Country followed her, too. In the distance she heard clanks, grating, and rumbling.

"You're going to kill everyone," said a voice in her mind. It sounded like coal and chocolate, like a great lady with copper curls. *"You're doing exactly what the Sly King wants, following his orders like another one of his Belusites. Like a* Whatnot." The voice spat the word.

"Be quiet," Hettie whispered, but her words were swallowed at once by the wind and the flapping wings. "I can't let him die. He's all I have, him and Mummy, and I *can't*."

She knew the voice was right. All those faeries would be here, and this wasn't their home. This was where the Sly King wanted them to be, but no one asked them what *they* wanted. She remembered the rebels in the Old Country, struggling weakly against the Sly King. She remembered Old Crow Alley and how the faeries there had seemed so dark and horrible to her. But she hadn't known a thing about faeries then. They were all trapped, in the smoke and the iron, and in someone else's plans. And so was Hettie.

She wished she had the mask again. All she would need to do was tie its ribbons behind her head and suddenly she would be strong. She would be wise, and she would know how to stop the Sly King *and* save her brother, both at once.

But she didn't have the mask. She didn't have anything.

Whatnot, she heard Piscaltine saying, and she heard the Sly King saying it, too, and the reflection of the old Peculiar in the water. *Whatnot, Whatnot. You're nothing but a useless little Whatnot. Better do as you're told.*

London loomed. The black wings swelled, a great wave about to descend.

Hettie broke into a desperate, stumbling run.

"Mi Sathir?" Florence whispered. "The Peculiar is in London."

The Sly King flinched. It was very small, just a tiny click of his fingers. But Pikey saw.

"Who?" he croaked. "Who reached London?"

Bartholomew wasn't listening. *"You lied to me!"* he shouted. "You never knew! You never did!" He tried to duck under the blades. One of the beaked ladies swatted him back, and another swatted Pikey, though he hadn't moved.

Pikey tried not to cry out, tried to ignore Bartholomew. "Who reached London?"

The Sly King glanced at him. "Nobody," he said. And then, addressing the beaked ladies, "Kill them."

Pikey shouted, struggling. "Is it Hettie? Is it Hettie in London?"

The beaked ladies drew back their swords.

"You lied!" Bartholomew yelled, and then Pikey kicked him, hard, and they both fell rolling and wrestling to the ground. The blades sang together over their heads.

Bartholomew tried to scream again. Pikey kicked him again. "Shut up," he snapped. "I'm sorry I lied. I wish I hadn't, but it's your own fault. You can't just give up. You can't just stop, just because things are bad. You don't know what's going to happen, but I do, and I'll *tell* you. We're going to get Hettie and—"

A blade buried itself in the stones between Pikey's fingers. Another pegged his hood. He tore away, just in time to kick at a blade about to take off Bartholomew's ear.

"And everything's going to be grand!" Something sharp grazed his thigh. He barely felt it. "Anyway, what if the faery's the one lying? Why d'you only believe the bad things? I don't care if you hate me and if you leave me behind, but you can't *give up*!"

"Oh, kill them and stop that infernal noise," the Sly King groaned.

Florence La Bellina shoved past the ladies. A knife glinted in her hand.

Pikey's eyes widened. "Barth?" he said shakily.

Bartholomew didn't even glance at the doll-woman. Her blade flew. And Bartholomew caught it, right out of the air, spinning with the force of the throw. He leaped to his feet. The knife flashed again. Florence let out a screech. He had the knife in his hand, and its tip was against her heart.

"Get back," he said. His voice was ragged and low. Savage. "Get back, all of you, or I'll kill her." When he said it, Pikey knew he would.

The beaked ladies retreated a step. The Sly King stayed perfectly still.

"You, too," Bartholomew said, gesturing to the King.

The Sly King smiled. "No," he said. "Go on. Kill her. I have a better servant now."

In one smooth motion Bartholomew kicked the legs out from under her. She crashed to the ground. Bartholomew pressed the knife to her back and the red velvet parted such a little bit.

"Back," he said.

"No!" the Sly King said gleefully. "I *do* have your sister, you see. The London Door. Henrietta Kettle. She is the trick and the whip hand. She will be the turning point of this endless war. But she doesn't know. She doesn't know what she's worth. Servants never do."

Bartholomew whirled, hurling the knife at the Sly King. The faery smiled wider. He raised a finger and the knife stopped, midflight.

"It's too late to stop her. She is going to destroy London. She is going to destroy your entire kingdom, and she is doing it for *you*. Because she wants to save you."

Slowly the knife turned in the air. "But she can't." It pointed to Bartholomew. It shot forward.

Bartholomew ducked. "Run!" Pikey shouted, but the beaked ladies were moving in again, surrounding them. Florence La Bellina was on her feet.

Bartholomew stooped. He began fiddling with his boots.

"You idiot, stop—" Then Pikey saw.

The buckles. The silver feather buckles on Bartholomew's boots. They were sparking, and Bartholomew was pressing them and twisting them and mumbling frantically. Then he lifted them, two fistfuls of glinting metal feathers, and they seemed to struggle out from between his fingers. He tossed them. They exploded into hissing puffs, and when the steam cleared they were delicate clockwork creatures, like insects. Each had a stinger, and each stinger carried an emerald bulb of poison at its tip. They swarmed the beaked ladies and the Sly King.

Before Pikey could see what they would do,

Bartholomew snatched his arm, and he and Pikey pelted away along the cliffs.

Ahead was the hole into England. Behind them, shouting. And then a tinkling as the stinger-insects dropped to the stones. Pikey looked over his shoulder. The Sly King's hands were raised, his mouth moving. Florence and the beaked ladies were flying after Pikey and Bartholomew, leaping along the cliffs like deranged marionettes. Pikey saw the hole ahead, a black speck among the rocks. He reached it. He dove in, headfirst. He didn't wait for Bartholomew. He pushed deeper and deeper, felt the old roots coiling, and the endless weight of stone and dirt above him.

The first thing he smelled of London was the burning, and a wind heavy with smoke and coal.

The faery prisons were almost free of the trenches. They rolled up the banks slowly—a thousand tons of iron and spikes—and the faeries pushing them screeched in anguish. Guns bombarded them. Aether cannons shot sprays of greenish-black orbs, compacted gases that burst into gales of fire upon impact, but the globes never faltered. They eased up onto the lip of the trench. Soldiers scattered. Faeries whooped and yelled as English guns were ground into the muck. The globes began to roll. Slowly at first, but quickly gaining speed, thundering over the winter fields.

High overhead, a tiny clockwork bird flapped. It flew straight and true, a dull gleam of brass over fields, then rooftops, to Westminster Palace. An old gentleman stood in one of the upper windows. The bird alighted on his hand. Behind him other gentlemen waited, lords and dukes and the last brave members of the Privy Council. Mr. Jelliby was there. His face was gray, but his jaw was set. They all saw the brass capsule attached to the bird's leg. They all knew what was inside. The old man took out the slip of paper and read it silently. He handed it to the others. They read it, too. Some looked grave, some fearful, some determined. Then they all shook hands and began to descend to the street, one after another.

The window was left open. The paper lay discarded, drifting over the floor. There were only three words on it, scrawled in splattered ink: *We are lost.*

Hettie was on a road into North London, walking as fast as she could. Her eyes were pinched shut. Tears seeped from them, but she didn't try to stop them anymore. A barn shattered behind her. Wood flew by her face, puffs of white feathers that might have been chickens, and splinters of metal as long as daggers. She did not flinch. She did not open her eyes. On and on she walked, stumbling toward the sooty skirt hem of the city.

Something in the city was on fire. She could smell it, and when she opened her eyes she could see the orange flames dancing on the clouds above. Ahead was Bishopsgate. Broken wagons and discarded furniture made a barricade in front of it. As if that could stop her. Beyond were the crooked streets and leaning houses of London. And somewhere was Wapping and an old, burned-out warehouse. Once, in that warehouse, a faery by the name of John Wednesday Lickerish had tried to do just what Hettie was doing now. He had tried to destroy all of London. Hettie had been afraid then. Afraid because the wings had been so loud and the wind so cold. How different she had been then. How small and empty-headed.

Do they lead home? she had asked the faery butler, that night on the boat. Do all these horrid things lead someplace good?

And the faery butler had said, *Perhaps, if we make them to.* But she couldn't. She couldn't make them to, not now, not for her.

She climbed over the wagons, under the stone archway, and into High Street. Behind her, Bishopsgate blew up in a shower of stone.

The globes were hurtling toward the city, churning the new snow into mud. *Fifteen miles, fourteen miles.* The smoke of the city came into view, then the first houses, already smashed beyond repair. The globes picked up speed.

Pikey burst from among the roots of the tree, into the court behind the butcher's shop. He spun, expecting to see Bartholomew clawing up after him. He waited, heart thudding. Wind whispered across the roofs. Somewhere in the distance, a roaring.

"Bartholomew?" he called, as loud as he dared. "Barth?"

No answer.

"Barth?" With a stab of panic, Pikey went down on his knees and began scrabbling back into the hole. *"Barth!"*

He felt a hand, hot breath against his face.

"Pikey." It was Bartholomew. His fingers tightened around Pikey's wrist. "Pikey, something's got my leg. Go get Hettie. She's here and she's alive; go get her."

"No!" Pikey dragged at Bartholomew's hand, wrenching him up.

"Go," Bartholomew gasped. "Go, please!"

"No, you have to get out. She's *your* sister, and she needs you, not me."

Bartholomew was halfway out now, his whole upper body in England. They both saw the feathers at the same time.

They scudded down into the court like black snow. The distant roaring grew. Pikey saw the wings, a vast cloud of them, boiling up in the distance, over the gable of the butcher's shop, darkening the moon.

Bartholomew started shouting. "Hettie! It's Hettie, she's opened the door! *Hettie!*" Pikey joined in, and they yelled until their voices were hoarse.

But there was no way she could have heard them. She could have been a mile away. And suddenly Bartholomew was jerked back underground. Pikey saw a pale hand in a red sleeve wriggle up Bartholomew's neck and clamp over his eyes.

"Pikey, she's opened the door! She'll destroy the whole city!" Bartholomew clawed at the hand. He was slipping, disappearing back into the hole. "Stop her. Tell her not to, no matter what. Tell her I'm all right. I *will* be all right."

All Pikey saw of Bartholomew now were his fingers, stark against the black coiling roots.

"Pikey?" Bartholomew's voice was muffled. His hands scrabbled frantically. "Pikey, GO!"

Pikey let out an angry cry and shot to his feet. He

looked up. The wings were pouring across the city, seeping over the rooftops and slithering between chimneys, crumbling them. They would kill him. He had heard enough stories of Bath and the faeries to know that. He spun back to the tree. Bartholomew was gone.

"No," he whispered. He took a few steps toward it. He felt the wind plucking at his cloak. "No!" he said louder.

But he had to move. They had such a slim chance, Hettie and Bartholomew, and that chance was him.

Pikey stood for a second, looking up at the inky storm of wings. He closed his eyes . . . and leaped.

A dog was tearing through Leadenhall Street, whimpering. Hettie followed it. Furniture littered the cobbles. Sofas and desks and shattered portraits. Envelopes and nightgowns spilled out of drawers, wafting over the wreckage. A steam coach had overturned coming around the corner of an alley and lay abandoned now, its door open, pointing to the sky. The people of London had fled in a panic.

Somewhere ahead was the river. After that was more London, then villages, and then, Hettie imagined, winter fields.

It's not the right way! It's not the way to go! the voice in her head screamed, and she knew it wasn't, but it was the only way she could see. She passed the Bank of England, Cannon Station with all its engines gone, and the clock frozen at eleven o'clock. An automaton stood slumped at the loading curb, its eyes watching her as she went by. The wings swallowed it.

Suddenly Hettie stopped, staring up the street. For a second she imagined she was in Old Crow Alley. It was full of broken furniture, too. The sky was black, and the stars were falling, and a wild laughter was on the icy wind. Miserable, angry faery faces looked down at her from the broken windows, their branch-hair growing into the walls and knotting them to the earth.

The image faded. She was back in London. *Cross the river*, the Sly King had said. *Cross the river, or you'll die.* But she was dead either way. Even if she did everything he said, she would never see Mother or Bartholomew again. She would be a Belusite then, and after she had destroyed the whole city and brought the faeries into England, she would join all the other Belusites and wander about in beautiful clothes, working schemes for the Sly King. There *had* to be another way. *I wish I could see it,* she thought. *I wish I knew.*

And then she heard the shout. A word, echoing louder even than the wings. Was somebody calling her? She took a few steps back the way she had come.

"Bartholomew?" The wings formed a wall in front of her, filling the street, gutter to gutter. *"Barthy?"*

The flood of wings almost smashed Pikey sideways. He fought his way forward, desperately, one foot after another, headfirst into the screaming wind. Fingers pinched him. Something cold and stinging slid against his bare hands, but he didn't stop. He wasn't dead—not yet—and he wasn't going to stop.

"Hettie?" he shouted into the blackness. "Hettie, where are you?"

Whispers filled his ears. He felt strange suddenly, hazy, and when he looked down he saw that the ground beneath his boots kept flickering between London cobbles and the shattered stone of a gray ruin. He was *in* the door, right in between, in the Old Country and England both. Somewhere he heard a steady beat, like the marching of soldiers, coming toward him. He heard the wings and the whispers. And then, above it all, he heard a voice. A child's voice, shrill as a whistle.

"Bartholomew?" It was faint, whirling among the feathers. "Barthy?"

Pikey switched directions, following the sound. "Hettie!"

"Bartholomew?"

Ahead Pikey saw a break in the wings. He hurried toward it. And then he was out of the blackness and hurtling toward a small, pale child. She stood in the middle of the street, next to a red chair. Her back was toward him.

"Hettie!" he shouted. She turned. Her eyes widened. The chair billowed away in a flight of ruby-bright flakes.

Pikey rushed to her, gasping and swatting at the

feathers. "Hettie," he said, "I'm Pikey, and I'm your brother's helper, and you have to stop this. You have to stop those faeries."

Hettie stared at him. "What?" Her cheeks were wet, and Pikey saw that her eyes were dark and dripping. "My brother? Bartholomew?"

"Yes! I was just—"

"Is he all right?" Hettie took a step toward Pikey, but it was as if something were holding her back, as if hands were dragging at her. "They said they'd kill him, but he's not dead, is he? He's safe?"

For an instant everything became silent. A piece of paper curled overhead, so calmly Pikey could see the picture on it—pen-and-ink, an illustration of a summer country and a cottage just peeking over the hill.

Yes, he almost lied. *He's safe. He's just sitting, waiting for you.*

But of course Pikey didn't know if Bartholomew was safe. He didn't know how he possibly could be, wounded and dragged back under the Gallows Tree. And Pikey was done lying.

A gust of roof tiles whirled passed them, and the silence shattered. "I don't know!" he shouted. "I don't know if he's safe, but we've got to hope he is, right? We've got to hope for it. Me and him, we got away from the Sly King and we got to London, and he said he'd be all right, and if Barth says something he means it. So you need to stop all this. You need to, because no one else can and nothing'll be all right if you don't get rid of these blinkin' *faeries!*" The wings rose into a gale along with Pikey's voice, almost drowning him out.

Hettie stared at him, not moving.

"Can you?" he shouted. "You're the only one who can, so you can't say no!"

"I don't know!" she yelled back. They were inches apart, but the black feathers made a pillar around them. They could barely hear each other. "I don't *know* if I can!"

"Yes, you do! You can, because you've *got* to!"

And all of a sudden it was as if he could see through those huge dark eyes into a quick and click-ing mind. He saw sadness, then doubt, then wonder and determination. "All right," she said, and she wasn't crying anymore. "But you have to leave now. You have to run, and you can't stop. Go that way! Go!"

And then she shoved Pikey, and he went stumbling and leaping away down the street. Fingers and wind pulled at his cloak, then let go. The wings fell away behind him. Ahead was the river, a bridge, and the great, silent city.

Bartholomew kicked free of the roots and limped over the scattered cobbles, gripping his cloak with both hands. The red woman had cut him. He had felt a knife, or a jagged fragment, cold as iron. And then, all at once, she had let out a terrible cry and had lost her grip on him. He limped faster. Behind him, he could still hear her shrieking. The black wings were everywhere, flooding over him. Feathers scraped his skin and fingers prodded, but he felt no pain. The sylphs would not kill him. Not a Peculiar and a faery-touched.

He looked back over his shoulder. Florence was

dragging herself out from under the tree, like a ghoul climbing from a grave. Her face was cracked, and she looked oddly disheveled, She stood. Behind her, the tree opened. Its branches swayed and writhed, and inside stood the Sly King.

"Florence!" the King cried, but she did not look at him. Her empty eyes had grown into huge, round pits. She was facing north, her hand extended, as if reaching for someone who was not there. The wings swooped around her, up the tree. The Sly King lunged out of it. A second later, it was uprooted. It whirled into the air. The branches lashed. And then the tree smashed down again, full force, and the cobblestones leaped.

The tree had fallen exactly where Florence La Bellina and the Sly King had been standing.

Bartholomew did not wait to see the aftermath. He dashed from the court, into the street, stumbling and fighting through the wings. Houses were falling around him, tipping forward like packs of cards. The cut hurt. A pain in his stomach, slowing his steps.

"Hettie?" he shouted. "Pikey?"

The wind swallowed his voice. He took a few more halting steps. Then he collapsed under an archway. The house it belonged to groaned and went down. Only the arch stood, Bartholomew under it clutching his stomach and pulling his legs away from the thundering rubble.

The last thing he saw was the blood seeping between his fingers, dripping like claret onto the cobbles.

Outside of London, the snow in the fields had begun to tremble. It shifted and shook across the frozen earth, a thunder cracking the still air.

Slowly a body tipped out of a huddle of apple trees. The body struck the snow with hardly a sound. Florence La Bellina lay faceup, her pale skin a web of cracks. Her eyes were wide and her hand was reaching, up and out toward London, grasping for her other half, grasping for her sister. Then the globes came and the trees were gone, and so was she.

⌣⌣

Hettie looked at the mass of wings towering above her, arching over the whole city, and she knew what she had to do.

We've got to hope, the boy had said. Well, Hettie was going to hope she could stop the Sly King until she *had* stopped him. She was going to hope Bartholomew was alive until she saw him again. But she didn't have to hope she was strong and brave, because just then she knew she was.

She whipped around and began walking back the way she had come, quick and purposeful. She thought of the great lady, proud and lovely, looking at her out of the mirror. She thought of Piscaltine, always trying to keep her small and telling her what she wasn't. But once, just once, Piscaltine had told the truth. *This is the creature that is your soul,* she had said, and it was. The hideous old Peculiar in the water hadn't been her. It might have been, but she wasn't going to let it. Hettie was the one in the mirror, even if no one else knew.

"Stop!" she shouted at the top of her lungs, to the wings and the door and the writhing darkness. She could see the faeries in the distance, marching rank upon rank. They carried weapons, swords and clubs and long, cruel spears with tips like the claws of beasts. The first ones would be in London soon.

Only they wouldn't.

It was her door. She *was* the door, wasn't that what Mr. Lickerish had said? Well, then she would make it do as she said.

"Stop!" she shouted again, and this time she sensed a response. *Surprise? Fear?* The whispers of the sylphs grew louder, swirling around her. She walked faster. "Stop!"

She felt the door, a thousand feet high, as if it were her own skin. She twisted her hand and high above her the sylphs twisted, too, screaming. She began to run. The Old Country was behind her suddenly, and she was pulling it, dragging it in the direction of the wide open fields. The wings skimmed the rooftops, sending tiles flying like flocks of crows. She labored back up High Street, now only a thread of cobbles between the rubble. She clambered over a sofa, over the tumbled stones and broken wagons of Bishopsgate. She was almost there. The faery army was close at her back now, so close she could hear the jingle of their armor and the scrape of steel. Her legs pumped over grass, over the flattened boards of the barns she had destroyed. And then she stopped.

Ahead, twelve massive iron globes loomed. They were coming at full speed, straight for London. Straight for her. They would be upon her in seconds. Ten. Five.

You were wrong, Sly King, she thought. *Maybe I am a Whatnot, but I'll stop you cold.*

She planted her feet and lifted her hands. There she stood, one small girl in front of twelve great globes. Behind her, the army neared. Ahead, the globes bore down on her, deafening. She spread her arms. The door went wide, shooting out a mile on either side. She felt its edges far, far away, as if they were her fingertips. The globes' shadows fell across her. The wind thrashed her twigs and tore at her nightgown. And then the globes whirled past, so close she might have touched one. They rolled straight through the door, into the Old Country—twelve faery prisons, rattling away over the rubble. The faery army shrieked and scattered. They dropped their weapons. They dropped helmets and armor and fled back to their great houses and hollow hills.

Hettie didn't know how long she stood there. She didn't know how long she held the door and pressed it open. Vaguely she glimpsed faeries passing her, some going in, some going out, soft and sly and merry in their strange faery way. There were families of goblins and gaggles of piskies and solitary spriggans in waistcoats and hats. They touched her as they passed, her branches and her face, and some of them smiled, wide, toothy smiles, but Hettie wasn't afraid. *Thank you,* the faeries said. *Thank you, thank you.* And after the moon went down and up and down again, after she felt she had done her job, she let her arms fall and watched as the great door dissolved in a wisp of ash.

Epilogue

THEY met outside London, in that wide winter field. Bartholomew and Pikey climbed down from a carriage and set off across the snow. Hettie hobbled, her feet dragging through a hundred thousand black feathers.

They all went as fast as they could, but their steps were weighted by wounds and weariness. They did not call out to one another as they approached.

Hettie looked different from when Pikey had seen her last. She had been small then, and frightened. She was still small, but she didn't look frightened anymore. And her branches . . . They were no longer bare and smooth. They had bloomed sometime in the night, little white flowers as soft as milk. They were beautiful.

"Hello, Hettie," Bartholomew said when they were face-to-face. His voice was low. He looked different, too. He was dressed in fine clothes, a velvet coat and gray woolen stockings. A bandage was wrapped around his midsection.

"Hello, Barthy," Hettie said.

They stood there a while, just staring at each other. Pikey hung back, shuffling. Then, without a word, Bartholomew picked Hettie up so that her feet went right off the ground and hugged her. Hettie started to cry and then to laugh, and then Bartholomew started laughing, too. Even Pikey laughed a little bit, and then wiped his face quickly.

Behind him, he heard the creak of a hinge— Mr. Jelliby stepping from the carriage, standing by it and smiling somewhat sadly. Pikey looked toward the carriage and looked toward the road, a shattered road leading into the winter sunlight. Bartholomew had set Hettie down. They were murmuring to each other, saying all the things Pikey supposed brothers and sisters would say after years and years. He began to back away. He still had his cloak. He still had his boots. It had been a good adventure.

He started to walk. But he hadn't gone far when he heard a shout. Bartholomew and Hettie were hurrying after him, hand in hand.

"Where are you going?" Bartholomew yelled across the field. "You can't wander off now!"

"I can!" Pikey shouted back, but he stopped.

They caught up. "No," Bartholomew said, slightly out of breath. "I said that when we'd found Hettie we'd all go back to Bath, and I meant it. You did it all. I don't think anything would have been the same without you."

Hettie nodded. "People should say thank you to you. All of *England* should say thank you."

Pikey imagined that for a second—all of England saying thank you to the boy from the cracker box. He felt a glow filling him from the top of his head to the bottom of his boots. He grinned at Hettie and

Bartholomew. They grinned back.

"Come on," Bartholomew said, taking Pikey's hand. Hettie snatched his other one. Together, the three of them turned toward the carriage. "Let's go home."

THE END